TIED
WITH ME

BOOK SIX IN THE WITH ME
IN SEATTLE SERIES

KRISTEN PROBY

TIED WITH ME
Book Six in the With Me In Seattle Series
Kristen Proby
Copyright © 2014 by Kristen Proby
ISBN: 978-1496026064

The following story contains mature themes, strong language, and sexual situations as well as light BDSM themes. It is intended for adult readers.

Cover Art:
Photography by: Dylan Duvall
Models: Dustin and Stephanie Culp
Cover Artist: Okay Creations

For L. Thanks for encouraging me to write this story, this way.

A NOTE FROM THE AUTHOR

This book in the With Me In Seattle series is a bit different from the others. Each of the stories are sexy, sensual, and feature an alpha man with a strong woman, and this book is no exception. However, Matt Montgomery isn't just a run-of-the-mill alpha male. Matt also dabbles in the world of BDSM. The scenes that explore this lifestyle are respectful, sane and always consensual, as should always be the case in this world. The heart of this story, like the others, is the romance. The discovery of love and deep affection for another person is paramount.

I hope you enjoy Matt and Nic's journey.

Best Wishes,
Kristen

PROLOGUE

"Why are we here?" I ask Bailey for the fortieth time since we arrived at the Seattle Arts Center.

"Because you need some excitement in your life," she informs me with a sly grin. "And I didn't have anyone else to come with me."

"*This* is the kind of excitement you think I need?" I ask incredulously and take in the scene before me.

Bailey, my best friend, talked me into attending the Seattle spring erotic festival. How she managed, I have no idea. I'm the least-kinky person on the planet.

I'm so vanilla, I smell of it.

Or maybe that's just because I bake with it all day.

"Don't be such a prude," she admonishes me with an eye roll. "It's fun."

"It's not my thing," I reply and step aside as a man wearing nothing but leather and chains brushes against me.

The main room has been transformed into a large dance club. There is a DJ on stage, loud music pumping out of the speakers, and lights flash as bodies move and grind on the dance floor.

There are many different levels of dress. And undress. Nudity isn't allowed, but many have pushed the boundaries, covering only the most necessary parts of their bodies. In a smaller room off to the right is a smaller dance floor with softer music and a stage, where a burlesque group is about to perform. There is also a fully stocked bar in that room.

To the left of the main dance area is another large room that is broken into segments, where different kinks are demonstrated for the crowd.

"We'll go in there later, after we get some drinks into you," Bailey informs me and pulls me in the direction of the bar and burlesque show.

Bailey has dark blond hair that falls to her ass, stick straight. The highlights are natural, damn her. Her eyes are wide and deep brown, and when she smiles she has dimples that have long labeled her as *cute*, which she hates with a passion.

When we approach the bar, we both order 7&7s from a bartender dressed in booty shorts and orange suspenders then find a seat near the stage.

"What do you think so far?" Bailey asks with a grin and takes a sip of her drink.

"There are way more people than I expected." And they're of all ages and sizes, different sexual orientations. What surprises me the most is how open and comfortable everyone seems, smiling, happy to be nearly naked and unapologetically exploring their kinkier sexual side.

"This community is larger than you'd think," she agrees and lets her eyes wander over the room. "You look great, by the way. It's a nice change to see you out of that white jacket and hat that always hide your body."

"It's called my work uniform," I reply drily.

"That's just it. You're always at work, friend. You're either in that hideous, body-hiding outfit or in pajamas."

I shrug and look away. There's nothing to say. She's right. I glance down at the short denim miniskirt and thigh-high stockings, heels and red strapless top that Bailey insisted I wear. I can't help but admit that it feels good to dress up a bit.

Reminds me that I'm a woman with needs that go beyond a hot kitchen and chocolate frosting.

Bailey helped me apply my makeup of dark liner, fake eyelashes and bright lipstick, and teased my long dark hair into ringlets that fall down my back and over my breasts, which have also been teased to be high and pushed together, showing off what little cleavage I have.

God bless, Bailey and her girlie secrets.

"You have a kickin' body, Nic. You should show it off more."

"To who?" I ask with a laugh. "My clients want cupcakes, not my boobs in their face."

"Depends on the client," she replies with a laugh just as the lights fall and loud, thirties swing music erupts into a seductive pounding rhythm and a young blond woman saunters out onto the stage in a sailor's uniform, dancing about vigorously.

Within thirty seconds, she's left wearing pasties and a G-string.

I'm not even sure what happened to her clothes, they came off so quickly.

I tilt my head and watch her move effortlessly across the stage, smiling, biting her lip, flirting with the guys—and girls—in the audience.

Four more girls perform, much to the crowd's delight, before they take a break, rearranging props and giving the crowd a chance to refresh their drinks or go explore other parts of the event.

"Okay, let's grab another drink and go check out the exhibits." Bailey claps her hands and pulls me to my feet.

"Do we have to?"

"Yes!" She rolls her eyes again and drags me behind her. "You don't have to participate. Just watch. It's fun, Nic."

"If you say so," I murmur and greedily sip my fresh drink as we walk through the dance room to the fetish exhibits, where the music is gone and instead there is laughter and moans of pleasure.

"You didn't say that people participate." My voice is three octaves higher than normal, and I don't care.

"Of course they participate. But *you* don't have to."

The first demonstration we come across has me sucking down my drink in one long sip of the straw and pulling Bailey's drink out of her hand to suck hers down, too.

A woman is lying on a massage table, face up, with a blue satin sash over her naked breasts and pelvis. A large, shirtless, gorgeous man is standing over her with a metal wand in his hand. It's attached to a machine, and when he touches her skin, it shocks her.

"Electro play," Bailey informs me.

My eyes can't move away from the woman as she writhes and moans on the table. The man leans down and murmurs in her ear, but she smiles and shakes her head. "He's checking in with her, to make sure she's okay."

"Kind of him," I reply sarcastically.

He resumes pulling the wand over her breasts, making her nipples pucker even more than they were, which didn't look possible, down her stomach and finally between her legs, sending her into a screaming orgasm.

"Dear God."

Bailey laughs at me. I didn't even realize I'd spoken the words aloud.

"You're into that?" I ask her.

"No, it's not for everyone, and it takes a lot of trust and someone very practiced to dive into that world." She smiles as she watches the couple on the small stage.

The man has turned the machine off and pulled the woman into his arms, soothing and petting her as she shakes and pants. He kisses her cheek and whispers lovingly in her ear. Watching them together, so intimate, so loving, makes my chest hurt.

It's beautiful.

"Those two are married. She's been his submissive for about three years."

"Submissive?" I ask.

"Are you really that naïve?" Bailey asks with a shake of her head.

"I had no idea that stuff happened in real life. I thought it just made for a fun romance novel."

"It happens."

"Are you submissive?"

She smiles at me then shrugs her slim shoulder. "Unfortunately, no. I tried, but my mouth kept getting me in trouble. My ass was sore for a month."

I swallow hard as we move along to the next demonstration.

I jump when I hear the crack of a whip. "Holy shit!"

Bailey laughs and tucks her arm through mine as we watch another tall, lean, shirtless man wield a bullwhip. A woman is suspended by the wrists to a chain in the ceiling, her arms pulled high over her head. She's wearing black panties and a bra.

The man circles the whip over his head and cracks it in front of him, leaving just a tiny red mark on the woman's shoulder blade. She moans, as though it's the sexiest thing she's ever felt.

The man circles her, his focus completely on her, and when he gets to her back, he repeats the motion, leaving another, identical mark on the other shoulder blade.

He approaches her, grips her red hair in his fist and pulls her head back so he can whisper in her ear.

"Yes, sir," she replies breathlessly.

He grins and kisses her deeply before releasing her hair and raising the whip above his head, the leather kissing her skin, leaving one, two, three more red marks on either side of her spine.

"How can he do that and not break the skin?" I ask in awe.

"Lots and lots of practice," Bailey whispers back. "That's Master Eric."

"Is she his submissive?" I ask, proud of myself for understanding the lingo so quickly.

"No, she's not with anyone that I know of. But she is a masochist, and Master Eric is happy to oblige her."

"Jesus," I whisper, but can't deny the clench in my stomach when Master Eric cups her ass in his hand, pushing his fingers between her legs and pulling them away sopping wet, glistening in the soft light.

"See? She's happy. Master Eric would stop if she said her safe word."

Jesus, I think again. Safe words and whips and electrowands. Who would have thought?

When we move along, a woman is pouring ladles of hot wax on eager participants.

"Ah, we're moving on to the more vanilla demonstrations," Bailey explains. "Not that hot wax is vanilla, but it's no bullwhip."

I smirk and watch in rapture as a shirtless man has wax poured on his chest, down his defined abs, and smiles in pleasure. A hard ridge beneath his blue jeans proves that he is enjoying himself.

"Want to try it?" Bailey asks me.

"No, thanks." I shake my head but can't look away as the next woman in line takes a seat and scoops her hair off her neck, giving the woman pouring wax space to drizzle the hot liquid over her collarbones and chest. It cools and hardens almost immediately and is peeled seductively off the skin.

It's actually kind of...*sexy*.

"Oh! The bondage area!" Bailey exclaims excitedly and pulls me over where a small line of women are waiting patiently as a handsome man ties long lines of ropes around their torsos, arms, legs, leaving a trail of intricate knots around their bodies.

Wow.

"I had no idea that ropes could look so artistic," I murmur.

"It's definitely an art form," Bailey agrees and eagerly steps forward when the man motions her to join him.

He crosses her hands over her lower back and begins looping and knotting a blue rope over and around her. The color of the rope looks amazing against her little black dress and accentuates her curves.

She's stunning.

The man plants a kiss on her forehead and grins when she thanks him and bounces over to me.

"You should do it, too."

"You can't move your hands," I respond, pointing to where her arms are restrained behind her.

"You don't have to have your hands bound," she replies and nudges me forward. The man is grinning, but then is interrupted by another man.

I stop about a foot away and watch as the second man whispers in the other's ear. They both nod, and the new guy grins at me, and suddenly, he and I are the only ones in the room.

He has ice-blue eyes. The kind of eyes that pull you in and drown you in their depths. His hair is light brown and cut relatively short.

His face is shaved clean, and his full, sexy lips are pursed in a smirk.

"Are you coming or not, little one?"

CHAPTER ONE

Weddings really aren't my thing. Well, baking the cakes for them, that is. I own a successful little cupcake bakery in downtown Seattle, and cupcakes are what I enjoy most.

But when Brynna Vincent, now Montgomery, asked me to bake a cake for her wedding, I couldn't refuse her. She rushed into my shop just about two weeks ago, her eyes bright with happiness, and asked me if I could bake a cake for her because my cupcakes are her very favorite.

Yes, it was a nice stroke of my ego.

And when she assured me that she just needed a simple two-tier cake for a small wedding, I was in. It didn't hurt that she had her adorable six-year-old twin daughters with her, and they bought a dozen chocolate cupcakes to go with them.

But now that I'm in the thick of it, arranging the cake, making sure it's displayed perfectly, while the last of the vows are said and the large family behind me cheers with delight and joy, I'm reminded why I never ventured into the wedding cake business: It's too damn stressful.

Brynna has been a dream to work with. No bridezilla here, thank God, and I'd even be willing to say that she and I have become friends in the past few weeks while putting our heads together for her beautiful cake.

But the actual execution the day of the wedding is torture for me. I have to be sure that every tiny rose, the placement of the cake topper, *everything* is perfect.

Because if I were the bride, that's how I'd want it to be.

I make a mad dash out to my car to gather the last of my supplies and hustle back to the cake table behind the home where Brynna and her husband were married today.

The house isn't terribly large. It's in an average neighborhood and probably boasts three or four bedrooms. But the backyard is something out of a *Better Homes and Gardens* magazine.

Brynna had mentioned that her new father-in-law is an avid gardener, and she wasn't kidding. The yard is blooming brightly with fragrant summer flowers. There are ponds and paths scattered throughout the large property, giving it a park-like feel.

Kids from toddler to the twins' ages are running about, enjoying the warm day. Soft music has been piped in, from where I'm not sure.

"When do we get cake?" a man asks from behind me.

I turn and have to crane my neck back to see the man's face. He has bright blue eyes and dark blond hair, and he's smiling down at me.

He's one of the largest men I've ever seen and, for some reason, looks very familiar.

"That's the bride and groom's call. I'm just putting the finishing touches on it."

I grin back at him and fuss with the last of the baby-pink rosebuds on the top of the pretty white cake.

"Will you tell if I steal a slice?" he asks with a chuckle.

"I will," a stunning redhead replies drily and rolls her eyes. "Don't mind him. He's always hungry."

"You caught me," he murmurs and nuzzles the redhead's temple. "I'm Will. Brother of the groom."

He holds his big hand out for me to shake.

"And this is my beautiful fiancée, Meg."

"Nice to meet you both." And then it hits me. "Holy crap, are you Will Montgomery, the football player?"

"Yeah," he confirms almost shyly. "But today I'm just a brother."

"Cool." I grin, proud of myself for maintaining my composure. I had no idea that Brynna's in-laws were *those* Montgomerys.

Will and Meg wander away, and I finish the cake, then look around for Brynna to say congratulations and leave the party, relieved that my job is just about finished.

I look out over the yard and see Brynna standing with a group of her guests, waving at me. I grin as I wipe my hands on my jacket and join Brynna, standing on my tiptoes to hug her close.

"Congratulations, friend!" I murmur. "Where is your man?"

"Right here," Caleb announces with a wide smile as I pull away from his bride. "The cake is beautiful, thank you."

"My pleasure," I reply happily, relieved that they're happy with the end result of many hours of planning.

"You make the best cake in the whole world," a blond woman next to Brynna tells me, but as I turn my head toward her, I swear to God above, I have a hallucination.

Someone slipped me a roofie, and I'm suffering from side effects.

That's the only explanation I can come up with for why I'm standing here looking at the one man I can't seem to shake from my memory, no matter how hard I try.

I blink once, but he's still there, in khaki pants and a white button-down, his light brown hair combed into a tidy style, rather than the messy waves they were in the last time I saw him.

But those eyes...those eyes that are bright blue, narrowed and fixed on my face, watching my every move, are exactly as I remember.

"Holy shit," I whisper and try to take a step back.

"Do you know each other?" Caleb asks.

Stay professional!

I shake my head and offer Brynna the best smile I can manage. "I'm so happy that you like the cake. It's ready to go for you. Congratulations again."

And with that, I turn to leave, but before I can even take one step, I hear, "Stop."

As much as it totally pisses me off, my body halts and I stand still, my hands folded in front of me, and watch him warily. Just the sound of that one word out of his sexy-as-hell mouth has my nipples puckered.

Thank God no one can tell since I'm wearing this baker's jacket.

I refuse to cause a scene here in front of all of these people, but what I really want to do is tell him to kiss my ass and stomp off.

Pinning me with his gaze, he grasps my arm and leads me away from the others.

"I'm happy to see you, Nic. You look beautiful. The new haircut suits you."

His nose pressed to my ear, the clean, masculine scent of him surrounding me, has me turned inside out, and frankly, I can't deal with it.

I can't deal with him.

I'm breathing hard, and my cheeks are flushed as I wrench my arm out of his grasp, toss him an angry glare and storm away.

I'm not sure, but I think I hear him mutter, "Spank her ass," behind me, making me move faster, praying that he doesn't follow me.

And just like that, memories I've been fighting to forget come barreling back at me...

"Are you coming or not, little one?"

Bailey pushes me with her shoulder, and I stumble toward him, not able to look away from those incredible blue eyes.

"So, you want to give it a try?" he asks, holding my gaze.

I swallow hard and nod slowly.

Where the hell did my voice go?

"I need a verbal response, please," he replies with a knowing smile.

"Yes, please."

"Don't worry," he whispers as he leans his face close to mine. "This won't hurt a bit."

I offer him a small smile, and he surprises me by pulling his fingers gently down my cheek, then brushes his thumb over my lower lip, sending my body into overdrive.

My nipples have puckered, and I swear to God I need to change my panties.

And he really hasn't even done anything yet!

He drags a black duffle bag across the floor to his feet and rummages inside, drawing out a long length of white rope.

"White will look beautiful against your clothes," he murmurs, deep in thought. He scrubs his fingers over his mouth as he thinks, bouncing his attention between me and his bag of tricks.

I giggle at the thought, then cover my mouth with my hand as his head snaps around and he raises an eyebrow as he watches me.

"Something funny?"

I shake my head no, but he grips my chin between his thumb and forefinger, making me meet his hot gaze.

"Try again."

"I thought it was funny that you were rummaging through your bag of tricks." My voice is soft. Why do I feel the need to please this guy?

His lips twitch, and he releases me, and I'm shocked at the feeling of loss at having the contact of his skin gone from mine.

God, get a grip. I obviously need to get laid. It's been…way longer than I am comfortable admitting.

"Wrap your arms behind your back and grab your forearms with your hands."

"I don't want my hands bound," I reply quickly.

He stares at me for a moment and then steps to me, leaning in so his mouth is near my ear. God, he smells amazing, like spicy body wash and hot, unadulterated man.

"I can cut you out at the drop of a hat, little one. This won't hurt you. Trust me."

He pulls back, watching me, and I nod hesitantly, putting my arms around my back like he asked. I don't know why I trust him, but I do. He's not going to hurt me.

I'm rewarded with a bright smile, and if my panties weren't already wet, they would be now. Holy shit, this man is amazing. As he turns away from me to gather his rope, I let my eyes wander down his body. He's very tall, over six feet. His shoulders are broad and covered by a black button-down shirt, the cuffs rolled on his corded forearms. The shirt is tucked into black slacks, and he's wearing black shoes and a belt as well.

The black should give him a daunting appearance, but it's just plain hot. It fits him. I suddenly want to lick him.

Down girl, you're just here to try out the bondage thing.

Beside us, the other man has resumed tying his ropes around the other girls who were in line behind me. I look around for Bailey, but she's nowhere to be seen.

"She's not far," the stranger murmurs, reading my mind.

"What's your name?" I ask softly as he turns to me and reaches around me, tying my wrists behind my back. My nose is practically pressed to his chest, and I can't help but breathe him in again.

He just smells so good.

"Matt." He pulls the ropes around my arms and torso and smiles down at me. "You?"

"Nic," I respond, watching as he begins looping and knotting the rope over my chest and stomach, making a perfectly symmetrical design over my chest, around my breasts, the ropes looking amazing against the red and black material. His hands are long and lean, and his fingers work deftly, quickly, easily making the knots and loops in the rope.

"You're good at this," I murmur.

He grins and continues to watch his hands as they move against me, the backs of his fingers brushing against the sides of my breasts, over my stomach.

My breath comes faster and my heart rate speeds up as he continues to work. My torso is done, and when I try to pull my hands, they're tied tightly in place.

"Does it hurt?" he asks softly.

"No," I reply honestly.

He nods as he reaches between my legs and threads the rope, loops it around my back and back through my legs again. I have to bite my lip to keep from moaning aloud.

Dear God, how is it possible that I'm this turned on just because he's wrapped me up in some rope?

Finally, he ties a knot, making it blend in with the rest, so you can't tell where the rope begins or ends, and stands back, crosses his arms over his chest and gently runs the tip of his forefinger over his bottom lip as his eyes rake up and down my body. His bright blue eyes are hot with lust and need as they meet mine. His breath is coming faster, matching mine, and I swear to the bondage gods, I feel an inexplicable pull from my gut to his.

If he doesn't touch me—truly touch me—soon, I'm going to spontaneously combust.

Finally, he slowly moves to me, cups my face in his hands and kisses my forehead, before whispering, "Do you belong to anyone?"

The question should piss me off, but I'm so caught up in his spell, I can only shake my head no.

"Nic," he whispers and kisses the corner of my mouth, then sweeps his lips down my jawline to my ear. "I don't typically come on this strong, but I want to fuck the shit out of you right now."

My breath catches and eyes widen as I lean back to look him in the eye.

Tell him no! Run away! Jesus, what kind of sick pervert says something like that?

But, instead, I find myself licking my lips and leaning toward him. "I live three blocks away."

He tears his gaze away from mine and nods at his colleague, grips my upper arm in his strong hand and leads me beside him, not behind him, toward the door.

"Wait! My friend…"

"Is right over there," he says calmly, pointing through the crowd. Bailey is watching us with a knowing grin and gives me a thumbs-up and an obvious wink. "See? She's fine."

"Hold on." I dig my heels in and pull us both to a stop. "You could be an ax murderer. A junkie. A rapist."

His lips twitch, and he sighs as he sinks his fingers through my long hair, pushing it off my shoulder. "Good girl."

"So, I'll see you around…"

"Stop," he commands softly, and I immediately obey, my feet betraying every instinct I have to keep going.

He walks to me, wraps one arm around my back and grips my bound wrists, holding me close to him. With just that one touch, my body flares to life, and I can't help but press myself even closer against him.

He chuckles and brushes my nose with his. "I haven't felt this physically attuned to anyone in a very long time. I promise you, I'm no criminal." And with that, he covers my lips with his and sinks into me, exploring my lips, nibbling and tasting me, and I melt against him, submitting to his every desire.

I can't move my arms, and I desperately want to circle them around his neck, grip his hair in my fists and hold him to me. Instead, I press my chest to his and moan as his tongue plunders my mouth. He wraps his other arm around me and presses his pelvis against my stomach, making me well aware of his erection.

Fuck, he's sexy.

"It's your call," he whispers.

"Let's go."

He doesn't need to be told twice as he leads me out to his BMW and settles me into the passenger seat, buckling me in with my arms pinned behind me. It's uncomfortable, and I have to lean away from the back of the seat, but I'm so damn turned on right now I don't even care.

He smiles wolfishly before kissing my cheek. "I like seeing you restrained like this."

Before I can respond, he shuts the door, hops into the driver's seat and speeds away.

"Three blocks down on the left," I instruct him.

"Above that bakery?" he asks and points.

"Yes. Nice car."

"It was a gift," he replies carelessly as he parks.

Who in the hell gives someone a car as a gift?

He finds parking and leads me up the stairs at the side of my building.

"You'll have to pull my key out of my purse," I murmur, turning so he can access my purse.

"Digging in a woman's purse always makes me nervous," he confesses with a grin. "My mother would have cut our hands off if we dared open her bag."

"Well, I'm a bit tied up here," I respond with a smile.

"That you are," he replies as he finds my keys and opens my door. He lays my bag and keys on my table and leads me deeper into my apartment toward my bedroom.

"A couple of guidelines," he murmurs gently. *"If you say 'no' or 'stop,' it all ends immediately. I'm not a sadist, so I don't want you to hurt. But you will do as I say, without question."* He leans down and pins me in those ice-blue eyes. *"Are we clear?"*

"I don't have a say?"

"I didn't say that. If you are in pain or uncomfortable, you say so. But I'm going to make very sure that you're not." He grins, pushes a finger in the ropes that cross between my breasts and tugs me to him.

"Do I need a safe word?" I ask.

"'No' is your safe word, little one."

"Okay," I whisper just before his mouth finds mine again. His mouth is hard and frantic, urgent. This is going to be fast and hard, and oh my God, I can hardly wait.

We reach my bedroom, and he flips on the bedside lamp, sending a soft glow through the room.

"I can't take my clothes off with these ropes around me."

Standing before me, he leans his forehead against my own and brushes his hands down my upper arms and my sides, down my thighs to where the edge of my thigh-highs meet my skirt.

"I don't need you naked to fuck you. It would be preferable, but I enjoy seeing you in my ropes."

I grin and tilt my head to the side. *"Why?"*

He shakes his head and covers my mouth with his as he unbuttons his shirt and tosses it aside. He steps away from me to open his belt and pants, steps out of them, and I'm shocked to see that he wasn't wearing any underwear.

How that can shock me after everything I've seen tonight, I have no idea.

His eyes drift down my face, my neck to my breasts to where my nipples are pressed against the material of my shirt. He cups my breasts in his hands and bends over to pull the hard nubs into his mouth, shirt and all.

My head falls back as I feel the pull all the way down between my legs where the ropes are nestled against my folds. All he has to do is tug them and my panties to the side and he can easily slide right inside me.

"Want to touch you," I whisper. I desperately want to grip his hard dick in my hand, make him as crazy as he's making me.

He lays a hand on my shoulder. "On your knees," he murmurs, guiding me down before him.

I greedily open wide, taking the head of his hard cock into my mouth, sucking and lapping at him like my life depends on it.

And damn if I don't feel myself grow wetter when he growls deep in his throat.

I look up to find him watching me, his jaw clenched tightly and eyes narrowed, glowing bright blue.

"Fuck, you're good at that," he groans and gathers my long hair in his hands, pulling until he's just tugging, not quite hurting me, and begins to guide himself in and out of my mouth. He never pushes in hard enough to choke me. He's in complete control, enjoying my mouth on him.

"There is nothing sexier than this. You, on your knees, in my ropes, with your sexy mouth wrapped around my dick."

God, I love his dirty mouth.

I moan in agreement and slide my tongue over the long vein on the underside of him. I can't help but grin to myself when I feel the fingers in my hair shake.

Suddenly, he guides me to my feet and bends me over the bed. He hikes my skirt up over my ass, parts the ropes and pulls my thong to one side. Instead of pushing inside me like I'm expecting, he kneels and buries his face deep into my folds, sucking and licking and making me see stars.

"Holy shit!" I squeal and try to stand, but he plants one large hand between my shoulder blades and holds me down as he assaults me with his mouth. It's the most incredible thing I've ever felt.

He presses two fingers inside me and massages my clit with his thumb as he stands behind me, opens a condom with his teeth and manages to roll it down his length one-handed.

He quickly pulls his fingers out of me and replaces them with his cock, pushing in until he's seated balls-deep, making us both moan. He grips my bound hands and begins to ride me, hard and fast.

"God, you feel so good." His voice is rough and broken. "So fucking tight. How long has it been?"

I shrug. Jesus, he wants me to think now?

"Answer me," he commands and slaps my ass with his hand, making me squeal.

The pain surprises me but is quickly replaced by an erotic heat that makes me want to squirm beneath him.

"I don't know. A year?"

"Fuck me," he whispers and continues to pound inside me, as though he's running a race, and the finish line is in sight. He keeps his hand tightly gripped to my wrists, and with the other, grips on to my hair and pulls me back until my chest is off the bed and I'm completely at his mercy.

"Does this hurt?" he asks, his mouth pressed against my ear.

"No," I gasp. God, this angle makes him feel even bigger. I want to rotate my hips, to push back against him, but I'm defenseless with my arms pinned and my torso being held off the bed.

"Am I pulling your hair too hard?"

Yes.

But I like it.

"No," I reply and gasp when he pushes into me even harder, bucking his hips against my ass. I feel the tension building, settling in the small of my back.

"Do not come until I tell you," he commands, his teeth clenched.

"But…" I begin, but he grips my wrist tighter.

"You heard me."

I swallow and try to concentrate on something else. Grocery shopping. The orders I have to fill for tomorrow. What to send to my grandmother for her birthday next month.

But it's no use. My body is on fire, and there is no turning back.

Finally, with a roar, he pushes inside me and yells out, "Come, Nic!"

And I do, succumbing to the most intense orgasm of my life. My hips jerk against him as he comes inside me, our bodies moving in sync, perfectly attuned to each other.

Finally, he plants a gentle kiss between my shoulder blades as he releases my hair and wrists and begins to untie me.

"You could just cut me out," I whisper, resting against the soft cotton of my duvet.

"I prefer this," he replies softly.

As he loosens the knots, he massages my skin gently, and my body is just one big ball of sensation, from the intense sex and the sweet way he's touching me now.

When my arms are free, he helps me to my feet so he can finish untying his intricate knots.

"I liked it," I murmur, watching his hands.

"Did you," he responds with a half smile.

I nod shyly, feeling my cheeks heat.

"No need to get shy on me now."

I chuckle as he pulls the last of the rope away.

"Thank you."

His eyes find mine, and he frowns. "For what?"

I tilt my head to the side, finding the words. "For this…new experience."

Matt smirks and raises my hand to his mouth where he plants sweet kisses on my knuckles, then yanks me against him. He's still naked as can be, and I'm fully dressed, but I finally get to touch him. His skin is warm and smooth beneath my hands as I glide them up and down his back, his arms, up into his thick hair.

"Your hands are dangerous," he murmurs against my lips.

"You feel amazing."

He smiles down at me and catches my hands in his, kisses my nose and moves away.

"I'm going to need your phone number."

As he speaks, his phone rings in his pants. He frowns and pulls away from me to retrieve his phone and answers.

"Yeah."

He scowls and begins to swear a blue streak as he yanks his clothes on. "I'm on the way. Are the girls okay? I'll be there in ten minutes."

He snaps his phone shut and gazes at me with regret.

"You have to go."

"Yeah." He kisses me quickly, his mind already somewhere else. "I'll call you."

And with that he runs out of my apartment. He's gone before I can remind him that he never got around to taking my number.

It's probably for the best. He's into shit that I have no concept of. This will just be one night that I'll never forget.

I shower and dress in my pajamas, grab a bag of chips out of the pantry, and settle on the couch, not paying attention to what's on TV.

I wonder who the girls were that he mentioned. Could he have kids?

Oh. My. God.

I just had random sex with a married guy with kids! I'm so fucking stupid! Just because a guy is hot and says, "Trust me, baby," doesn't mean that I can, in fact, trust him.

I toss the bag of chips aside and hang my head in my hands. And what the fuck was I doing, playing at the whole submissive-girl-who-likes-to-be-tied-up thing? That's not me.

Now I wish he had taken my number so I could tell him off when he calls.

"Nic, stop."

His voice is hard and close behind me.

Damn it.

I almost made it to my car.

"Why?" I ask and whirl around, turning on him. "What could you possibly have to say to me?"

CHAPTER TWO

~Matt~

"First, I think I need to apologize for something, based on your less-than-warm reaction to seeing me, but I'm not sure exactly what I did wrong, except forget to take your number before I ran out of your apartment."

A mistake I've been kicking myself for ever since. That one night with this gorgeous dark-haired, green-eyed woman has haunted me since I had her beneath me, wrapped up in my ropes.

"I'm quite sure your wife and kids would have had an issue with you taking my number. I can't believe I was so stupid." She clenches her eyes shut and shakes her head while I scowl down at her.

"What wife and kids?" I ask, dumbfounded.

"Yours," she replies.

I feel my eyes widen in surprise. "I'm not married, Nic."

She whips her green gaze up to mine, and her jaw drops.

"Why did you think that?" I ask as I step closer to her.

"Because when you took that call, you asked if the girls were okay."

I nudge her chin up with my fingertip, making her meet my eyes. That she's been convinced for weeks that I am a married man who cheated on my wife with her pisses me off beyond words.

"Brynna was in a car accident that night, and she had the girls with her."

She gasps, her eyes go even wider, and then she frowns, looking toward the house. She obviously wants to go to Bryn, to check on her.

God, she's amazing.

"So you see, I'm as single as they come, Nicole."

"Nic," she replies absently, then shakes herself and focuses back on me. "It doesn't matter." She pulls away.

My eyes travel down her petite little body, currently covered in a crisp white baker's jacket and black slacks. A simple red bow is tied around her head. She's beautiful in anything, whether it be a small skirt and barely there top, or this boxy jacket.

Fuck, she'd be beautiful in a burlap sack.

And I haven't even seen her naked yet.

Yet.

"Why?" I ask calmly.

"Because I'm not your type, Matt." She smirks and opens her car door, throws her bag into the back seat and turns back to me with sad eyes that contradict the stubborn set of her jaw.

"Why?" I ask again. "What type is that?"

"Submissive. I don't have a submissive bone in my body." She spreads her arms wide. "I have opinions, and I like to assert them. I don't like being told what to do."

She's definitely not suitable to be a full-time sub. There's no way in hell that she's slave material. And I don't give a fuck about that anyway.

I'm no slave master.

But she was perfect in the bedroom, the way she communicated freely but let me push her limits, her fear of having her hands tied, and bringing her just to the edge of her pain threshold, gripping her hair in my hand and holding her up off the mattress.

Goddamn it, just thinking about her flushed cheeks and the way she looked back at me while I pounded inside her makes my dick throb.

Her breathing increases and her cheeks redden as she watches me, as though she can read my thoughts. She drops her arms and twists her hands together at her waist.

"I beg to differ."

"I'm the one who's supposed to beg, right?" She shakes her head and lowers herself into her car. "It'll never happen. Leave it be, Matt."

And with that she drives away.

Not a chance in fucking hell am I going to leave it be.

***

"So, I know you're ugly as fuck, but you don't usually scare the women off. What happened?" Will smirks at me as I join the others in my parents' backyard.

"Fuck you," I reply under my breath and yank a bottle of water out of a cooler, twist off the top and take a long pull.

"Seriously," Will responds, his face sobering. "Is everything okay?"

"I don't know," I shake my head and turn to watch my family.

Caleb is dancing on the grass with Brynna. They're grinning at each other and talking softly amongst themselves. Their daughters, Maddie and Josie, are dancing around them, their pretty white dresses flowing around their legs as they giggle and skip, their dog, Bix, joining in the fun.

Our parents all have their heads together at a long table. My mom is holding Liam, my oldest brother, Isaac's baby boy, who is drooling profusely and chewing on his fist. My dad is listening to her tell a story to Luke's parents, smiling at her as if she hung the moon.

And as far as we're all concerned, she did.

Our family has grown by leaps and bounds in the past few years. Now that Caleb is married off, Dominic and I are the only ones who have managed to stay single, and I don't plan to change my status any time soon.

Our baby sister, Jules, is rubbing her barely there belly and leaning on her husband of almost a year, Nate. They're chatting with Natalie, Jules' longtime friend and who we all consider to be our sister, and her husband, Luke Williams, along with Luke's sister, Sam, and their younger brother, Mark.

At a nearby table, Will's fiancée, Meg, is chatting with her brother, Leo, and our oldest brother, Isaac, with his wife, Stacy.

Dominic, a brother we recently discovered we had as a result of a brief affair on our father's part more than thirty years ago, is talking quietly with Alecia, the event planner who pulled this wedding together at a moment's notice.

"So you chased off the baker," Caleb comments as he approaches Will and me. The song is over, and Brynna has returned to chat with Jules and Nat.

"I didn't chase her off," I growl.

"How do you know her?" Isaac asks as he also joins us.

"Jesus, don't you all have anything better to do?"

"Than nose into your personal life?" Will asks and shakes his head as he stuffs some appetizers into his mouth. "No way."

"She's just someone I met a few weeks ago."

"You like her," Isaac comments.

"What are you, a girl?" I smirk and glance over at Brynna, who is laughing at something Jules just said. "Are we going to talk about our feelings now?"

"This is a wedding, dude," Will replies. "Feelings are running rampant around here."

"Well, in that case, now's as good a time as any to give a toast."

And get your focus off of me, for fuck's sake.

I walk to the center of the yard and motion to Alecia, who speaks into her wrist, and magically, the music hushes.

"Okay, everyone, it's time for a toast," I announce in a loud voice. Everyone turns to me, and I tuck one hand in my pocket and shift awkwardly.

I've never been comfortable being the center of attention. That's Will's job.

"First, I want to say congratulations to both of you." I turn my eyes to Caleb as he stands behind his bride and wraps his arms around her waist with his chin resting on her shoulder. "You each went through your own private hell to get where you are. To find each other. And, honestly, I can't think of two people who deserve to be happy more than you."

Brynna's eyes fill with tears, but I keep going.

"Brynna, you've been a part of our family for a while now. I know that I've thought of you as a sister for quite some time. Your daughters, despite being little extortionists, are beautiful and wonderful, just like their mother. You have the strength and humor to put up with this sometimes overwhelming family, and we love you. It's my pleasure to officially welcome you to our family."

There are whoops and hollers as everyone applauds. When the noise dies, I continue.

"Caleb, you're not just my little brother. You're my best friend."

"Hey!" Will interrupts, but I ignore him and continue.

"You're here, whole and healthy, thank God, because you were meant to make Brynna and her girls yours. I believe that. I'm just glad you pulled your head out of your ass and realized it yourself."

"Love you, too, bro," he replies softly.

"You're my hero," I tell him earnestly and with a strong voice. Our brothers and Jules all nod and murmur in agreement. "So, to Brynna and Caleb." I raise my water, and everyone follows suit. "May you always be as happy as you are today."

"Here, here!" our father exclaims.

"And now for the gifts!" Jules announces and claps her hands.

Dom steps forward with a grin. It's still surreal to look at him and know that he's my brother. Where the rest of us are all fair, with blond to dark blond hair, Dom is dark, with black hair. But he shares our blue eyes.

"You know that I own a villa in Tuscany," he begins. Brynna's eyes widen, and Caleb laughs. "I'd like for you to spend two weeks there. Enjoy it. You'll have Maria, who will come in to cook your meals, but other than that, it'll just be the two of you."

"We're keeping the kids!" Bryn's dad calls out.

"Is Maria a good cook?" Will asks, earning a punch in the arm by Meg. "What? Maybe we should go there, too."

"Thank you so much," Brynna replies and blushes when Dom plants a kiss on her cheek, earning a growl from Caleb.

"That's not all," Luke adds. "You're going to need to get there. We," he gestures to the rest of the siblings, "have all pitched in to charter a private jet, so you can go whenever it's convenient for you."

"You don't have to—" Caleb begins, but Nate interrupts.

"One thing you know about us, we don't do anything we don't want to. We want to."

"So you just decide when you want to go, and it's yours," Dom informs them.

"But until then," Natalie joins in, a wide smile on her beautiful face, "we've reserved a room for you at a bed-and-breakfast at the beach. You can go have as much sex as you want over the next four days."

"Thank you all, so much," Brynna replies with tears in her eyes, hugging everyone in turn.

"Let's dance, sweetheart." I hold my hand out to her and lead her to the grass where the music has started again. *Need You Now* by Lady Antebellum.

Appropriate.

I pull Brynna into my arms, and we begin to sway with the music.

"How are you feeling?" I ask her.

"Happy," she replies with a grin.

"That's not what I mean," I respond, and she nods. She knows I'm referring to the injuries she sustained in the car accident a few weeks ago.

"I'm good, Matt. Much better."

"Good."

"Are you going to tell me about her?" Brynna asks with a knowing smile.

I don't even bother pretending that I don't know what she's talking about.

"I hardly know her."

"Didn't seem that way to me."

"It's true." I look over her shoulder when Nate swings Maddie up onto his back and runs around the yard with her, making her giggle incessantly.

"She's a really sweet woman. I like her. Do you want her number?"

"I have it," I reply and smile at her warmly. I never got around to getting it from Nic when I ran out of her apartment two weeks ago, but it wasn't hard to track her down, since I know where she lives.

"You know where she works now," she reminds me.

"I'm not going to stalk her at her job."

"So you'll just stalk her during her private time?" Brynna asks with an innocent smile.

"Doesn't Caleb ever spank you?" I ask.

"Yeah"—she sighs and grins over at her husband—"he does."

"You've had your hands on my wife long enough," Caleb informs me as he cuts in.

"Possessive much?" I ask as I back away.

"Like you'd be any different."

I smirk, but he's right. If I found a woman I wanted to spend my life with, I'd be damn possessive.

"Thanks for the dance, sweetheart."

"Good luck." She winks at me just before Caleb twirls her away and into his arms.

***

I'm restless.

The reception wrapped up awhile ago. Caleb and Brynna are off to their weekend away on the coast, and everyone has gone home. I'm sitting in my Belltown apartment, watching the lights of my city.

And I can't seem to get a certain dark-haired pixie out of my head.

I'm not sure what it is about her, exactly, that has me so interested. I've fucked my share of beautiful women. Tied them up, had my way with them, and moved on with my life.

Her insisting that she's not my type should be a flashing neon warning sign that I should just stay away.

No means no, after all.

But she's wrong. She may not be submissive all the time, but she is beautifully submissive in the bedroom.

And damn if I don't want to show her how life-changing it can be.

Fuck it.

I yank my phone out of my pocket and dial her number. She answers on the third ring, sounding out of breath, and my cock immediately stirs to life.

All she did was *breathe*, for Christ sake.

"Hello?"

"Hello, little one," I murmur and smile when I hear her gasp.

"How did you get my number?"

"You made a cake for my brother, Nic," I lie, not wanting to admit that I've had her number for well over a week now but was too consumed with my family to call her. "It wasn't hard."

"You are tenacious, I'll give you that."

"Look," I begin and shove a hand through my hair, "I think we got off on the wrong foot today. I'd like to talk with you."

"I like you, Matt." She sighs before she continues. "And, honestly, I'm flattered. You seem like a really good guy. But I wasn't kidding when I said that I'm not your type."

"I don't think that's true," I counter softly. "Let me show you."

She's quiet for a long minute, and I wonder if I've lost her before she clears her throat.

"I'd like to be friends," she whispers. "But I think that's all I can give you."

That's a start.

"Okay, for now."

"You're hot, but you're not irresistible, you know."

"You think I'm hot?" I grin and lean my shoulder against the cold glass of the window, watching cars drive by below.

"I have to go, egomaniac."

"I'd like to see you tomorrow."

"I just told you…"

"As friends. Friends drink coffee, right? Do you serve coffee at your bakery?"

She chuckles in my ear, and the tension in my stomach loosens as I hear her softening.

"Yes, I serve coffee."

"Great, I'll see you tomorrow."

"Good night, Matt."

"Good night, little one." I hang up, change into my gym clothes and head for the door. I'm too restless to be home. I need to burn off some steam, and going to the club tonight holds no interest for me.

Which in and of itself should be another big red flag.

The ten-block jog to the gym is invigorating. Summer has settled nicely over Seattle, making the days warm and the nights just perfect.

I start on the weights, working my core and arms today. Just when I've finished my second set of bench press, I sit up and pull my T-shirt over my head, wipe the sweat off my brow and chest with it, and throw it on the floor. As I take a long drink of water, my eyes survey the room.

And that's when I see her. Jesus, we belong to the same gym? She's on a treadmill across the room, running at a fast clip. Earbuds are tucked in her ears, and her eyes are on the console of the treadmill, probably watching her distance.

She's wearing nothing but black shorts and a tight black tank top. More of her body is exposed now than it was when I was plunged deep inside her.

Her little body is firm, yet curvy in the right places. Her arms are defined, probably from all the manual labor she does while baking.

When she's finished running and climbs off the treadmill, takes a long drink of water and wipes her face with a towel, I walk toward her.

Shit, I must look like a fucking stalker.

I keep my eyes trained on her as I approach, eager to see what her reaction will be when she sees me.

And I'm not disappointed when her eyes widen and her mouth opens as she lets those gorgeous green eyes roam down my body. My cock tightens at her gaze, and I want to pull her against me and kiss her stupid. But I just stay where I am, watching her.

She quickly recovers and raises an eyebrow.

"Okay, Matt, it's called stalking now."

I grin and offer her a fresh bottle of water, which she accepts, unscrews the cap and takes a sip.

Fuck, she has beautiful lips. Lips that look amazing wrapped around the head of my cock.

"It's not a crime to belong to a gym," I reply.

"*My* gym?"

"Do you own it?" I ask with a grin.

She laughs and shakes her head. "No."

"It's not far from my apartment, and it's convenient to work, too, so here I am."

She nods and glances down, not sure what to say next.

"The cake was delicious today," I comment casually, giving her the opportunity to talk about her work.

"Oh, good!" She grins and joins me as I walk toward the smoothie bar, pull out a chair for her to drop into at one of the tiny two-person tables and sit opposite her. "I'm glad you enjoyed it."

"You do good work. Leo and Sam are always talking about your cupcakes."

"Leo and Sam keep me in business, I swear." She laughs, sending electricity down my spine. "They're very good customers."

I nod, watching her.

"I like your shorter hair," I murmur and reach out to brush the ends with my finger, enjoying the softness.

"Most men like long hair," she replies softly.

"I like long hair, too. You look beautiful in both."

She frowns and glances away from me.

"Why did you cut your hair, Nic?"

She shrugs and won't meet my gaze. "It was time for a change."

"Try again," I reply.

She turns her eyes to mine and squares her shoulders, firms her chin. "It was time for a change."

That's a lie.

I cross my arms over my naked chest and drag my finger over my lip, watching her squirm.

She isn't a good liar.

Good.

"Okay."

She sighs, relieved, before I continue.

"For now."

She scowls at me, making me laugh. "Friends don't lie to each other, little one. The sooner you remember that, the better."

"You've known me for three minutes, Matt. Don't assume you know all there is to know about me."

"You know what they say about assuming," I murmur with a grin.

"Well, you *are* an ass," she replies and then giggles.

I lean in and rest my mouth next to her ear. "This ass would love to smack *your* pretty little ass until it glows," I whisper so only she can hear.

She gasps and pulls back so she can look me in the eye, and I see it. The hunger. The lust. The awareness.

"Friends don't usually threaten to spank each other's asses," she murmurs softly.

I lean back in my chair, not answering her, and cross my arms again as she pulls herself together.

"I should head home," she says finally and stands. "I have to be in the shop early tomorrow."

"It was good to see you, Nic," I reply, allowing her to run. "I'll see you tomorrow."

She looks like she wants to say something more, probably to tell me not to bother coming into her shop, but she just shrugs and offers me a half smile before turning and walking away.

Yes, I'll definitely be seeing you tomorrow.

CHAPTER THREE

~Nicole~

This ass would love to smack your *pretty little ass until it glows.*

Christ on a crutch, who in the bloody hell says something like that?

I turn onto my side and stare at my alarm clock. 4:43. My alarm is going to go off in seventeen minutes, and I haven't slept a wink. Not even after a three-mile run and a hot, hot shower.

Instead, all I could hear was Matt's deep voice running through my head. His ice-blue eyes haunted me, the way they shine when he's happy and darken when he's turned on.

And they darken a lot when he looks at me.

I'd like to lick him.

Except, he would rather tie me up.

And the part that scares me is, I'd like for him to tie me up, too.

Dear God, what is wrong with me?

I sit up and turn off my alarm before trudging into the bathroom to begin getting ready for my day. When I go down to the shop in the mornings to bake the cupcakes for the day, I forgo any makeup in favor of comfort, then run upstairs about thirty minutes before we open to primp and be presentable for the clients. So it only takes a few minutes to pull on clothes, push my hair back with a headband—the one reason that I regret cutting my hair is no more ponytails—and I'm on my way down to the kitchen.

My work space is my pride and joy. I attended countless used commercial kitchen auctions, biding my time until I found the perfect equipment for just the right price. The stainless steel counters gleam under the fluorescent lights. My ovens are almost orgasm-inducing.

I love this place.

The front of the house was designed with the same care. I have a long glass display case that can hold roughly fifty dozen cupcakes at any time. I have an industrial espresso machine that would make Starbucks proud.

The color scheme is red, white and black. The floor is covered in black and white tile. The tables are little black wrought iron bistro tables for two covered in red tablecloths, and there is a long pub-height table by the front windows where people can stand with their treats and watch the traffic or the many musicians who come and go out of the nondescript recording studio across the street.

I've been open for just over a year, and I couldn't be happier with the success of the shop. Succulent Sweets has made a profit from the first month, which I know is rare.

I work my ass off for it.

I set out my ingredients for the different flavors of cakes and dig in immediately. It's a Sunday, so I'm open only half the day, from nine to one, but I still have orders to fill for two birthday parties, a baptism and a baby shower.

Thank God cupcakes are all the rage these days.

After the cupcakes that will be sold in the shop are all baked for the day, I let them cool while I bake the special orders. Just as I'm about to begin decorating, Tess, my part-time employee, bounces into the kitchen.

"Good morning," she sings and smiles widely.

"You are very chipper for this early on a Sunday morning," I respond with a smile. "And good morning."

"I went out last night," she announces as she ties her white apron around her trim waist. Tess is tall and thin, with thick blond, red and *pink* hair. She wears black-rimmed glasses that are almost as big as her face, but she insists they're very cool.

And, I have to admit, she looks adorable in them.

She pulls her hair back into a ponytail and grabs some frosting out of the fridge, ready to help me finish up today's baking.

"Who is he?" I ask.

"His name is Sean…" She scrunches up her face. "Sean something."

"Geez, Tess."

"Oh stop, I had a bit to drink. He's tall and built, and he has his nipples pierced."

"Ouch," I reply with a laugh.

Tess laughs with me as she frosts the lemon cupcakes with lemon frosting.

"How was your night?" she asks.

"Fine. I just went to the gym."

"Oh." She sighs and looks at me like I'm an old maid.

"Don't look at me like that."

"I just wish you'd go out and have fun," she replies and arranges the lemon cupcakes on a long plastic tray, ready for the glass case.

"I do go out and have fun," I reply.

"Going to kitchen auctions is not having fun," she responds sarcastically.

I send her the stink eye, and she visibly shrinks before holding her hands up in defeat. "Okay, okay, I'm sorry. I'm sure the kitchen auctions are totally fun and full of really hot guys."

"You're a smart-ass." I laugh and put the finishing touches on two dozen It's A Girl treats for my client.

"You love me," she replies and kisses my cheek before she bounces out to arrange the glass case out front.

"Okay," I announce when she returns, "these special orders just need to be boxed up. Do you mind doing that while I run upstairs and shower? I'll finish up with the daily special when I come back down."

"No problem. Take your time. We're ahead of schedule, boss lady."

I shake my head and chuckle as I climb the stairs to my apartment, shedding clothing on the way.

Tess is young, only in her early twenties and still in college, but she's a hard worker. She loves the shop, and I enjoy having her around. There's never a dull moment when she's working.

It doesn't take me long to shower and dress in my uniform of black slacks and red T-shirt with a white apron, tie the red ribbon in my hair like a headband and brush on a bit of makeup.

When I return to the kitchen, we still have forty-five minutes until we open, so we spend that time frosting the daily special—white chocolate mocha—and preparing batter for the next morning.

At nine a.m., Tess unlocks the door and immediately a small crowd of guests pours in to order a treat and coffee.

When the crowd finally dies down at about twelve thirty, I have a moment to slip in the back and quickly eat a banana and string cheese before consolidating the cupcakes in the glass case and tidying up the seating area.

The bell over the door rings behind me as I'm tucking chairs under a table.

"It smells amazing in here."

I'd know that voice anywhere.

It was in my head all night long.

I turn to find Matt and a slightly shorter, dark-haired man I've never seen before standing just inside the door. Matt has his hands in the pockets of his jeans and is smiling at me. The man with him has already crossed to the case, practically drooling over the cakes inside.

"Hi," I murmur, smoothing my hands down my apron.

"How's business today?" Matt asks as I walk behind the case, putting a good three feet between us.

"It's been busy. It just started to slow down."

"Montgomery has lost his manners," Matt's friend informs me with a smile. "I'm his partner, Asher."

"Hi, I'm Nic Dalton."

"I've driven by this place a hundred times and have always meant to come in." Asher grins as he peruses the case. "What do you recommend?"

"The chocolate," I reply, my gaze still stuck on Matt.

He's remained quiet, hanging back, watching my every move.

It's unnerving and yet comforting in a way I can't explain.

He's in a dark blue button-down shirt with the sleeves rolled, and it suddenly occurs to me that he's wearing a holster at his waist with a handgun and a badge clipped to it.

Glancing at Asher, I see he's wearing the same.

I raise an eyebrow at Matt. "I don't sell doughnuts here."

His lips twitch. I had no idea he's a cop!

"Maybe we need a change of pace," Matt replies. "Besides, I told you I'd be in today."

I nod and smile at Asher. "You sick of doughnuts, too?"

"I never get sick of doughnuts. But I'll take that chocolate cupcake right there."

I place his treat on a plate and hand it to him. He peels the paper off and takes a bite, his eyes rolling back in his head.

"Marry me," he announces and stuffs the rest in his mouth. "Marry me right now. We'll go to Vegas."

I laugh and shake my head. "What can I get you, Matt?"

"Dinner tomorrow night," he replies smoothly.

"Dude, you're good," Asher compliments him. "But she's marrying *me*."

"Who's marrying who?" Tess asks as she returns from the kitchen then stops in her tracks. Her eyes widen as she takes in the two very attractive—okay, gorgeous—men chatting with me.

"Nic is going to marry me," Asher announces with a wink.

"Or, I can just keep baking cupcakes and you're welcome to stop in from time to time. That way, there are no messy contracts or things like commitment," I suggest with a laugh.

"Yes, that'll work," Asher agrees.

"Tess, could you please box up a couple of the chocolate for Asher to go?" I ask her and then turn to Matt. "What would you like?"

"I told you. Dinner tomorrow night."

My heart skips a beat then shifts into overdrive.

"I meant…"

"I know what you meant. I'll take a dozen of the special and dinner tomorrow night."

"Yes, she'll go," Tess answers for me.

"You, I can fire, you know."

She waves me off like I just announced that she has something in her teeth.

Matt laughs as he accepts the cupcakes from me. "Can I talk to you somewhere more private?"

The shop is still empty, so I nod and lead him back into the kitchen.

"You didn't have to buy a whole dozen just to ask me to dinner," I inform him softly.

"I bought them for the guys at the precinct." He shrugs and grins at me. Is this really the same man who had me tied up in knots—literally and figuratively—not long ago?

"So, you're a cop."

"I am." He nods.

"So, if I need to file a stalking complaint, you're the person to call?"

Matt takes a step to me and drags his index finger down my cheek to my jawline. "There's a number you can call for that, but I hope I'm not the one you're thinking of turning in."

I smirk and watch him, waiting for him to dictate to me what we'll do next or where we'll go to dinner, but he just waits for me, watching me just as I am him.

"I'll go to dinner with you tomorrow," I finally murmur. My stomach clenches and nipples tighten when he offers me that megawatt smile and leans in to plant his lips on my forehead.

"Excellent. What time will you be finished here?"

"Four in the afternoon."

"Pick you up at six?"

He's asking, not telling!

"Sure."

He cups my face in his hands and sighs as he looks in my eyes. "We will need to talk, little one."

"That is usually a part of going to dinner with someone," I reply with an innocent smile.

He laughs and plants a chaste kiss on my lips then turns to leave. "See you tomorrow." He winks, and then he's gone.

I lean on the countertop, trying to catch my breath. Good God, he barely touched me and I was ready to tear my clothes off and attack him right here in the kitchen.

That's so not gonna happen.

I busy myself by wiping down the already clean countertops, trying to clear my head before I can face Tess or any potential customers.

One thing I can say about Matt is, he always leaves me off balance, not necessarily in a bad way.

Would it hurt so much to go out to dinner with him? To get to know him better? I lean my hips against the countertop and scrub my hands over my face.

"Did you forget to eat again? Are you okay?"

I whirl at the sound of Bailey's voice to find her standing in the doorway, her hands on her hips and her pretty face pulled into a frown.

"I'm fine."

"Are you closing soon?"

I check the time, surprised to see it's already almost one, which is my closing time on Sunday.

"Yes, in just a few minutes."

"Good, we're going out for appetizers and wine," she informs me.

"Nic has a date!" Tess shouts excitedly as she bursts into the kitchen. "With a hot cop!"

"Really?" Bailey asks and watches me speculatively. "We are definitely going out for wine."

"I wish I could go, but I just got a call from Sean." Tess grins as she grabs her purse and shucks her apron. "I already closed up, boss, so you're good to go."

"That was quick," I reply.

"It was dead out there, so I closed up while the other cop—Asher—chatted with me. He placed an order for a dozen strawberry shortcake cupcakes for Saturday. It's his daughter's birthday."

"That's sweet," I respond as I close up the kitchen for the night.

Tess waves and takes off, leaving Bailey and I. me.

"Talk," she commands.

"I need wine first." I sigh as I grab my wallet.

I lock the door behind us, and we walk down the block to Vintage.

"Your usuals?" our waiter, Dan, asks after he seats us.

"Yes, please," Bailey responds and then giggles after the handsome college student leaves to fill our order. "I think we come here too often."

"No, it's just right," I disagree. "We'd have to train someone else if we went to a different place. Besides, they have happy hour all day on Sunday, and that's hard to find, too."

"Good point." She nods.

"One glass of pinot noir and one glass of merlot and a basket of fresh bread." Dan winks at me then rubs his hands together. "What would you like to eat?"

"We'll take the spinach dip with chips and calamari," Bailey responds.

"Oh, and the cheese and cracker platter, too, please," I add enthusiastically. I'm starved, and that's not a good thing.

"You got it, ladies."

We both watch Dan's firm, young ass as he walks away and then sigh as we take sips of our wine.

"So, who's the cop you're going out with, and why am I just now hearing about it?" Bailey asks.

I feel my cheeks heat as I swirl the wine in my glass. Bailey is the only person I told about my night with the handsome man. "I ran into Matt yesterday at the wedding I did the cake for."

"Matt, as in the guy who tied you up and rocked your world, Matt?"

"The same," I reply with a nod.

"Small world."

I snort. "Right."

"He seems nice."

"He's kinky," I respond without thinking, then bite my lip and shake my head.

"He's into bondage, so what?"

"Do you know him?" I ask, hoping she says yes so I can drill her for information.

"Not really. I've seen him around before, but I've never spoken to him." Bailey cocks her head, takes a sip of her wine and watches me closely. "What's your hang-up?"

"I'm not submissive, Bailey."

"Okay."

"Trust me when I say, he's pretty dominant in the bedroom."

"Okay."

I growl and glare at my best friend. "Stop saying okay."

"Look, you're overthinking this, Nic." She squirms a bit across from me, getting comfortable. "You two had a good time together. Did he scare you?"

"No."

"Did he hurt you?" She's watching me very carefully, reading my body as well as my words.

"No," I reply immediately.

"Then what makes you hesitate to see him again?" she asks, confused.

"Well, at first I thought he was married with kids," I remind her and glare when she bursts out laughing. "But I found out yesterday that it was a family emergency, and he's single."

"Dramatic much?" she asks, still laughing. "I told you it probably wasn't that."

"Look, he lives a lifestyle that I know nothing about, and I *can't* lose control of my life, Bailey. You know that better than anyone."

"Who says he wants to control your life?" Bailey asks, her expression clearly confused.

"Please, he's a Dominant, right?"

She grows quiet, frowns and fidgets with her glass for a moment before pinning me in her gaze. She looks…*hurt*.

"I never figured you as a snob, Nic."

"What?!"

"Every person is different, no matter their circumstances. You're a baker, but I bet another baker doesn't make cupcakes the exact same way you do. Matt likes bondage and, yes, he's dominant in the bedroom, but you haven't even given him a chance to talk to you. He may not be looking for a full-time sub. Maybe he just wants to tie you up and boss you around in the bedroom. He's obviously into you."

I don't know what to say. I'm still stuck on "snob."

"He didn't hurt you, and he had a valid reason for leaving that night. Give him a chance. See where it leads. Maybe it won't be for you, but you won't know until you try."

"How can you be a part of this community and not be a little afraid of it?" I ask honestly. "I know you. You're not weird or some kind of whack job."

"Um, thanks. I think." She wrinkles her nose and then giggles. "Most people who enjoy sex on the kinky side aren't whack jobs. We're just a little different. I'm not sure where I fit in yet. I'm not submissive. There isn't one particular fetish that I enjoy more than others. I guess I'm still figuring it out."

"Since when are you so smart?" I ask.

"I just don't want you to throw away something that could be good just because you have preconceived notions about a lifestyle you know nothing about. This isn't fiction, Nic. He's just a guy. If it turns out that you don't like it, you can end it and move on."

"I did like it," I admit softly. "And maybe that scared me."

"Did he check in with you?"

"What do you mean?"

"When he was with you, while you were tied and whatever else he had you doing. Did he check to make sure you were okay?"

I think back to that night in my apartment, to the way he asked me if he was hurting me.

"Yes."

She nods and smiles at me. "I'm excited for you."

"It's just dinner tomorrow night," I remind her.

"But you're gonna give it a chance, right?"

I drain my wine glass and watch my best friend for a moment and feel the excitement spread from my belly, out my arms and into my throat.

And it has nothing to do with the wine.

"Yeah, I definitely am."

"Attagirl!"

***

Why did I agree to go out to dinner with him?

Do *friends* go out to dinner? Well, girlfriends do, and I guess I've been out to dinner with Ben once or twice when I was back home visiting.

Even though he's my ex-boyfriend, he's just a friend now.

And I'm overthinking this.

I'm in black capris and a white top with the shoulders cut out, showing off the ink on my right shoulder.

The doorbell rings just as I finish primping my short dark hair. I slide my feet into black sandals, grab my handbag and open the door to the finest specimen of man I've ever seen. He's in faded denim and a blue T-shirt that molds to his torso, defining every ab, making me want to pull him inside this apartment and say screw it to dinner.

"Hey." He grins.

"Hi yourself." He steps back, allowing me to pull the door closed and lock the deadbolt.

"You look great." He motions for me to lead him down the stairs to the sidewalk below.

"Likewise," I reply and then giggle. "Seriously, it should be illegal to look like that in a T-shirt."

He cringes and then laughs. "I'll have to look that law up."

"Do that," I reply. "So, where are we going?"

"There's a great place over by the Seattle Center. It's not far, and it's gorgeous tonight. Let's walk."

"Sounds good." I fall into step beside him as we head down the dozen or so city blocks to the Seattle Center, where the Experience Music Project, Space Needle and KeyArena all are. It's always a bustling place, lots to see.

"How did you find your building?" he asks as we wait for a stoplight to change.

"It took months," I inform him. "I think my Realtor was ready to throw me into the sound by the time we found it. But I was picky." I shrug and then shiver when he rests his hand on the small of my back, leading me across the busy intersection. "I knew when I saw it that I wanted it."

"It's an awesome location."

"It really is. Plus, Leo Nash comes in on a regular basis. That's one piece of eye candy that never gets old."

Matt laughs next to me and steps around the opposite side of a tree, dividing us.

"Bread and butter," I mumble.

"What?" he asks with a smile.

"When you're with someone, and you both walk around the opposite side of something, you're supposed to say 'bread and butter' so you don't have bad luck." I giggle and glance up at him. "At least, that's what my great-grandmother used to tell me. But she was very superstitious."

"I'll have to remember that," he replies with a grin. "So, back to Leo, did you meet him at the wedding?"

"No." I shake my head. "I saw him there. I don't usually talk to the guests. Actually, I don't do many weddings."

"Why not?"

"Because they're stressful and most brides are certifiable."

Matt leads me past the EMP, and we stop to watch a juggler for a few moments.

"I prefer to be in my shop."

"Do other musicians come in?"

"Sure. I've had Adam Levine in. I thought Tess was going to pee herself." I laugh at the memory. "Bruno Mars, Eddie Vedder, Blake Shelton...they've all been in."

"That's cool. But Leo's your favorite?"

"He's nice. His girlfriend is always really nice, too. Sam, right?"

He nods, watching me, and I'm suddenly mortified.

"I'm sorry. They're your family and I'm chattering on about them like a fan-girl."

"It's fine. They're just normal people. You'd like them."

"Are you taking me to the Greek place?" I ask with enthusiasm.

"Is that okay with you? They have great food."

"I know! It's my favorite." I grin at him as he holds the door open for me. We're seated quickly by the windows with a great view of the Space Needle.

"Tell me about your tattoo." He's watching me over his menu, his eyes calm and ice blue.

"Rebellious stage."

"Can I get you both something to drink?" the waitress asks as she approaches the table.

"I'll take a Diet Coke, please."

"Water for me," he replies. "Tell me more."

"I had a few years where I gave my parents a run for their money. I got this"—I point to the bright flowers on my right shoulder—"on my twentieth birthday."

"It's beautiful."

"Thank you. I'm glad I wasn't stupid enough to get something like Tweety Bird or something."

"Do the cherry blossoms mean something to you?"

"I thought they were pretty. And, trust me, that was a time in my life when I didn't think much about me was pretty."

He tilts his head to the side and narrows those blue eyes on me, but I look down at my menu, avoiding his gaze.

Why did I say that?

Rather than push for more, he turns his attention to his menu, and the waitress returns with drinks and to take our order.

Twilight is just beginning to set in, and the lights on the Space Needle begin to glow.

"I love the Space Needle at night," I murmur.

"The view from the top is amazing," he agrees.

"I've never been to the top."

His gaze whips to mine. "Never?"

"Nope." I shake my head and take a sip of my drink. "I've only lived here for about five years."

"Where are you from?"

"A small town in Wyoming."

"Is your family there?"

"Yeah." I nod slowly and drag my fingers down the beading condensation on my glass. "My parents and sister are all there. I have lots of extended family, too."

"So why are you here?"

"Because I like the city. I came here for culinary school and never went back."

"Do you visit?"

"Sure, about once a year. My mom spends the whole week I'm there begging me to move back, giving me the guilt trip for being so far away."

"So she does the mom thing," he replies with a wink.

"Big-time." I nod. "I love them, but there are only about twelve hundred people in that town. What would I do there forever? I like it here. This is my home. I can visit them."

His eyes are warm as he watches me. "I'm glad you came here."

His voice is soft and low and like warm honey. He's such a nice guy. He hasn't been pushy or demanding at all.

Is this really the dominant man I knew a few weeks ago?

Our food is delivered, and we continue with small talk throughout the meal, and when we're finished and we step out in the warm Seattle evening, I take a deep breath and rub my belly.

"God, I'm full."

"You eat like a champ," he replies with a wide grin.

"I know." I scrunch my nose. "I'm gonna need an extra mile on the treadmill tomorrow."

"Let's work some of it off now." He leads me toward the heart of the center. The whole space is lit up, and people are milling about. Kids are skipping, yelling, crying. Cotton candy stands, ice cream stands and candied nut stands are positioned about.

"How about an ice cream?" he asks.

"We're supposed to be working calories off, not adding to them," I remind him with a laugh. "How about an iced tea?" I suggest, pointing to a nearby barista.

"Good idea."

"Officer Montgomery!" a little middle-aged woman exclaims from behind her espresso machine. "I haven't seen you in a long time. You never visit me anymore."

"It's detective now, Mrs. Rhodes." He grins and winks at the older woman. She's old enough to be his mother.

And she looks completely smitten with him.

"Who is your lady friend?" she asks with a soft smile.

"This is Nic." Matt settles his hand on my back, introducing me to the kind woman. "Nic, this is Mrs. Rhodes. She makes the best coffee around."

"Of course I do," she replies. "But you don't ever come to get any."

"Well, you said you were going to leave Mr. Rhodes and run away with me, but you never did that either. You broke my heart."

"Oh, now you stop that, young man!" She shakes her finger at him, but her eyes are shining with humor. "You're going to make people talk."

I can't help but giggle at their banter. Matt is charming and most likely making Mrs. Rhodes' year.

"What can I get for you, darling?" she asks me kindly.

"Just an iced tea, please."

"Do you want me to sweeten it?"

"No, thank you," I reply.

"And for you, troublemaker?" she asks Matt, who laughs delightedly.

"I'll have the same."

She fills our drinks, and when she tries to pass them over the counter, Matt steps behind and takes them from her, then leans in and kisses her cheek.

"If you ever need anything, you have my number."

"You're a good boy, detective."

He smiles softly and hands me my drink, waves at Mrs. Rhodes, and we are off again, wandering around the Seattle Center.

"She is smitten with you," I inform him.

"Jealous?" he asks me with a wolfish smile.

"No." I giggle. "I liked her."

"She's been serving coffee in that same spot for years. This used to be my beat when I was a beat cop."

"Oh, cool. Do you miss it?"

"Just Mrs. Rhodes." He laughs. "She and her husband are good people."

I nod, not knowing what to say. I'm learning that not only is Matt Montgomery sex on a stick, but he's just plain…*kind*.

I'm in trouble.

"Where are we going?"

We've stopped by the base of the Space Needle and thrown our empty cups into the trash.

"Up the Needle," he replies with a raised brow. "You've never seen it."

My mouth drops for a moment, and then I clap my hands and bounce on the balls of my feet. "Awesome!"

"Come on."

He buys our tickets and leads me into the elevator.

"Have I mentioned that I'm afraid of heights?" I ask as we climb higher and higher.

Matt laughs and then wraps his arm around my shoulders, hugging me against his side. "Don't worry, I'll protect you."

The doors open, and I forget my fear of heights.

"Oh, it's so beautiful."

I walk to the railing and gaze out at the city that I've come to love so much. It's dark now, and there is a sea of glowing lights below us. The air is still warm. There's a light breeze, making the ends of my hair tickle my cheek.

"Come this way." Matt holds his hand out for mine and leads me around to the opposite side of the deck that looks out over the sound. We can see lit-up ferries and boats floating over the water.

"Gorgeous," I whisper.

"Yes," he murmurs.

I glance up to find him looking down at me.

"You're a charmer," I inform him with a laugh.

"One thing you'll learn about me, little one, is that I rarely say what I don't mean."

We're standing side by side, not touching, watching the city around us. It's amazingly quiet up here.

Peaceful.

Suddenly, Matt reaches over and grasps my hand in his, linking our fingers. He doesn't look down at me, just holds my hand as we watch our city.

I take a deep breath and let it out slowly.

Okay, maybe Bailey is right. I need to give this a chance.

CHAPTER FOUR

~Matt~

It's been a long fucking night.

Asher and I caught a case that kept us up all night long, bouncing from the crime scene to the hospital, interviewing family members and speaking with the doctors.

Domestic disputes are rarely this bad, but when they are, it's exhausting.

I arrive home at just before nine Saturday morning. The only thing I can think of is taking a hot shower and climbing into bed, succumbing to oblivion.

I strip my clothes off, leaving a path of dirty laundry behind me on my way to the bathroom. I turn on the shower and step in before the water even has a chance to heat up all the way, scrubbing the night at work off my body. Just as the water hits scalding level, I shut it off, towel myself dry and pad into my bedroom as my cell phone rings.

I scowl when I see Asher's name on the display.

"Yeah," I answer and sit on the edge of the bed.

"Hey, I just picked up the cupcakes for Casey's birthday party tonight, and I thought I should call you."

"What's wrong?" I ask, my body already on alert and the fatigue forgotten.

"Nothing's wrong, but I thought you'd like to know that your girl is swamped in her shop today."

"My girl?" I ask drily.

"I'm not stupid, man. I don't know what you have going on with her, but I can tell there's something there. She's shorthanded and running ragged today. She seems okay, just thought I'd give you a heads-up."

"Thanks, partner. I'll go check on her."

"See you tomorrow," he responds and hangs up.

I glance longingly at my comfortable bed and resign myself to being awake for a few more hours.

There's no way in hell that I'll leave her to fend for herself today. Not if I can help her.

I dress quickly in jeans and a black T-shirt and drive quickly to the bakery.

Sure enough, it takes me five minutes to find parking, and when I finally step inside, there is a line to the door. Nic is smiling widely but clearly overwhelmed, bustling behind the glass case, back and forth between plating cupcakes and ringing up customers.

This is a two-person job.

She hasn't even noticed I'm here when I slip back into the kitchen and grab a spare white apron, pull it over my head and tie it around my waist.

Oh, we're going to have fun with her apron very soon.

Before I can spend too much time daydreaming of tying her up with her apron and fucking her blind here in her kitchen, I join her behind the counter, startling her.

"Matt!"

"How can I help?" I ask calmly.

Her cheeks are flushed and her hands are shaking as she brushes a piece of hair off her face.

"You don't have to," she replies but swallows hard.

"Clearly, I do. We'll talk later, just tell me what you need." I smile reassuringly and brush her soft cheek with my fingertip.

"Can you fill cupcake orders while I make coffees and ring them up?" she asks.

"I can do that," I reply.

"I need two minutes," she informs me and disappears into the kitchen.

I'm just filling a white box full of a half-dozen carrot cake cupcakes when she returns, chewing on something.

"Better?" I ask.

She nods and returns to the cash register, attending to her customers. That red ribbon is tied around her head again. It seems to be a part of her uniform. I do believe we'll find a way to have fun with that as well.

God, she's fucking beautiful.

We work side by side for the better part of the morning without a break. I can't believe how busy her little shop is. I grin in pride when an elderly man approaches Nic to ring up his sales.

"My Margaret and I sure do love your sweets, girlie."

"Thank you, Mr. Larsen. How is your pretty wife?" Nic asks with a grin.

"She's been a little under the weather, but these will brighten her right up."

"I hope so," Nic replies and drops some chocolate-covered cherries into a bag to give to him as well. "These are new. I'd love it if you two would let me know what you think."

Mr. Larsen winks at Nic and grins before walking out with his purchase.

Nic knows most of her clients' names and deals with them all with humor and grace.

At two thirty, there is a lull in customers, so Nic slips in the back for a few minutes and returns with more trays of cupcakes to fill empty slots in her case. She has a stick of string cheese hanging out of her mouth, chewing away on it.

"So what happened?" I ask as she arranges the case.

"Anastasia, my other part-time helper, called out sick this morning," she replies with a sigh. "Tess is in college, so she can't help during the week. So that left me."

"Maybe you should hire someone full time to help out," I suggest, but she glares at me from across the space.

"Trying to tell me how to run my business now, Matt?"

"Hey," I reply, holding up my hands, "it was just a suggestion."

"I'm sorry." She sighs and rubs her forehead with her fingertips. "I haven't had enough to eat today. It makes me grouchy."

"You close at four?" I ask. I walk behind her and begin kneading the tight muscles in her shoulders.

"Yeah," she replies and sighs deeply, leaning against me. "Jesus, that feels good. Why did you come in?"

"Asher called me. Said you were pretty busy, so I decided to come check in on you."

She spins around, her jaw dropped in surprise. "But he said you two worked all night."

I smile patiently and step closer to her, needing to be next to her. She smells of vanilla and sugar, and it's the most alluring smell I've ever experienced.

Who knew sugar could be so fucking sexy?

"You needed me," I reply simply. "And I've missed you this week."

Her green eyes widen, and suddenly she's in my arms, wrapped around me, hugging me hard. Her head is tucked against my chest, and she turns her face to bury her nose against me while taking a long, deep breath.

"Thank you," she whispers before pulling back, but I hold her tight and keep her with me for a few moments, giving us both a moment to settle.

"You're welcome."

The bell above the door sounds as a customer walks in, and for the next forty minutes—ten minutes past closing time—we are busy with customers again, cleaning out the glass case except for one cupcake.

Nic locks the door, takes a deep breath and laughs. "I can pay you with a crème brûlée cupcake," she says.

"I'll split it with you," I reply.

"Nah, I don't eat them." She waves me off after she hands me the cupcake, stacks the trays from the case and carries them into the back.

"Why not?"

"Can you imagine if I ate everything I baked?" She laughs and shakes her head. "I'd have to live at the gym."

"You don't sample anything?" I ask and take a bite of the cake. Dear Christ, these are amazing.

"Once in a while, if it's something new," she replies and pulls her apron over her head, throws it in a hamper and watches me enjoy the treat. "Good?"

"Amazing."

"I'm glad." She tilts her head, watching me. "You're tired."

"I'm exhausted," I confirm and swallow the last bite.

"Come upstairs with me." To my surprise, she holds her hand out for mine and then leads me up to her apartment. "We'll have dinner and you can crash for a while."

"I don't live far," I respond.

"I would rather you didn't drive when you're this tired," she replies. "Plus, you saved me today, so the least I can do is save you back."

Save me.

Why do I get the feeling that Nic will save me in more ways than she'll ever know?

***

"So how did you become a baker?" I ask and take a bite of meat lover's pizza.

We are seated in her living room, shoes off, facing each other from opposite ends of the couch, the pizza box between us.

"I always liked to bake," she replies. "Couldn't afford to go to a university and actually, didn't go to culinary school until I was about twenty-three. I got a job out of high school, partied a little too hard, basically gave my parents gray hair until I pulled my head out and saved my money so I could attend the Art Institute here."

I nod and stretch my legs out in front of me and rest them on her ottoman. "That's right, you were rebellious."

"What about you?" she asks.

"What about me?" I reply and grin at her. Which part of me are you asking about, baby?

"How did you become a cop?"

"Oh, that. I did two years in the Army." I wince and shake my head. "Caleb was much more suited for the military."

"Don't like being told what to do, huh?" she asks me with a wink, making me chuckle.

"That wasn't it, actually. I don't want to move around all the time. I like it here. I want to be near my family. So, when my two years were up, I came home and worked my way through college and then applied to the academy."

She closes the pizza box, sets it aside and lays her cheek against the back of the couch, a soft smile on her full lips. If I had the energy, I'd lean over and capture those lips under mine and kiss her mad.

Instead, I pull her feet into my lap and begin to rub the arches of her feet. She sighs and closes her eyes.

"God, that's nice."

"Just relax."

"You should be the one relaxing. You worked all night and then worked all day in my shop."

"Don't worry about me," I reply with just enough of an edge in my voice to make sure she knows I mean it.

"What about the other stuff?" she asks softly, and when I raise my eyes from her feet to her face, I see her watching me. I raise an eyebrow, and she snickers. "The ropes."

"I responded to a domestic violence call in my second year on the force. It happened to be at a local BDSM club, which is actually very unusual, as I've come to find out since then." I pause and check her to make sure that I haven't already scared her off, but she's just reclined comfortably, listening, so I continue. "While

I was there, I saw someone I recognized and saw that he had tied this girl up in ropes, and I thought it was hot as hell, to be honest."

She smiles, and for just a moment, I forget what I was saying.

I shake my head and pull her other foot into my lap.

"So, when I saw him a few days later, I asked him about it. It's called Shibari. It's an ancient form of Japanese bondage, and this friend is a master."

"Had you tied girls up before?" she asks softly.

"I'd played with handcuffs before, sure. And restraining a woman was always fun, but once I started learning Shibari, I also learned that it comes with responsibility. Trust."

"What about the dominant stuff?"

"Are you asking just because you're curious, or have you decided to change your mind about our friendship status?" I ask quietly.

Her cheeks flush as she meets my gaze. "I'm not just curious."

"I need you to say the words, little one."

"I want to see where this might go," she admits.

I release her feet and pull her into my lap, unable to keep from holding her any longer, and let's face it, talking about this stuff is a huge turn-on for me. I settle her against me but arrange her so I can still look in her eyes while I talk.

This conversation could make or break us, and I am not going to fuck this up.

"What are you afraid of?" I ask gently.

She shrugs and looks down, but I catch her chin with the tip of my finger and tilt her head back up.

"Talk to me."

"I don't like losing control," she whispers. "I have to have control of my business, my financial life, my health, everything, Matt."

"Okay." I nod and push my fingers through her soft, short, dark hair. "What about when we had sex before? Did you hate giving up the control of that to me?"

"No," she answers, and I grin.

Jackpot.

"There are different kinds of Doms, Nic. Some Doms want a full-time sub. Some even have slaves."

She gasps and covers her mouth, her eyes wide in terror.

"Not that kind of slave, little one. Everything is always consensual and sane."

"So these women voluntarily allow someone to call them a slave?" Her brow is pursed in a frown, and she's suddenly overcome her fear, and curiosity has set in.

"Not just women," I reply and laugh when her jaw drops again. Oh, it's going to be so fun introducing her to my world.

"Wow, I had no idea."

"When you were at the erotic ball with your friend, was that the first time you'd been anywhere like that?"

"Yeah, she dragged me," she replies.

"I'm sorry, baby." I kiss her forehead and nuzzle her nose with mine. "If I'd known, I would have done things a little differently. I thought you were just shy."

"I didn't want you to do anything differently." She frowns.

"So you enjoyed yourself?"

She nods and then bites her lip before saying, "I'm no one's slave, Matt. Voluntarily or otherwise."

"I'm not a slave master, Nic. That doesn't interest me at all. As I was saying, some Doms are into the slave thing. Some are happy with a submissive in the bedroom, and ask that their sub obeys their rules out of the bedroom as well, especially in a club atmosphere."

"What are the rules?" she asks.

"Good question," I reply with a smile. "They vary with the couple, based on their desires and hard limits."

She swallows and then nods. "Okay."

"But then there are other Doms who are perfectly happy to be sexually domi-nant but have a normal vanilla relationship outside of the bedroom." I grin down at her. "That's the category I fall into. The restraints are my kink. I love that you're a business owner and a strong-willed woman. But behind closed doors, I would like to pursue a relationship like the one you tasted a few weeks ago."

I sit back and wait while she processes this information, chewing on her bottom lip. "So, you won't try to tell me how to run my shop?"

"Why would I do that?" I ask with a raised brow. "The only thing I know about cupcakes is that they're delicious."

"You won't choose my clothes for me?"

"No." I shake my head. "That's too much, in my opinion, but it works very well for other couples."

She nods again, deep in thought.

"It's a lot of information." It's not a question, and she blinks a few times before meeting my gaze.

"Yeah," she agrees. "It is. Why no safe word?"

"In clubs, safe words are mandatory, so if we ever go to one together, your word will be 'red.' The second you say 'red,' everything stops, no questions asked. But, honestly, the way I feel about safe words is, you shouldn't need one with me. It's my job to learn what you can handle and what you can't, and I'm a firm believer in 'no means no.'"

"I beg to differ," she interjects with a laugh.

I laugh with her and pinch her round ass, then smooth it with the flat of my hand. "Sassy girl."

"I don't have a problem saying 'no.'"

"So I've learned, and I'm glad. It's imperative that you always communicate with me. I'll always be watching you for signs of any distress, but I can't read your mind, so you have to be honest."

"I can do that. Okay, another question."

"Anything," I reply and yawn.

"I can ask tomorrow. You're so tired." She rests her palm on my cheek.

I turn my face and press a kiss to her cool hand, enjoying her touch. "I'm okay, let's get this all talked out so we can move on."

"I noticed some girls called their Doms sir or master. Do you want me to call you that?" Her eyes say, *Never in a million years, dude.*

I offer her a smile and shake my head. "I'm not your father, and I won't insist that you address me as sir or master. I'm Matt or any other sexy-as-hell nickname you might come up with for me. But if we *do* go to the club, you should know that I'm known as Master Matt there."

"Why?"

"Because I'm a master in Shibari, and I've achieved Master Dom status within the club. So the subs address me as such." She frowns, but I reassure her with, "It's just the protocol, Nic. It's respectful."

"Will I have to kneel?"

"If we're at the club, yes, but I don't expect you to kneel when we're alone."

She exhales deeply and then turns tired eyes to me. "Is that it?"

I chuckle and drag my knuckles down her cheek. "Honestly, I'm shocked that we're having this conversation so soon."

"I was just curious," she responds with wide eyes, but I stop her before she gets the wrong idea.

"I'm happy, Nic. I was going to suggest that we pursue this, but I thought I'd have to be a bit more persuasive."

"Well, I am curious, and I do like you, Matt. But I need to be clear with you, this is new to me, and I'm not okay with being told how to live my life."

"That's fair." I nod. "And this also needs to be said: I don't share, Nic. Ever. I won't let other Doms touch you. They may watch"—her eyes widen at that—"but they'll never touch you."

"I don't share either," she whispers.

"Good, then we're on the same page."

I stand with her in my arms. "Let's go to the bedroom."

"Wow, that was quick," she replies sarcastically.

"We are both exhausted, baby. I'd like to curl up around you and sleep for about eight hours and then wake up and bury myself inside you for another eight."

She checks her watch and grins. "I have to be at work in thirty-six hours."

"You have tomorrow off?"

She nods happily.

"Then we'd better get started."

She laughs and points in the direction of her bedroom.

I like her apartment. It's small, but there's little clutter. The furniture is updated but not too fancy.

But her bedroom pulls at my heart. It's pure woman. The bed is a king-size four-poster with sheer curtains hanging at each corner.

"We're going to have fun with this bed, sweetheart."

She grins and lays her head on my shoulder as I look around the room. I was here before but admittedly was too busy looking at her to take in her bedroom. Her bedding has small pink roses on it. A vanity in one corner of the room is covered in makeup and hair stuff, and there is a pile of shoes in another corner.

"You don't have enough storage space," I comment.

"It's an older building, so it doesn't have much for closets."

I set her on her feet and strip her down to her black panties, pull the ribbon out of her hair and lay it on the bedside table, and take a deep breath.

Fuck me, she's gorgeous.

She has more ink, which I intend to fully explore later. Her body is petite. Thin, but not too thin. She has round breasts with dusky nipples that tighten as I continue to watch them.

A glimpse of silver winks at me from her navel.

"Matt…"

"Shh…I just want to look for a moment."

Her skin is tanned. Her thighs are slim, but they still touch when she's standing. She's a *real* woman, through and through.

I lick my lips and hold her gaze in mine. "You are amazingly beautiful."

She fidgets, and I immediately pull her to me, kiss her softly and draw the linens back on the bed and lay her gently on the soft pink sheets. She watches with sleepy eyes as I also shed my clothing, leaving just my boxer-briefs on, and join her. I turn her back to me and tuck her against me, bury my face in her soft dark hair and inhale the warm scent of vanilla.

"Sleep, little one."

"Sweet dreams," she whispers.

CHAPTER FIVE

~Nic~

Someone is planting soft kisses on my right shoulder, over my tattoo. Fingertips drag lazily up and down my arm, sending shivers down my body, pulling me out of a deep, restful sleep. I wiggle back, tucking my ass even closer to Matt's hips, enjoying the way his hardness feels against my back. He's warm and hard, *everywhere.*

"Good morning," he whispers against my ear, then nuzzles it with his nose.

"Mornin'," I reply softly.

His hand drifts down to my breast, and his fingers thrum gently over my nipple, making it pucker under his soft touch.

This is the most amazing way to wake up. Slow. Sexy.

He drags his nose down my neck and kisses my shoulder again.

"I'm going to spend the next hour or so exploring every inch of your delectable little body," he warns me with a whisper, making me grin.

This does not sound like a bad deal at all.

"Is that a threat?" I whisper, teasing him.

"If you like," he agrees. "But here's how it's going to work."

His hand drifts down to my wrist, which he brings up to his lips. He kisses the sensitive skin on the inside of my wrist and then loops the red ribbon I use for my hair around it. He scoots back so I can roll onto my back, and I'm wide awake now, watching him curiously as he repeats the motion on the other wrist, then makes a series of loops and knots to tie them together.

He slips a finger under the satin to make sure that it's snug but not cutting off my blood flow and then grins down at me with excitement shining in his gorgeous blue eyes.

"We're going to start easy today, little one." He kisses my cheek, not a quick peck, but plants his lips on my skin and inhales deeply, as if he's pulling my scent inside him, memorizing me.

I have one hundred percent of his focus, and it's completely intoxicating.

"Your hands are to stay over your head." He guides my arms up, so they are lying comfortably bent on either side of my head, my wrists joined. He drags the backs of his fingers down my arm and to my breast, barely touching just the tip of my nipple, but the electricity shoots down my belly and my panties are already soaked.

"But I want to touch you," I whisper.

He pinches my nipple, hard, making me squirm.

"I didn't ask you." He raises an eyebrow, reminding me that this is where I'm supposed to surrender to him, to let him do as he wishes.

No means no.

I offer him a half smile, and he kisses my lips sweetly. "That's better."

His lips travel down my jawline, to my neck and finally down to my breasts, where he licks and laps at my tender nipple then pulls back and blows on it, watching it pucker in the cool air.

"You're so responsive," he murmurs.

I begin to squirm, but he pins me in his gaze and says sternly, "Keep still."

His bossiness makes me want to rebel and makes my skin hot with lust at the same time.

He returns his attention to my breasts, teasing them into hard, pink tips and then nibbles his way down to my navel.

"Another part of your rebellious years?" he asks, referring to my piercing.

I have a simple pink barbell through the skin there.

"No."

"No?" He sweeps his nose across the metal and then tugs it gently with his teeth. "Tell me."

"It was a reward," I reply, breathless now. His fingers are still taunting my nipples, and that, coupled with the tugging on my piercing, has my pussy pulsing in need.

I desperately want to open my legs, but he's laid across my thighs, holding me still.

On purpose, I'm sure.

And he says he's not a sadist!

"Reward for what?"

I don't want to tell him this. It's embarrassing. In an attempt to switch his focus, I pull my arms down and bury my hands in his soft dark blond hair.

His head jerks up, his eyes narrow in malice, and in a move so fast it steels my breath, he raises up, pins my hands back over my head and covers my body with his, holding me beneath him, his face an inch from mine.

"Reward for what?" he repeats quietly.

"For dropping weight and having a flat stomach," I whisper.

He smiles widely and plants a deep kiss on my lips, nibbling and exploring my mouth thoroughly. He wiggles his hips between my own, settling his still-covered cock against my center, and rolls gently, just barely feeding my hunger to feel more of him.

"See? That wasn't hard," he murmurs and brushes my hair off my forehead with his thumbs as his fingers caress my scalp. "When I ask you questions, I want you to answer me honestly. Every time."

His face is passive, sober, waiting for my answer.

"Understood."

He rests his forehead against my own and takes another deep breath before kissing my nose, down my cheek to my ear. "I'm going to worship your body for a while, baby. It's not going to hurt. I just want you to keep your hands where I put them. Got it?"

I nod and sigh as he trails those magical lips of his back down my body to my piercing.

"I love this," he murmurs, then travels farther south.

"I haven't showered since yesterday morning," I remind him as he peels my panties over my hips and down my legs, discarding them on the floor.

"You're fine."

I bite my lip as he settles between my legs, nudging me open with his wide shoulders. "Fuck, you're beautifully wet for me already."

He glides a fingertip over the soft bare skin of my pubis, down the crease where my thigh meets my torso, then back up and over the other side, without actually touching the sensitive skin that's screaming for him.

"You have a freckle right here," he murmurs and plants his fingertip just to the right of my lips.

I gasp and have to consciously keep my hands over my head.

"Good girl." His voice is full of approval, and part of me glows brighter.

I love hearing his voice like this, the feel of his hands touching me as he pleases, pleasing me in turn. I'd keep my hands over my head for a week to keep his voice just like this.

His finger moves in, sliding in my wetness, from my slick entrance to my clit and back down again, slowly, leisurely.

Jesus, the man has the patience of a saint.

Finally, he leans in and plants a chaste kiss over my clit, then drags the tip of his tongue down into my folds, wraps his lips around them and sucks, hollowing his cheeks.

My hips buck up, and it takes everything in me to keep my wrists planted on the mattress over my head. His hands grip my hips, hard, and I settle, letting him take me wherever he wants to go.

Happily.

Freely.

He buries two fingers inside me and makes love to my clitoris with his mouth, sending me over into a mind-numbing climax. I plant my heels in his back and scream his name as I come against his mouth, my world shattering spectacularly around me.

As I return to planet Earth, I'm surprised to find my hands still over my head. Matt has continued his journey down my legs, kissing and massaging my muscles as he goes.

"Sometime soon I'll tie your feet up as well."

My eyes find his smiling down at me. "Then you'll be completely at my mercy."

"I think I am already," I reply breathlessly.

"Perhaps." He shrugs. "I have so much more to show you."

He turns me onto my stomach, then checks to make sure my arms are at a comfortable angle above my head and I can breathe comfortably. "Okay?"

"I'm good," I reply.

He kisses my cheek and then buries his face in my neck, tugging the flesh with his teeth.

"Tell me if the ribbon starts to pull too tight, or if you can't breathe freely," he instructs, then begins another journey with his lips down my back. He kisses the tattoo on my shoulder, making me grin.

I'm glad he likes it so much. I think it's pretty, and I like to wear clothes that show it off.

My entire body is one big tingle as his lips and fingers journey over my skin. I can feel his warmth against me, and every once in a while, his erection will press against me, making me swallow hard, remembering how it feels to have him buried so deep inside me.

"Tell me about this," he whispers, kissing the ink over the left side of my ribs softly.

"I got it when I opened the shop," I tell him, loving the flutter of his lips over my skin.

"Recite it to me," he demands.

I frown. He's looking right at it. He can read it.

"I want to hear it from your lips," he clarifies.

"You never know how strong you are until being strong is the only choice you have."

"Why these words?" he asks.

I bite my lip. Jesus, he's stripping me bare, body and soul here, and I love it and am afraid of it all at the same time.

Suddenly, he slaps my ass, and whispers in my ear, "What did I say about answering my questions?"

"Opening Sweets took everything I had. Failure isn't an option for me."

"Ah, baby," he murmurs.

I hear the crinkling of a wrapper and the dip of the bed as he sheds his briefs before his hands glide down my back to my ass, over my hips and thighs. "You are an amazing woman, Nicole."

"Ni—" I begin to correct him, but he interrupts me.

"We're going to have to work on your stubbornness in the bedroom, baby." He chuckles and bites my shoulder, then returns me to my back, covering my body with his. His eyes are on fire as he gazes down at me, his elbows planted on either side of my head, under my arms, holding me even more immobile. "Your body is fucking gorgeous. Every inch."

His nose sweeps against my own as his pelvis rests on mine, his cock lying nestled in my slick pussy lips.

"I want you," I whisper against his lips.

He sucks in a breath and lets it out in a shaky sigh, pulls his hips back and then slides slowly inside me until he's completely buried.

"So fucking tight," he growls and begins to move.

I raise my legs around his hips, opening myself up wider, allowing him to push inside even farther, and it's pure fucking heaven.

I've never felt anything like this, never had this kind of physical and emotional connection to a man in my life. I bite my lip as he begins to move faster, harder, an unseen force driving him on, as though he just can't help it. He crushes my mouth under his own and devours me, fucking me and kissing me voraciously.

Suddenly, he rears up, holding my knees out to the side, watching his cock move in and out of my wetness. He slides one hand down my inner thigh and plants his thumb against my clit, sending me into another plane of being.

I cry out just as he sends me over the edge into another orgasm, even stronger than the one before.

The head of his cock is dragging against my sweet spot, and his thumb continues to press against my clit, and it's amazing.

Crazy.

Fucking unbelievable.

"Look at me," he demands.

My eyes find his above me. He pumps into me twice, three times and then stills, groaning with his release.

He's panting and sweating, still inside me as he pushes his hands up my arms to my wrists and pulls them down. He methodically unties the ribbon—I won't be wearing that one in the shop again—and gently massages my wrists, hands and shoulders, then pulls out of me and climbs off the bed to take care of the condom.

When he returns, he doesn't join me in bed. He simply holds his hand out to me with a smile, and when I take it, he pulls me out of the bed and into his arms for a long, soft kiss.

"How was that?" he asks quietly.

"It was…" I tilt my head to the side, thinking about the amazing experience we just shared. "Yeah, it was good."

He grins, relieved. "Good. For me, too." He grabs my robe from the end of the bed and wraps it around me, bundling me up, then pulls on his boxer-briefs and grabs my hand in his, lacing our fingers.

"Come on, I'll make you breakfast."

"You cook?" I ask with a raised brow.

"Quite well, actually."

"I like all of these hidden talents," I reply with a smirk.

"Oh, honey, you haven't seen anything yet."

***

"Tell me about your ink," I request as Matt bustles about my kitchen.

I'm seated at the breakfast bar, wrapped in the robe that Matt draped around me, holding a cup of steaming coffee, an empty glass of orange juice at my elbow, also thanks to my bossy cop. He refused my offer of help, instead insisting that I sit and keep him company.

If this is what's involved in being submissive, I should have signed on long ago.

Although, maybe it's just this guy who works this way.

"This"—he points to the tattoo on his side, over his ribs—"is the Chinese symbol for truth."

I nod, admiring the black symbol, having an excuse to allow my eyes to roam over his perfect body. His arms are thick, the muscles clearly defined. When he lifts the pan to flip the pancakes, the muscles flex and bunch, and I can't help but squirm in my chair.

God, I want to touch him.

I wonder if he'll ever let me touch him when we have sex.

He turns his back to me, and my jaw drops. Jesus Christ on a motor bike, his back is blessed with more muscle, and it tapers down to his hips, where of course he's sporting two of the hottest damn dimples sitting right over his tight ass, currently covered in his low-riding shorts.

I could most likely bounce quarters off that ass.

It's something to write home about, that's for sure. Of course, my mom might not want to hear about my guy's ass.

Then again, maybe she would.

He's talking as he moves about, cracking eggs and checking on the bacon in the oven, but I have no idea what he's saying.

"Nic?"

My gaze whips up to his.

He's smiling, watching me. "Where were you?"

"Um." My cheeks heat, and I dissolve into a bubble of giggles. "Sorry. I was checking out your ass."

He chuckles. "First time you've seen a man mostly naked?"

"This is the first time I've gotten a good look at *you*." I shrug. "It's nice."

"Nice?" he asks and pulls the eggs away from the heat.

"You don't like nice?"

"Hmm…no. Nice isn't the word I'd like to hear you use to describe me."

"Well…" I tilt my head, like I'm pretending to come up with something, enjoying this banter. "I guess I could say sexy. Or crazy hot. Or even better yet, oh my God."

He walks around the breakfast bar and kisses me silly, his hands in my short hair, holding on tight as his lips nibble and explore mine. I plant my hands on his back and let them roam over his skin down to his ass, where I slip them under the waistband of his shorts and grip him firmly.

"So you're an ass girl."

"I am now," I agree with a laugh.

He laughs with me as he lets me go and finishes preparing breakfast, then loads only one plate of everything onto a tray and motions with his head for me to follow him.

His eyes are warning me not to argue, so I quietly climb off my stool and follow him back into the bedroom, where he climbs onto my bed, sits against the headboard and pats the space next to him.

"Join me."

I plant my knee on the edge, but before I can climb on, he adds, "Without the robe."

I bite my lip, watching his face, as I slowly pull the tie loose at my waist and let the satin fall open, push it off my shoulders and let it fall to the ground, leaving me naked.

Matt sucks in a breath, his eyes wide as they rake up and down my body. "Jesus, Nic."

"Can I join you now?" I ask sarcastically.

"We're in the bedroom, so watch yourself, little one."

I grin and climb on the bed, sit next to him with my knees pulled up to my chest, and wait for him to decide what to do next. He takes a bite of bacon and then a sip of OJ, and then offers me a bite of pancakes.

I blink in surprise and open my mouth, allowing him to feed me the pancakes, and then chew as he continues to also feed himself.

"Bacon?" he asks.

I nod, and he feeds me the bacon, patiently waiting while I chew. Finally, I start to laugh.

"Something funny?"

"This is incredibly funny," I confirm. "You're feeding me."

"I am," he agrees and then smiles widely. "It won't happen often, but I feel like spoiling you a bit. Humor me?"

"You're the boss." I shrug and lean back, letting him feed us both. "How are Brynna and Caleb doing?"

"They are almost a week into their honeymoon, so I would think they're fucking like rabbits and having a great time."

"Oh! Brynna said she didn't think they'd be able to get away."

Matt offers me some juice, and I gratefully accept.

"It was a gift from the family."

"That's awesome." I lean over and kiss Matt's bare shoulder, then remember myself and ask, "Am I allowed to do that?"

"To kiss me?"

"Yeah. You didn't give me permission."

"We're just sitting here, having breakfast and chatting, Nic. You can touch me whenever you want, unless I give you direction that says otherwise."

"Oh. I like that."

"Good." He grins and offers me some scrambled eggs.

"So, where did you all send them?" I ask and refuse the next bite, too full to eat any more.

"Italy," he replies casually and finishes the rest of the breakfast himself.

"Italy," I repeat with a snort. "Holy crap, that's some honeymoon."

"I know." He nods. "Dominic owns a home there."

"He seems nice."

Matt's eyes narrow on my face.

Is he jealous?

"He's a good guy. I haven't known him long. Just a few months."

"But he's your brother."

"Half brother," he clarifies and sets the empty tray on the bedside table. "We didn't know he existed until about five months ago."

"Wow."

"What do you have planned for today?" Matt asks, effectively changing the subject.

"I could use a trip to the grocery store, but other than that, I don't have solid plans."

He looks uncertain when he meets my gaze and says simply, "I'd like to spend today with you."

"Okay," I agree. "What do you have in mind?"

"Anything you want," he replies. "Let's get out of this apartment for a while, and then I'd very much like to spend tonight here with you."

"I'd like to go down to Pike Place Market for some produce for the week." I tap my lip with my finger, contemplating all the possibilities. "Maybe pick up some fresh chocolate from the chocolate place just up the hill from there."

"You use fresh chocolate in your cupcakes?" Matt asks.

"Of course. I buy all my chocolate from them. It's the best."

"Okay. I might have a surprise before the Market and the chocolate place." He checks the time, then leans in and kisses me softly. "Thank you for this morning."

He kisses me once more and pulls me from the bed. "Let's shower and then head out. We need an early start."

He picks me up in his arms and marches into the bathroom.

"Are we going to get dirty again before we get clean?" I ask with a laugh.

"Oh, definitely."

***

"God, I love Seattle in the summer!" I exclaim and lean on the railing of the ferry, breathing in the salty air and enjoying the breeze in my hair and on my skin.

It's a gorgeous sunny summer day in Puget Sound. Matt surprised me with a ferry ride over to Bainbridge Island, which is only about a forty-minute ride, but the view is spectacular.

"I do, too," he agrees and leans on the rail, watching the Olympic Mountains grow smaller as we drift away from the island toward Seattle. "Did you enjoy the town?"

"It's a cute place." I nod and smile. "The bagel shop makes one hell of a sandwich."

"Next time we'll rent bikes and ride around the island."

"Sounds fun, too."

He steps behind me, wraps his arms around my shoulders and rests his lips on the top of my head, holding me snugly against his chest as we enjoy the spectacular views around us.

I haven't known him long, and I've already placed so much trust in this man. More than anyone in my life before. His quiet calm is soothing.

I hope I'm not making a mistake.

When we dock at Seattle, we walk up to Pike Place Market, one of the most famous outdoor/indoor markets in the world.

"Our first stop is the doughnut guy," Matt informs me with a grin.

Because it's a beautiful Sunday, the market is bustling with tourists and locals alike. We join the line for doughnuts and wait.

Matt's eyes never stop roaming, watching the people who pass by, listening to conversations around us. His hand holds on to mine tightly, as if I might get scooped up into the flow of bodies and disappear.

His protectiveness is a new side of him that I can't help but enjoy. It makes me feel...wanted.

When it's our turn, Matt places his order and then offers the plain brown paper bag to me, steaming with hot, fresh doughnuts the size of a baby's fist.

"No, thank you," I murmur, secretly yearning for just one. *Just one.*

"Are you sure?" he asks incredulously. "These are the best doughnuts in the city."

I nod, my mind made up. I don't want to pay for it later. "I'm sure."

"If you're worried about the calories—"

"I'm not," I interrupt. "I'm still full from lunch."

He watches me closely for a moment and then shrugs, tosses a sugar and cinnamon doughnut into his mouth and leads me farther into the market. Despite the throngs of people, Matt stays close and patiently waits while I choose fruit for this week's cupcakes, as well as produce for my own kitchen.

"Fish for dinner?" Matt asks in my ear, pointing to the fresh fish on display from one of the vendors.

"Sure."

He leaves me to buy some fish, so I also buy fragrant herbs to go with the fish and the makings for salad.

"Hey, baby."

I frown and turn at the familiar voice, praying I'm wrong.

Please, God, don't let it be who I think it is.

Nope, I'm just not that lucky.

"Don't call me that, Rob." I roll my eyes and keep moving down the line of produce.

"Hey, you haven't returned my calls in a while," he responds, ignoring my request completely.

"Nope, I haven't."

"Why not?"

"Because I'm not interested, Rob. Look…" I turn and catch Matt watching us over Rob's shoulder. He raises an eyebrow, but I square my shoulders and look Rob right in the eye.

He's short, only a few inches taller than I am, but he's a good-looking guy with black hair and brown eyes, a crooked nose.

"I don't mean to hurt your feelings, but I'm just not interested in seeing you. Good luck to you."

I turn to go, but he grabs my arm. "Wait."

"I think she already said no," Matt growls from behind him.

There's really not enough room to have this kind of altercation here in the middle of the market. There are too many people bustling around us, bumping into us.

"This isn't your fucking business," Rob snaps back with a sneer, and Matt's eyes narrow into deadly slits.

"She's with me," he states calmly. "She said no. That's all you need to know."

Rob's gaze slides to mine. "Seriously."

"That's right."

"Fine." He backs away, his hands up in surrender, but I can see anger and embarrassment in every line of his body. "See you around."

"A former boyfriend?" Matt asks as he watches Rob's retreating form.

"Used to," I confirm and pay for my purchases. "I'm finished here."

"Chocolate place next?" Matt asks.

"Yes, please." I sigh in relief that Matt doesn't press the subject of Rob as we exit the market and begin to climb the hill that leads up into the heart of downtown. This hill is a bitch.

"I hate this hill," I grumble, earning a chuckle from Matt.

He links his fingers through mine and takes the bag out of my other hand, carrying both the fish and produce in his spare hand. "So tell me about that guy."

"I was hoping that subject was closed."

"It will be after you spill it." He grins down at me, then places a kiss on my forehead. "Please."

"He's a guy I met in school. I went out with him once or twice, but he's not really my type."

"And that is?"

"Well, let's just say Rob is pushy and selfish and really enjoys talking about his truck."

Matt chuckles. "Yeah, I know the type."

"So not someone I enjoy spending time with," I assure him and shake my head. "I just stopped returning his calls. It wasn't even worth telling him to go away, because we'd only gone out a couple times. There was no physical relationship. I just let it fizzle out."

"But he seems to still be into you," Matt comments.

"I guess. I don't really care." I wince and bite my lip. "That makes me sound like a bitch."

"No, it makes you sound honest." He pulls me to a stop on the hill, until I'm standing up higher on the hill than he is, making his eyes level with mine. He leans in and kisses my lips softly, cradling my cheek with his free hand. "His loss."

"Let's go get some chocolate."

"Good idea. I might have a plan." He winks and leads me into the decadent chocolate shop, Rob already a distant memory.

Chapter Six

"Oh my God, you really can cook." I sit back in my chair and push my finished plate of poached salmon and salad away from me and sip my water, watching Matt across the table.

"You doubted me?" he asks with a raised brow.

"Not at all." I shake my head and laugh. "I'm just offering you a compliment."

He nods and stands to clear the table, and I join him. "You cooked, I'll clean."

"We can do this together," he offers, but I shake my head adamantly.

"No way. You've been spoiling me all day. I can do this." I take the plate from his hand and stand on my toes to kiss his warm cheek.

His eyes are soft and happy as he smiles at me. "Okay, while you do this, I'll be in the bedroom."

"Taking a nap?" I ask drily, earning a light pat on my ass.

"No, smart-ass. You'll see." He kisses my forehead and then leaves the room.

Matt is an excellent cook, but oh sweet Jesus, is he ever a messy one, too! My kitchen looks like a bomb went off in it, and he only poached fish and made a salad! Although, some of the mess is from breakfast, too, because we didn't have time to clean up before we left for the day.

Which drives me nuts, because of all the rooms in the house, the kitchen is the one I get a bit obsessive about.

I can't help it.

So I dig in, loading the dishwasher, hand-washing what won't fit and sanitizing the countertops. By the time I'm finished, the kitchen sparkles and smells like lemons, and I'm mortified to see that I've been cleaning for more than a half hour.

Some hostess I am.

I wander back to the bedroom to find Matt sitting in the chair by the window, reading something on his iPad.

On the way back from the market today, Matt stopped by his place to grab a change of clothes and a few of his things for another night away from home.

He's lit a few of my candles and shut off the bright lights, giving the room a soft glow.

"I'm sorry I took so long," I murmur and lean against the doorjamb, taking in the handsome man in my bedroom.

"I'm sorry I'm such a messy cook," he responds with a wry grin. His eyes are warm as they travel down my body. He stands and walks slowly to me. "Your eyes look amazingly green in this candlelight."

"Thanks," I reply as my heartbeat speeds up.

He's predatory now as he slowly crosses my bedroom to stand directly in front of me. He doesn't touch me, not yet. He leans his forearm on the doorjamb above my head and kisses my forehead gently.

"I want to show you what I can do with my ropes tonight, little one."

I pull in a deep breath and clench my thighs at the sudden pulse of electricity that just his simple words send through my core.

"You can always tell me to stop if it's too overwhelming," he reminds me tenderly, still not touching me.

He's still wearing his soft gray T-shirt and faded blue jeans from today, and my fingers are itching to touch him before he immobilizes me. I push my hand under his shirt, over the tight skin of his abs. The muscles jump under my hand, and his jaw ticks as he watches me, letting me explore his skin.

"I just want to touch you for a minute," I whisper softly.

He kisses my forehead again and then tips my chin back, watching me intently as my hands explore his belly and chest, under his shirt. I move my hand around his waist to his back and step close to him, wanting him to kiss me.

Finally, *finally*, he cradles my face in his hands and kisses me. Lazily but thoroughly, sweeping his lips over mine, nibbling at the side of my mouth and then sweeping across to the other side before sinking in and taking over, kissing me in that intense way that only Matt can.

He pulls away, takes my hands in his and leads me out of the doorway toward the bed.

"How do you feel, sweetheart?" he asks.

"Fine."

He raises a brow, and I swallow, thinking about how my body feels. "Excited. Nervous."

"Better," he replies and tugs my top over my head.

He kisses my body as he disrobes me, brushes his fingertips over my skin, leaving me humming in anticipation of what's to come.

When I'm completely nude, Matt scoops me up and lays me gently in the middle of the bed.

"I've added something to your bed," he informs me with a satisfied grin. He takes my right hand in his, kisses my palm, and then is suddenly looping soft rope around my wrist, tying beautiful knots. He lays my hand above my head and then circles the bed to the opposite side and pays the other wrist the same attention before linking the two with loose loops.

He reaches up, and pulls the same kind of rope down from the rail along the top of my four-poster bed, ties it to my linked hands, and cinches it, hoisting my torso up off the bed until my shoulders no longer touch the mattress.

"Is this painful on your shoulders?" he asks calmly.

"No," I reply breathlessly, watching him with wide eyes. Just as he reaches for another length of rope—I didn't even see him grab that when we were at his apartment!—his cell phone rings in his pocket.

"Damn." His eyes are still pinned on mine. "I'm sorry, baby, this is work."

He yanks out his phone and takes the call. His eyes narrow, still watching me closely.

"What?!" Now he paces away and stands at the window, looking blindly out at the street. "When? Fuck! Hold him there! What do you mean you don't have cause? I'll give you fucking cause! Fine, I'll be there in twenty. *Do not* let him leave, understood?"

He ends the call and grabs his iPad, pulls his keys out of his pocket. "I'm so sorry, Nic, but I have to go."

"Uh, Matt?" My voice is full of humor as he turns to look at me, and his eyes glass over. "I'm kind of tied up here."

He drops his keys and iPad into the chair and swiftly returns to me, untying me quickly, rubbing my wrists and lifting me into his lap. He caresses my hair, my face, kissing my forehead and cheeks softly. "I'm so sorry, little one. I wouldn't have left you like that."

"I know." I giggle and burrow into his lap deeper. "You obviously need to go to work."

"I do." He sighs regretfully. "We might have just caught a break on a case that we thought had gone cold."

"I understand," I murmur and kiss his cheek.

"But, first, we'll sit here for a minute." His hand glides down my side to rest on my hip. "It's torture to leave now. You looked gorgeous in my ropes."

"We can finish what you started another time," I assure him.

"Damn right." He chuckles. His eyes roam down my chest, my nipples still puckered in anticipation.

I'm breathing faster than normal, and my body is humming. His hand travels from my hip to between my legs and cups my sex. "Fuck, you're wet."

"I like it when you tie me up," I whisper.

He growls as he plunges two fingers inside me and begins to fuck me with his fingers, quickly, not taking his time, but moving rapidly. His thumb presses against my clit, and he buries his face in my neck, biting and licking me. "I'm not leaving here until you come, baby."

His words and hand send me into a tailspin. My hips rock up, pressing into his hand, as I cry out, my arms wrapped around his shoulders. I ride through the orgasm and then settle against him, panting and spent.

"Better?" he asks, his lips turned up in a half smile.

"Hmm," I agree and cup his face in my hand. "Thanks, detective."

He laughs and sets me on my feet. "I'm sorry I have to go. I'll text or call when I can."

"Okay. Be safe."

He tilts his head, watching me. "Interesting choice of words. Good night, baby. Thank you for today." He kisses me gently and then takes off, pulling his phone out of his pocket before he's out the bedroom door.

"Asher, we caught a break…"

*** *

"You can head home, Anastasia. Things are quiet today." The pretty mother of three grimaces and pulls her apron off as she glances at the time.

There is still an hour before closing time, but it's dead in here. I could have closed at noon today.

"Yeah, it is. Unusual for a Thursday," she agrees.

I nod, already mentally tallying how many cupcakes are going to have to go to the homeless shelter down the street tonight. I never serve day-old cakes, so at the end of the day, the leftovers are sent to the needy.

Even the needy deserve a sweet treat.

"Have a good night." Anastasia waves and heads through the kitchen to her car parked out back.

Just then, the door opens, the bell above tinkling, and in walks Leo Nash. All six-foot-plus of his tattooed hotness. He grins at me in that cocky rock-star way and saunters over to the counter.

"Please tell me you have lemon and chocolate left."

"You're in luck," I reply as I pull down a two-cupcake box and gently lay one of each inside. "How did it go over there today?" I ask, gesturing across the street to the recording studio.

"It went well, actually. The new album is coming along great."

"A new album already? *Sunshine* just came out."

"Well, we record when we can." He grins and shrugs. "We have a few weeks off from touring, so we're getting a few songs down before we head out again."

I nod, pretending to understand the life of a rock star.

"You did a great job on the cake for Bryn and Caleb," he mentions casually.

"I'm glad you liked it."

"I did. In fact, I mentioned you in an interview."

"*Me?* Why?"

"It was one of those lame 'so tell us about yourself' interviews, and they wanted to know about Sam and I." He cringes and looks half-pissed for a second. "The only thing I was willing to share was that we love your cupcakes. So, I hope it drums up business for you."

I don't know what to say. Leo Nash told an interviewer that he loves *my* cupcakes.

"Wow."

He laughs and takes the box from me. "I hope that was okay."

"Uh, I think cupcakes are on the house from now on."

His eyes light up, but he still drops a twenty in the tip jar. "Sounds like a fair trade."

"So much for free cupcakes," I reply drily, eyeing the money in the tip jar.

"They're worth it." He shrugs and turns to leave, winking at me on the way out.

My heart might beat right out of my chest.

God, the man is just so…*hot*. Samantha Williams is one lucky woman.

I shake off my close encounter with the sexy Leo Nash and lock the door before putting cupcakes in boxes and cleaning up for the day.

My phone buzzes in my pocket with a text. I grin and dig it out, excited to see it's from Matt.

How was your day?

I miss him. I haven't seen him since he left my apartment Sunday night. Four whole days, which really isn't that long, for crying out loud. He's been busy working and sleeping and little else this week. But he's managed to find time to send me messages, just checking in, and called me last night just after I'd climbed in bed to say good night.

I've already gotten used to having him in my world, and it's only been a couple of weeks.

Slow. Closing up early. How was yours?

God, I'm such a... *girl.*

It's been a long four days without you. Can you please come unlock the front door?

What? He's at the front door! I race through the kitchen to see Matt leaning against the door, grinning at me. I run over and let him in.

"I wasn't expecting to see you today." I lock the door and then launch myself into his arms.

He catches me easily, wraps my legs around his waist and kisses me long and hard as he carries me back into the kitchen. His body is tight. Energy is coming off him in waves. He's edgy. Rough.

"Are you almost done here?" he asks.

"Yeah, I just have to get stuff ready for tomorrow. Shouldn't take long."

He sets me on my feet and kisses me once more, his hands fisted in my hair, before reluctantly letting me go and leaning his hips on the countertop.

I quickly clean the counters, stack my trays and take a quick inventory to make a mental list of what will be on tomorrow's menu.

"Don't take your apron off," he commands quietly. His voice has that edge to it, the one he uses in the bedroom, and a chill moves through me as I look at him over my shoulder.

"Ever?"

"Four days without you, Nic. It's been a motherfucker of a week, and I'm a bit on edge today."

It's a warning. He's in full bossy dominant mode, and it's such a damn turn-on I don't know what to do with myself. I bite my lip and nod then turn back to the task at hand, if a bit off-kilter and shaky. Finally, when I'm finished, I face him, standing across the room, my hands at my sides, waiting for him to tell me what comes next.

It's as natural as breathing, which is something I might want to ponder later, but all I can think about right now is that I'm happy to see him, and he needs me for this.

Whatever it is he's about to do to me, do *with* me, I'll give him freely.

"Come here," he commands.

I obey, walking to stand just a few feet in front of him, my eyes trained on his.

"Undress but leave that apron on."

"Can I lower it off my neck long enough to take my shirt off?" I ask, no sarcasm in my voice.

His eyes soften, but he doesn't smile. "You may."

I pull the loop of the apron over my neck, letting it hang at my waist so I can pull my shirt and bra off, then pull my pants and panties over my hips and down my legs. Just as I move to replace the apron around my neck, he interrupts me with, "You can leave it down."

It falls out of my hands, and I'm standing before him, naked except for the apron wrapped around my waist.

His sea-blue eyes travel over me, hot and full of lust. His hands are clenching in and out of fists, itching to touch me, but he waits.

How he ever learned to be this patient, I have no idea. I've never been patient. So this is slow torture.

Finally, he steps to me and drags his knuckles down my cheek before bending to kiss my lips. "This isn't going to be soft or gentle, Nic. I don't have that in me right now."

"Okay." Oh God, yes, please.

He takes both of my wrists in his hands, yanks me against him and kisses me again, the way he wants to. The way he needs to. With fire and control and *need*.

Suddenly, he turns me away from him and bends me over the stainless steel counter top. It's cold against my breasts and torso, and I gasp when my flesh meets it. There's no time to brace myself with my hands because Matt pulls them behind my back and ties them with my apron strings, making me immobile.

"I've wanted to play with this apron since I first saw you wearing it." His voice is hard and excited, and he turns me back to him and lifts me onto the countertop, keeping my hips at the edge, and off balance. He steps between my legs, his arms wrapped around my back, keeping me from falling back. "I won't let you fall."

"I know," I whisper, watching him, waiting to see where this goes, the excitement coursing through me. "Although, this is really unsanitary. If the health department walked in, they'd shut me down."

He grins. "This may not be the answer you want to hear, but right now I don't give a fuck."

With one arm bracing me, he unleashes his hard cock and pulls a condom out of his pocket, rips it open with his teeth and guides it down his length. He pushes a finger through my folds, testing me.

"So wet." His eyes meet mine, and he pushes inside me in one quick thrust, filling me completely.

My head falls back, but he grips my hair in his fist and holds me there, hands tied behind me, in his firm grip, as he begins to pound in and out of me, fucking me harder than I've ever been fucked before. My legs clamp around his hips as he rides me, his molten blue eyes pinned to mine, mouth open as he pants and murmurs incoherently.

Fuck, he's so damn sexy I can hardly stand it.

He pushes all the way in and pauses, grinding his pubis against my clit, and the friction, the fullness of his cock inside me, pushes me into an orgasm that makes my toes curl.

"Eyes!" he barks when my eyes close with the force of the energy moving through me.

I open them and watch him as he continues to push and grind against me, joining me as he comes inside me, jerking and yelling my name.

As he settles, he wraps his arms around my shoulders and pulls me against him, kissing my forehead, rocking back and forth, soothing us both while he's still inside me.

Finally, he pulls out and unties my hands while kissing me, as though he just can't get enough of me. When I'm free, I push my hands into his hair and hold on to him, enjoying the soft strands between my fingers, then caress down to his neck and over his shoulders.

"Are you okay?" I whisper against his lips.

He sighs and nuzzles my nose with his before leaning back. "I'm much better now."

He tugs the condom off and wraps it in a paper towel before shoving it in his pocket. "I'll throw it away somewhere that food isn't made."

I giggle as I put my clothes back on. "Who knew that a simple apron could be used in kinky sex?" I examine the apron before tossing it in the hamper.

"You'd be surprised what we'll end up using as restraints," Matt replies with a grin. "I can tie you up with just about anything."

"Good."

"Good?" he asks.

I nod and then shrug. "I seem to have a newfound affection for being tied up."

He growls and yanks me to him again. "Say shit like that and we'll go upstairs now where I can tie you up for the night, little one." He nuzzles my temple. "I love that you've come to trust me this much so soon."

"Let's go upstairs." Did I just say that?

He chuckles and shakes his head. "I promised I'd have dinner with Will and Meg tonight, and I want you to go with me. That's what I came over here for."

"Oh," I reply with a frown. "Are you sure you want me to go? It's okay if you want to go and I'll see you another time…"

"Stop."

My eyes find his in surprise.

"Why wouldn't I want you to come have dinner with me and my brother?" I frown and fidget. "Well, I guess I'm confused." *my brother and me.*

"About?"

I swallow and look down, but he tips my chin back with his finger. "What are you confused about?"

"What are we doing, Matt? Is this just a sex thing? Because taking me to spend time with your family kind of pushes whatever we have going on into a different area."

"This is not a *just* a sex thing." He frowns deeply, watching my face. "I'm sorry if that's what you thought. The sex is amazing, but I want to pursue a relationship with you, Nic. Wherever that takes us. I thought that's what you wanted, too."

I nod, feeling foolish. "I do."

"So, are we on the same page here?" He looks sincerely concerned, and it softens me even more. I lean in and kiss his chest before smiling up at him.

"Same page." I pull away and stack my boxes of cupcakes. "You carry these out to the car while I wipe down the countertop and run up and change."

"Where are we taking them?" Matt asks with a laugh. "Meg and Will can't eat all these. Well, yeah, Will probably could."

"We will take one box to them and the rest to the homeless shelter down the street. That's where I take all the leftovers every day."

His jaw drops as I pass him the last box.

"What?"

"You continue to surprise me, that's all."

"Giving cake to the homeless is surprising?"

"Most people wouldn't think of it. They'd just toss them out."

I shake my head adamantly. "I don't waste food. It's too expensive. Besides, I worked hard on those. Someone should enjoy them."

"Okay, let's go make someone's day and then go to dinner."

"It's a date."

CHAPTER SEVEN

~Matt~

"Why are you nervous?" I ask as we pull up to Will's house.

"I thought we were going out to eat." She fidgets in her seat, looking out at the big, stone house.

"Meg likes to cook," I reply and take her hand in mine, holding it firmly. "Look at me."

She turns those wide green eyes on mine, and my heart stutters. How can she have this effect on me after just a few weeks of knowing her?

"You've already met these people."

She nods and bites her lip. "I'm being stupid. I'm just not great with people."

I laugh loudly and shake my head. "Are you kidding me?"

"No."

"You're awesome with people. You talk to every customer who walks into your shop without hesitation."

"That's different," she whispers. "That's work. I'm kind of shy."

My eyes narrow on her. I never would have guessed that she's shy, based on how outgoing and talkative she is when she's in work mode.

"You'll be great. Meg and Will are fun, and you'll be Will's newest favorite person, thanks to the cupcakes." I wink at her and step out of the car, open her door and take her hand, pulling her up next to me. "Trust me."

"I do," she replies softly and gazes up to me. "And that surprises me, too."

"We're going to talk about this later," I whisper to her, my stomach still in knots from hearing her say that she trusts me.

This relationship won't work unless we trust each other implicitly.

"You brought me cupcakes!" Will exclaims when he opens the door for us.

My brother is a cocky pain in the ass much of the time, but I can't help but love the douche bag.

"Cupcakes?!" Samantha squeals from inside.

"Sam and Leo are here?" I ask as I lead Nic inside Will's house.

"Yeah, Meg figured we'd have them over, too, since they're in town." He eyes me over the white cupcake box in his hands before leaning in and whispering in my ear, "You and I will talk about this later."

I shrug and grin and take Nic's hand in my own, lacing our fingers.

"You know Nic," I gesture to the small dark-haired woman at my side.

Will nods and grins. "Thanks for bringing these."

"My pleasure. It was either bring them here or take them to the homeless."

"We still dropped three more boxes that size at the shelter," I add with a laugh.

"Thank God," Sam exclaims as she runs into the room, her blue eyes shining.

"Uh, we already had some today, sunshine," Leo reminds her as he joins us. "Hi, Nic."

"Hey." She smiles and grips my hand in a death grip.

It seems Nic has a crush on Leo.

As long as that's all it is, we'll be fine.

"Where did everyone go?" Meg exclaims from the kitchen.

"In here!" Will calls back. "Matt's here with Nic, and she brought me cupcakes!"

"What?" Meg exclaims and comes running from the kitchen. Her eyes widen when she sees that I'm holding Nic's hand, and then she grins widely. "Hey! Welcome!"

"Hi again." Nic grins and reaches out to shake Meg's hand but is scooped up in a big hug, much to her surprise.

"I'm so glad Matt brought you," Meg assures her.

"Me, too. Gimme the cupcakes, Montgomery," Sam demands, her hands outstretched.

"Kiss my ass," Will replies and holds the box close to him.

"There are a dozen in there," Nic assures them all. "Plenty for everyone."

"Are you kidding?" Will laughs. "That's one serving for me."

"Seriously, you have to share, babe." Meg laughs and loops her arm through Sam's.

"Why did we invite them?" Will pouts, then opens the box. "What kind are they?"

"There are some carrot cake, red velvet and strawberry shortcake." Nic returns to my side and wraps her arm around my waist, as if we've been together for years.

I loop my arm around her shoulders and kiss the top of her head. She needs to be close to me right now to feel secure, and I'm happy to give that to her.

Fuck, I'll give her anything she wants.

"We haven't tried those." Leo grins. "You'll have to try something new, sunshine."

"Happily," Sam responds.

"Well, before you all get high on sugar, let's have dinner." Meg shoos us all into the dining room as she takes the pastry box from Will. "I'll put these in the kitchen until later."

"What's for dinner?" I ask loudly. "I'm starving."

"Chicken Parmesan with pasta," Meg calls back as we all sit around the table, and Will sets one more plate.

"Lots of carbs," I comment with a raised brow at Will.

"Fuck off, man, it's summer."

"Just saying. You don't want to ruin your girlish football figure."

Nic is watching Will move, his shoulders and arms. She appreciates men, and I can't find any fault in that.

"Will has the hardest body in this family," Sam mentions casually while sipping a glass of wine. "I don't think one meal of pasta is going to ruin that."

"Sam, do you want to run away with me?" Will asks sincerely. "You're clearly now my favorite."

"I'd have to kill you, and I can't make records from prison," Leo responds with a laugh.

"Sorry, football star," Meg replies as she returns to the dining room with a big bowl of salad. "You're stuck with me."

"No one else I'd want to be stuck with." Will sweeps Meg into his arms and kisses her soundly. "You sit. I'll go get the rest."

Meg sighs and drops down into her chair, a happy smile on her lips. "He's hot."

Nic lays her hand on my knee and squeezes. I love that she likes to have her hands on me, always touching me. It makes tying her up that much more fun.

She's smiling widely, enjoying the banter of my crazy family.

"They're fun," she whispers to me.

"Just wait until you're with all of us. It's never dull." I kiss her temple and turn to Leo. "When do you head back out on the road?"

"Not for a few weeks. We're taking some time off."

"Did you bring your guitar?" Meg asks hopefully.

Meg and Leo grew up together in several foster homes and have maintained the sibling relationship throughout the years. They didn't speak for a while, but they've recently been reunited and spend a lot of time together.

"Not tonight." Leo shakes his head. "I want to go over some lyrics with you after dinner. We just need one guitar for that."

"You write songs together?" Nic asks and passes me the pasta.

"We have for most of our lives," Meg confirms. "I'm better at it than he is, though."

"You wish," Leo tosses back.

"That's so cool."

"Do you play any instruments?" I ask Nic.

She nods and chews on some salad. "I'm classically trained in piano."

I lower my fork to my plate and stare at her in surprise. "Seriously."

"Yeah." She shrugs like it's no big deal. "My aunt was a concert pianist, and she taught me and my sister."

"Cool." Sam grins. "I play, too."

"I always feel so musically stupid when I'm around them," Will mutters with a laugh.

"I bet we can't throw a football sixty yards," Nic replies.

"And I can't bake cupcakes to save my life," Meg adds. "I can cook all day, but ask me to bake, and I'll end up poisoning everyone."

"What can Matt do?" Sam asks with a tilt to the head.

"He can…" Nic begins, but I clamp my hand over her mouth and laugh.

"I can arrest you for harassment," I reply drily.

Nic's eyes are smiling above my hand.

"Yeah, you scare me, Montgomery." Sam's voice is dry as she eats her meal.

"Have you heard from Caleb and Bryn?" Meg asks.

"I got an e-mail from him," Will responds. "But it was about a week ago. He said they're having fun."

"They head back on Friday," I reply. "I got an e-mail the same day you did. Sounds like Dom's place is nice."

"I'd love to take Meg there sometime," Will replies and grins at his fiancée.

"You won that silent auction for a trip to Italy, remember?" Meg reminds him.

"That's right." He nods.

"You could swing by and check out Dom's place while you're there," I suggest.

"Good idea." Meg grins and takes a sip of her wine. "So, what else has been going on?"

"Luke is throwing a birthday party for Natalie at their place next Saturday," Sam announces.

"At the new house?" I ask.

Sam nods. "Yeah, it's beautiful."

"It's not far from here." Meg grins. "So I can love on those babies any time I want."

"When is Natalie due?" Nic asks.

"Not until this fall," Sam responds. "Her belly is so cute. Nat is beautiful pregnant."

"Nat is just always beautiful," Meg adds.

"So is it going to be a pool party?" Will asks. "We can set up the pool volleyball."

"Yep, pool party," Sam confirms. "The parents are keeping all the kids, so it'll just be the siblings."

"Can you get Saturday off from the shop?" I murmur down at Nic.

"Oh, you have to come!" Meg agrees.

Nic blushes and bites her lip. "I think I can get coverage for the day."

"Excellent." I kiss her cheek and glance up to find Will staring at me with raised eyebrows.

"Would you be willing to bring some cupcakes?" Sam asks excitedly.

"Sure." Nic shrugs. "I've been thinking about coming up with some new flavors, too. Maybe I can do something brand new, just for her."

"That would be awesome," Meg exclaims. "She's a photographer. Can you decorate them fun and stuff?"

"Absolutely." Nic nods enthusiastically. "I already have some ideas."

"Great, I'll let Luke know that we have the cake covered." Sam pulls her phone out of her bra and quickly taps out a text message.

"You don't have to do that," I assure Nic, frowning at Meg and Sam. "I want you to take the day off and enjoy yourself. You don't have to work."

"Oh! No, really," Meg agrees. "I don't want you to work either. I just know that they'll be delicious."

"It's fine," Nic assures Meg and looks up at me. "I don't mind at all. It's fun."

"Are you sure?"

"Yes." She nods happily and squeezes my knee again.

"Good, because I've already confirmed with Luke." Sam smiles innocently.

"Okay, now I want cupcakes." Will stands and walks into the kitchen to grab the box full of Nic's cakes and returns to the table.

"Mmm…" Sam sighs as she bites into a strawberry cupcake. "Seriously so good. Can I have a bite of your carrot?" she asks Leo.

"Can I have a bite of yours?" Leo asks.

"Fuck no."

"Then, no, I'm not sharing either." He laughs and takes a big bite of the cake. Everyone but Nic is enjoying her efforts.

"You're not having one?" Meg asks before I can.

Nic shakes her head and smiles. "Nah, not tonight."

"You're missing out." Leo grins and winks at Nic. "They're delicious."

"Dear God, woman," Will moans and reaches for a third. "Run away with me."

"You say that to all the girls." Nic laughs. "But I'm glad you like them."

"You caught a good one." Will winks at me. "She can stay."

I smile and nod at my brother.

Fuck yes, she can stay.

***

"Talk," Will commands as we sit at the bar of his playroom. He has a full wet bar with tall stools.

Sam and Nic are chatting animatedly on a nearby couch. Meg and Leo have their heads together across the room, Meg with her guitar and Leo with a notebook and pencil, talking music.

"Since when do you have a piano?" I ask, pointing to the upright in the corner near where Meg and Leo are working.

"Leo plays, and he and Meg use it when they're writing," Will replies with a smile. "It makes her happy."

I smirk, but can't help but envy my brother just a little. He found a woman who loves him deeply. Meg doesn't give a shit about his celebrity. Hell, she almost loves him *despite* it, and that's something that we all worried about when it came to Will finding a woman. With his celebrity status, finding a true-hearted woman could have been a challenge.

But Meg fits him. She doesn't take his shit and supports him wholly. She also continues to pursue her own nursing career, even though she certainly could quit her job and be a housewife.

Just mentioning the idea to Meg might get you stabbed in the face.

And that just makes me love her more.

"Hey, Nic, can you come here, please?" Leo asks.

My eyes narrow as he crooks his finger at Nic, and she grins and walks over to join the rocker and Meg.

"What's up?"

"Can you play this?" Meg asks, holding the paper out to her.

"Uh, this is a bunch of squiggles." Nic laughs.

"Welcome to my world," Sam calls out and grins.

"Here, I'll show you how it's supposed to sound. We need to hear it with the guitar." Leo sits at the piano and gestures for Nic to join him and begins to play.

"Why don't you just play it?" Nic asks nervously.

"Because I need to write." He grins and shows her how the melody should sound, then sits and listens as Nic picks it up, playing beautifully.

She never stops surprising me.

"She's good," Will murmurs.

"I had no idea," I reply softly.

"So talk while she's preoccupied."

I glance at my brother, who's watching me closely, and then turn my gaze back to the powerhouse of a woman on that piano bench.

"What?" I ask.

"I've never, *never*, seen you with a woman," Will replies softly.

"That's an exaggeration, drama queen."

"High school doesn't count."

TIED WITH ME | 103

I shrug. I knew this was coming, and it'll come again Saturday when I take her with me to Nat's party.

"I like her."

"Jesus, you're stubborn," Will growls and shoves his hand through his hair.

Nic continues to play the piano, surprising Leo when she changes some notes, telling him that it sounds better like this.

Leo scowls, listens, and then grins.

"You're right." Meg nods. "It's smoother."

"She's amazing," I whisper to Will. "She's smart and kind. Sexy as fuck."

"She is pretty hot," Will agrees with a nod and then laughs when I glare at him. "Dude, I'm perfectly happy with my own hot woman." His face sobers. "But does she know…"

"She knows," I confirm. "And we're good."

Will nods. He and Isaac have never really understood my bedroom preferences, but they're as supportive of me as I am of them, which means they'd have my back no matter what.

Caleb gets it. I can't wait for him to get home so I can talk to him about all of this.

"I like her, man." Will clamps his hand on my shoulder. "She's sweet. I think she'll get along well with the family, if that's where you're heading with this."

"It's where I'm heading."

Will nods, watching the three of them play the music and smile and laugh together. "Meg's already marrying you off in her head. You know that, right?"

I laugh and shake my head. "Of course she is. Meg wants everyone to be happy."

"She's a lot like Nat in that way," Will agrees. "Jules might be a hard sell."

"Jules loves everyone, too," I disagree, thinking of my sweet baby sister. "She's just a little protective of her brothers. She never had an issue with Meg."

"No, but that's because she's known Meg since college," Will replies. "And Bryn's been around forever, too. It'll be interesting to see how she reacts to someone she doesn't know."

"I'm not worried about Jules," I reply drily.

"You will worry when she and Nat take Nic shopping." Will shakes his head ruefully. "Those two are responsible for keeping Seattle's commerce thriving."

"At least they're doing their part," I reply with a grin.

"Looks like your girl has a bit of a crush on Leo." Will gestures toward them with his chin.

Leo has hugged her, excited about the progress they made on the song, and Nic is blushing furiously.

"That doesn't worry me either." I smirk. "Leo's a rock star, and Nic's a fan. She'll get over it."

"I wonder if she knows who Luke is." Will says thoughtfully. "She doesn't seem to mind being around me."

"That's because you're a douche bag," I reply.

"Whatever, moron." Will laughs.

"I know what you're getting at. It's hard to be with our family. But I trust her." I scratch my cheek then cross my arms over my chest.

"Okay." He grins at me smugly. "I knew you'd fall in love eventually."

"I'm not..." I begin, but he cuts me off with a loud laugh.

"Right. That's what I said, too. Now look at me, so in love with her I can hardly see straight, and getting married." Will's face softens when he watches Meg play her guitar. "I wouldn't change it for anything. She's all that matters, Matt."

I take a deep breath and watch Nic at the piano, tickling the keys, singing under her breath, off in her own world.

She's all that matters.

CHAPTER EIGHT

~Nic~

"Thanks for taking me with you," I murmur to Matt as we walk up to my apartment.

I rub my temple, hoping to alleviate the dull ache that's been throbbing behind my eyes all day and has only gotten worse since dinner.

Matt lays his hands on my shoulders and rubs, making me moan in pleasure. "There's nowhere else I'd have you be."

I unlock the door and lead him inside my apartment, but turn and stop him from following me inside. "I'm not going to be the best company tonight, Matt."

He frowns as he takes my face in his hands. "What's wrong?"

"I've had a headache all day, but it seems to be getting worse, so I think I'll just take a shower and go to bed." I shrug and offer him a small smile. "I'm sorry."

"What are you sorry for?" He takes my hand, kisses my knuckles tenderly, sending electricity up my arm, before pulling me behind him to the bedroom.

"For ending the night early."

"Do you mind if I stay?" His voice is soft, gentle. He brushes his knuckles gently down my cheek before leaning in and kissing my forehead carefully.

"I don't mind," I reply.

"Have a seat." He gestures to the bed, but I shake my head.

"I really just want to take a hot shower and go to sleep, Matt. If you change your mind and don't want to stay, it's okay."

He steps closer and wraps his arms around me, pulling me in for a big hug.

I wrap my arms around his waist and hang on, close to tears, and I have no idea why. I had a great time with his family. He hasn't done anything wrong.

Damn hormones.

He runs one big hand down my back to my ass and back up again before sighing and whispering against my hair, "I don't want to go, little one. I want to take care of you."

I begin to shake my head no, but he chuckles quietly.

"Just relax and let me take care of you. Let go. I'm going to help you get rid of this headache."

It suddenly occurs to me that just having him here with me has helped. Who knew that a good, firm hug could ease a headache?

Matt kisses my hair and gently pushes me back onto the bed before marching into the attached bathroom. I hear water running in the tub and soft music begins to play, which must be coming from Matt's phone, before he walks back into my bedroom and pulls my shirt over my head. He undresses me slowly, careful not to jostle my head as the smell of jasmine fills the air.

"You used my bubble bath," I whisper.

"I like it," he replies calmly. His hands are warm but don't travel my skin the way they normally would when he has me naked. Instead, he's comforting.

Loving.

He leads me into the bathroom, and I'm surprised to see candles flickering around the room. The bathtub is my favorite part of the apartment. It's a large old-style claw-foot tub set against the wall and is currently full of water and bubbles. I step inside and lower myself into the fragrant water, sighing with relief as I lean back against the white porcelain.

"Water too hot?"

"Mmm," I murmur.

"Is that a yes or no?" he asks with a laugh.

"Feels good," I reply. My eyes slide closed, and I float weightlessly. The pain behind my eyes begins to fade.

"Can I get you something to drink?" he asks quietly.

"No, thank you," I whisper. "You can join me, though."

"No, this is just for you, baby. Relax. I'll be back."

I open one eye to see him walk out of the bathroom and shut the door behind him to keep the warmth in the bathroom. I sigh and sink down lower into the hot water. It is a bit too warm, but it feels fantastic.

I've never trusted someone enough to take care of me. I would have said that I don't need someone to take care of me. And, truth be told, I don't. I can take care of myself just fine, thank you very much.

But having someone around to pamper me a bit, just because he can, isn't a bad deal at all.

"How are you feeling?" Matt joins me, kneeling beside the tub.

"Better." I grin at him and raise a wet hand to cup his cheek. He turns his face and plants a kiss to my palm. "Thank you."

"We're not done yet," he replies, his clear blue eyes smiling.

"We're not?"

He shakes his head and holds his hand out for mine, pulling me out of the cooling water. He wraps a towel around my shoulders and dries me off, then leads me back into the bedroom, where he's lit more candles.

"Lie on your stomach," he instructs me, pointing to the center of the bed.

I shrug and climb up onto the bed, smiling at Matt's groan. "You okay?"

"You did that on purpose," he growls.

"Did what?" I look back over my shoulder and bat my eyelashes innocently.

"Stuck your ass and beautiful pussy in the air for me to see," he replies.

"I don't know what you're talking about." I giggle, lie on my stomach and sigh in contentment when Matt's oil-coated hands begin to knead my shoulders. "Oh God."

"Not too deep?" he asks.

"You can go deeper," I reply and melt under his touch. Instead of flaring to life in lust, my body settles, calms under Matt's magical touch. "You're good at that."

"Just breathe deeply and enjoy," he murmurs.

Being the object of a pampering Matt is perhaps the best thing I've ever experienced. My already relaxed muscles from the hot bath relax further, loosening until I'm simply a pile of mushy goo on the sheets.

"You're going to make me drool," I mutter.

"I hope that's a good thing." He chuckles.

"You have amazing hands," I reply as he finishes rubbing my shoulders and backs away so I can sit up.

"Here." He tugs the covers up over me as I snuggle down into my bed, yawning deeply.

"Are you leaving?" I ask with a frown. I don't want him to go.

"I'd like to sleep here with you, if that's okay."

I grin and pull the covers back in a silent invitation. "I think it's perfectly okay."

A smile spreads over his handsome face as he strips down to his boxer-briefs. I never tire of seeing his perfect body. A flare of recognition flows through me as my eyes travel the length of him.

"If you keep looking at me like that, sweetheart, I'll have no choice but to fuck you until we both pass out, and I've already made up my mind to simply cuddle you tonight, so be good."

"I'm always good." I grin.

Matt laughs as he climbs between the cool pink sheets with me and pulls me up against him, my head resting on his chest. "Did you have fun tonight?"

"I did." I grin, thinking of the banter between Matt and his brother, how the girls accepted me so readily. "They were really nice to me."

"They're good people," he murmurs. "I'm excited for you to meet the rest of the gang next weekend."

"How many people will be there?" I ask. My finger is making swirly designs across his chest, down his stomach and back up again, making his muscles twitch under my touch.

Fuck, I love touching him.

"Well, we are a big group. Let's see." He purses his lips in thought. "Luke and Nat, Jules and Nate, Isaac and Stacy, Will and Meg, Leo and Sam, Caleb and Bryn, Mark, Dominic, and you and I, so that's…"

"Sixteen people?!" I ask, shocked.

"Yeah." He grins and shrugs. "I told you, we're a big group."

"Wow. It must be fun to always have that many people around." I settle my head back on his chest and feel the tears threaten again. I don't know what it's like to have that kind of support system. I made the choice to live far from my family long ago, and I certainly don't have a circle of friends that big.

"It can be a pain in the ass, too." He laughs. "They're all nosy, so you'll get a lot of questions."

"How do you want me to answer them?" I ask.

"Honestly, of course." He tilts my head back and frowns down into my eyes. "Why would you ask that?"

"They're going to want to know how we met," I remind him. "Especially the girls."

He sobers, as though he hadn't thought of that. "Just tell them we met at a party. That isn't a lie."

"Okay." I nod. It's true, we did meet at a party. "So, your family doesn't know about your…preferences?"

"My brothers know some," he replies and pushes his fingers through my short hair. "Caleb knows more than the others."

"I won't say anything you don't want me to," I assure him.

"What happens between you and me behind closed doors is our business, Nic. It's no different than me asking Will if he likes to use toys when he fucks Meg. I'd never ask that. It's none of my business."

I wrinkle my nose at him and giggle. "I don't think I want to know."

"Trust me, neither do I. Although, I should warn you, the girls like to talk about orgasms and sex in general when they get together and alcohol is involved. But it's always in generalities, not specific to their relationships."

"Of course they do," I reply with a scoff. "We're women."

He closes his eyes and sighs deeply. "You'll get along fine."

I grin and kiss his chest.

"Are you sleepy?" he asks.

"A little."

"How is your head?"

"Better."

"What do you usually do before you fall asleep?" he asks and kisses my forehead.

"I read."

He glances around my room and spies my e-reader on my bedside table, picks it up and raises an eyebrow in question.

"You want to read to me?" I ask with a laugh.

"Sure." He wakes up the tablet, and the book I've been reading is immediately displayed. "Do you mind?"

I bite my lip and look from my book to his face and back again. If I remember correctly, things were getting very interesting in the story when I put it down the night before.

"It's a romance novel," I warn him.

"I don't mind."

"Okay." I shrug and settle in next to him, where I can watch his face as he reads. "Read on."

"What's this called?" he asks and looks into my eyes.

"*Kaleb*. It's by Nicole Edwards."

"One of your favorite authors?"

"Yes. Bailey recommended her to me a few months ago. She's excellent."

"Okay, here we go." He clears his throat and begins to read.

"Lean into me," Gage told her, and she did as she was told. It didn't take a rocket scientist—or someone who had done this before—to know what they were getting ready to do. Had she not been on the verge of begging them to fuck her into oblivion, she might've been worried.

Kaleb's warm mouth trailed kisses down her spine as she continued to impale herself on Gage's cock. She couldn't quicken her pace because both men were controlling her movements, and she was beginning to get frustrated. Then, just when she was about to tell them to get on with it, something cool slid down the crack of her ass, followed by a warm finger.

"Interesting," Matt mumbles. He tosses me a curious look and settles down deeper into the bed to keep reading. His voice is deep, and the sound of him reading the erotic images is turning me on.

Big-time.

Kaleb's big hand pressed down on her back, flattening her against Gage and holding her still. She was filled entirely with Gage's iron hard erection, and Kaleb was teasing her anus with a gel slicked finger.

"Oh!" Damn, it felt good. "More." Zoey wondered if she'd ever be able to look at either of them again after this. They'd turned her into a wanton slut in just the last hour, proven by her begging.

When Kaleb's finger slid into her, Zoey tensed momentarily, her body instinctively trying to force out the intrusion.

"Relax for me, baby," Kaleb said, his mouth shockingly close to her ear. "Let me fuck your beautiful ass, Zoey."

Matt clears his throat again and lowers the tablet to his side, watching me carefully. "Does this turn you on?"

"It's hot," I reply. Fuck, yes, it turns me on!

"Is a threesome something you're interested in?" His eyes are hot, watching me intently, and I wrinkle my forehead as I think of my answer.

"I think it's something that most women fantasize about, wonder what it would feel like. Having two men focus entirely on her pleasure." I shrug and blush. "But I'm way too shy for that."

He sets the tablet on the bedside table and rolls toward me, facing me but not touching me.

"There are other ways to feel what it would be like to have sex with two men at once."

I frown in confusion.

"Let me make this clear right now, little one." He cups my cheek in one palm and holds me in his intense gaze. "I will never share you. The thought of someone else touching you doesn't sit well with me, and I'm not interested in watching you with someone else. That isn't my kink, and I won't allow it."

He drags his fingertips down my cheek and over my neck then cups my breast in his palm, making my legs squirm against the dull ache that has settled between them. "But, I can use toys, or even my own fingers, to give you the same full feeling."

My eyes widen on his. Is he serious?

"Have you ever had anal sex, Nic?"

"No," I whisper.

"Are you interested?"

"Tonight?" I squeak.

"No." He chuckles and kisses my forehead. "No sex tonight. I'm enjoying just being with you. Holding you. But it's something we can explore if you want. I would love to push your boundaries a bit, help you learn more about yourself."

As I process his words, I'm shocked to discover that the possibility of exploring the kinkier side of sex doesn't scare me in the least. It excites me, especially knowing that it's Matt who will be with me every step of the way.

"I'd like that," I reply softly.

"Do you remember when I told you that I'm a member of a club?" he asks quietly.

I nod, wary of where he's taking this conversation.

"I'd like to take you there this weekend."

I swallow hard, watching his face. He's waiting patiently, watching me, his big hand petting me soothingly.

"Why?" I whisper.

"Because I want to share that part of my life with you, Nic." He frowns and glances up as though he's trying to gather his thoughts. "I can show you things that will excite you. Some might scare you. Turn you on. You don't have to be interested in all of it. In fact"—he grins wolfishly—"you might not like *most* of it. But some of it might interest you. I'd love to show it to you."

"Is it like the erotic festival where we met?" I ask.

"Not really. It's easier to show you than try to describe it to you. But I guarantee you this"—he pulls me closer, wraps his arms around me and nuzzles my nose with his own—"if you are uncomfortable at all, all you have to do is say so and I'll take you out of there. I'll be right beside you every second. I promise you'll be perfectly safe."

"I always feel safe with you," I reply honestly. "What would I wear?"

"The outfit you wore to the festival is perfect. Is that a yes?"

"Yes, I'll go with you."

He kisses me deeply, but before I can lean in and take it further, he pulls back, picks up the tablet and continues with the story.

She couldn't verbally respond because her breath was locked in her chest...

CHAPTER NINE

What am I doing here?

Matt parks the car, cuts the engine and takes my hand in his, laces our fingers and pulls in a deep breath while watching me closely.

"Look at me."

I bite my lip and find his bright blue eyes with my own.

"How do you feel?"

"Like I'm about to dive into a shark tank."

He laughs in surprise and smiles warmly at me. "Well, at least you're honest." He kisses my knuckles tenderly. "What are you scared of?"

I shrug and look out the window toward the seemingly harmless house to my right. It's a large house, but other than being big, it looks fairly normal. It's set back in the trees, away from nearby neighbors. There are about a dozen cars parked in a small lot to the left of the building, ranging from expensive Mercedes to simple Toyotas. For all anyone would know, a Tupperware party could be going on inside.

If only.

"I won't ask you again." His voice has hardened in warning, and it makes my stomach clench in warmth.

Jesus, I *enjoy* riling the man up.

"I'm not sure," I reply softly. "Maybe I'm just nervous because I don't know what to expect."

"You can expect to see people having sex. Some are into hard-core fetishes. Others just like to watch. Look at me," he repeats, and I comply immediately. "While we're here, you're mine to take care of implicitly. I won't leave you, not for a minute. Your safe word is 'red.' And it's important that you do as I say, not because I'm on a power trip, but because it could be for your safety."

I swallow and nod, watching his hard, stern face.

God, he's hot when he shifts into his role as Dominant.

"If you have a question, you ask me. I won't make you kneel tonight. My name is Matt, not sir or master."

"But you said…"

"Fuck what I said, Nic. This is you and me. Every relationship is different, remember?"

I nod and relax as I realize that I don't have to play a role I'm not comfortable with. Our dynamic won't change when we get inside.

"Will you want me to do…stuff?" I ask.

"I will want you to do whatever you're comfortable with. *With me.* I don't share, remember? And I'm not much of an exhibitionist." He clicks us out of our seat belts, pushes his seat back and pulls me into his lap, holding me closely against him. "This is not meant to scare you, little one. We're here to have fun, and if it's not fun, or interesting to you, just say the word and we'll go home."

"I want to make you happy," I admit and bury my face in his neck, breathing him in.

He's dressed in a black button-down and slacks, much like he was the night I first met him. He smells clean and fresh and like *Matt*, soothing me.

"You do make me happy, baby. After tonight, if this is something you can't or won't do, we don't ever have to come back."

But the thought of him coming here on his own freaks me the fuck out!

"Stop," he commands and tilts my face up so I have no choice but to meet his gaze. "*I* don't ever have to come back."

"But…"

"Enough talk for now. Let's go in." He smiles widely and kisses my forehead. "Trust me."

"My trusting you is the only reason I'm here."

He stills for a moment and then kisses me softly, longingly. My thighs clench as he pushes his fingers into my hair and holds on tightly. Finally, he withdraws and rests his forehead against my own.

"Thank you for that."

He leads me up to the door and rings the bell, and almost immediately a man answers. He's maybe the biggest man I've ever seen in my life. Well over six and a half feet tall, as wide as the door frame, and his skin is a dark, rich mocha. Diamond studs wink from his ears, and a single gold chain with a thick cross hangs around his neck. He stares at us for a moment and then breaks into a smile.

"You look good with a woman on your arm, Montgomery."

"I look good with *this* woman on my arm," Matt agrees. "Nic, this is Reggie."

"Are you security?" I ask with a grin and shake his hand as he leads us inside.

"I'm the beauty and the brawn around here," he replies with a chuckle and winks at me, immediately setting me at ease. "Welcome to Temptation. Have fun."

"Thanks, Reg."

Matt takes my hand and leads me out of the foyer into a large great room. It must have originally been a family room. Music assaults my ears. Rihanna is singing about diamonds in the sky. It's loud but not too loud that you can't hear a conversation right next to you. The floors are hardwood, but that's where the resemblance of a normal home ends. There is a bar along one wall with a tall man tending it.

There are deep-cushioned couches and chairs in reds and browns set about the dimly lit room in small groups, perfect for people to sit and chat. But in addition to that, there are stations around the edges of the room. One woman is naked, suspended from the ceiling and being smacked with a leather crop. I have no idea what the equipment is called, but it all has restraints attached, obviously to hold a person down while they get a good beating with some kind of instrument.

A shiver runs down my body.

"You're not a masochist, baby," Matt whispers in my ear.

My eyes whip up to meet his, and he smiles softly while brushing his finger down my jawline. "Your eyes are as big as saucers. Look"—he points to men in plain black T-shirts positioned about the room—"those guys are security. We call them dungeon masters. They make sure that nothing goes beyond what anyone is comfortable with. This is all consensual, Nic."

I take a deep breath and look around again. People are laughing, talking. Some women are kneeling at the feet of their partners, on pillows, hands resting on their knees and heads bowed. One Master feeds his sub fruit from his plate while he chats with a man sitting across from him, who is getting a blow job.

Holy shit.

"Let's get you a drink, and then we'll walk around." Matt leads me to the bar, my hand tucked firmly in his.

"Montgomery!" the bartender bellows and marches over to take our order.

"Hey, Sal. It's busy tonight."

"That it is." Sal nods with a grin. He seems like a happy man, with smiling hazel eyes and a lopsided smile. His lips are full. His hair is light blond, reflected in his light eyebrows and fair skin, and he's muscular. A white T-shirt hugs his torso, and black jeans mold his lean hips and thighs.

Sal's a hottie of epic proportions.

"Who is this beautiful little thing?" Sal asks Matt.

"This is Nic, my girlfriend. Nic, this is Sal. He's a Master here, and a gifted bartender."

"Hello," I murmur, my heart pounding at the sound of *girlfriend* falling so easily from Matt's lips.

"Nice to meet you, darlin'." He eyes Matt. "She's new."

"She is," Matt confirms.

"You can just call me Sal. We have a two-drink maximum here, darlin'. What can I get you?"

"I have a two-drink maximum myself, so that works," I reply with a wide smile. "I'll have a dry martini, please."

He cocks an eyebrow for a moment, and then he laughs, reaching for a martini glass. "What would you like, Matt?"

"Just water for me."

"Are you demonstrating tonight?"

"I hadn't planned to," Matt responds with a frown. "I'm just here to show Nic around tonight."

Sal nods and hands me my drink and a bottle of water for Matt. "I think Des needs a Shibari demo tonight, if you're interested."

Matt shakes his head and wraps his arm around my shoulders protectively. "Not tonight."

"Have fun then. Welcome, darlin' Nic." Sal winks and moves away to fill another order.

I sip my drink and sigh in happiness. "Sal makes a great drink."

"He does," Matt agrees with a chuckle and leads me through the room and up a wide staircase to the second floor, which is similar to the first, but there is no bar up here, the lights are dimmer, the music louder, and instead of couches and chairs, there are beds covered in red velvet around the edges of the room. In the center of the space are several platforms with more equipment I don't know the names of. Some have restraints hanging from the ceiling, and some are just simply beds.

All of it scares me and intrigues me at the same time.

But what catches my eyes are the people. The few dozen people scattered about the room are mostly naked. Some are fucking. Some are watching.

Directly to my right, two heavily muscled men are seducing a plump woman, caressing her body and whispering in her ear, kissing her nipples. There are hands and lips and groans everywhere.

My core tightens.

"Ah, just like the story the other night," Matt whispers into my ear. He's moved behind me, wrapped his arms around my waist, sliding his hand up my ribs to cup my breast in his palm. "Does that turn you on, little one?"

My breathing has turned choppy, and my heart is going to pound out of my chest.

If I'd worn panties, they'd be wet by now.

I nod, not taking my eyes off of the threesome. "Who are they?"

"That's Kevin and Gray. They're firefighters and always share their women."

My eyes widen further at the thought. "Always?"

"Yes."

"Are they gay?" I ask softly.

"No, they just enjoy sharing. They're best friends." The woman between them lets out a wail of ecstasy as Gray slips his head between her legs and laps at her center, while Kevin grips her hair in his fist and guides her mouth to his large, stiff cock.

Matt leads me farther into the space, past a couple kissing and caressing each other on a mattress, slowly undressing each other.

"Some couples like the idea of being watched," Matt murmurs in my ear, sending shivers down my spine. He continues to worry my nipple through my shirt. I'm stunned to realize I'd rather he just pull my strapless shirt down and unleash my breast to touch it properly.

Jesus, I'm becoming an exhibitionist.

"And others"—he nods toward the couple sitting not far away, lounging in each others' arms, watching the goings-on around them with content smiles on their faces—"others just want to watch."

"Do you have to have sex in public here?"

"No. That couple we just passed will most likely watch their fill then go to one of the private rooms to enjoy each other."

Oh.

"Did you ask permission to speak to Master Ethan?" a man not far from us yells in anger at a woman kneeling on a pillow on the floor next to him.

"No, Master." Her head is bent in submission and shame, and her shoulders are shaking.

I stiffen in rage.

Matt grips my waist tightly and whispers in my ear, "Just watch."

"Did I specifically tell you to be quiet?"

"Yes, Master."

"What happens when you defy me?" the man demands.

"I am punished, Master."

His eyes narrow on the woman next to him.

"Get punished, my ass," I whisper in indignation.

"Shh," Matt breathes into my ear.

Without another word, the man yanks the woman across his lap and lands a hard *smack* on one of her ass cheeks.

"Matt, he hit her!"

"Wait," Matt warns me.

"You'll get six, one for each word you said to him. Do you understand?"

"Yes, Master," she responds and moans in pleasure when he lands the second blow.

She likes it!

"Count!" He hits her for a third time, careful not to hit her in the same spot twice.

"Three," she moans.

And so it goes until the sixth blow. He shifts her, cradling her in his arms and whispering in her ear, then removes the pillow from the floor and makes her kneel without it.

"You'll get ten minutes without the pillow under your knees to make sure you don't do it again."

"Yes, Master." She smiles sweetly and kneels at his feet, seemingly content.

"She could have used her safe word at any time," Matt murmurs as he leads me away.

"She let him hit her."

"He spanked her, sweetheart."

"He left handprints," I argue.

Matt grins wickedly at me. "Yes, he did."

Holy shit.

"Excuse me, Master Matt." A woman approaches Matt, her head bent in respect and hands clasped at her waist.

Her very naked waist.

"Yes, Anna?" Matt answers.

"My Master and I would like to respectfully ask if you would like to restrain me," she responds softly. Her nipples are puckered. She's clearly very turned on at the idea.

Fuck that.

Matt raises his eyes over her shoulder to see a man leaning against the wall, arms crossed over his muscular chest, watching silently.

"Why did Master Alex send you over?"

"Because it was my idea, Master."

I just bet it was.

"I see. I will have to pass, Anna. I have a date this evening." Matt smiles at me. "This is Nic."

Anna frowns for a moment but then offers me a fake smile, nods at Matt and stomps away.

"You've clearly played with her before," I mumble. My body is stiff in anger and jealousy, which pisses me off more.

What he did before me isn't any of my business.

"Nic," he begins, but I shake my head and try to walk away. He grips my upper arm and pulls me around to face him. "I may not make you kneel and call me Master, but you will not top me here, do you understand? The past is the past, and the only woman I'm interested in touching is the one before me."

His jaw is clenched, and his eyes are deep blue and ice cold. His grip on my arm is firm, but he's careful not to hurt me.

God, I want him.

"Yes, *sir*," I mutter, stressing the word *sir*.

Matt shakes his head and laughs, rubs his hand over his mouth and watches me carefully. "Jealousy doesn't become you. I think I might have to teach you a lesson about who is in control here, little one."

He takes my hand and leads me over to an empty platform that has suspension chains hanging from the ceiling. He approaches one of the dungeon masters and murmurs in his ear, then turns to me with shining eyes.

"I'm going to undress you."

My mouth drops open in surprise, but when his eyes travel the length of me, undressing me with his gaze, I bite my lip and almost strip out of my clothes myself. I start to look around the room, but he grips my chin in his fingers and holds my gaze steady.

"You'll watch me and only me. There is no one else here but you and I, do you understand?"

I nod, but he pushes his face closer to mine.

"Words, Nic."

"I understand."

"What is your safe word?"

"Red." I swallow and watch his lips as he licks them. His thumb is tracing circles on my cheek, soothing me.

"Trust me."

"I do," I reply and know that I feel it, to my bones. He won't hurt me, and won't do anything to embarrass me. I can feel eyes on me around the room, but I focus on his voice and his blue gaze.

Focus solely on him.

A man drops a large black duffel bag at Matt's feet and discreetly backs away. Matt tucks one finger in my red, strapless top and pulls me to him, kissing me deeply, firmly. His tongue slips between my lips and laps at my mouth, exploring every inch, as his hands travel around to my back to unzip my shirt then discard it to the floor.

I'm not wearing a bra, so the cool air and Matt's kisses, the intensity of this crazy evening, have puckered my nipples to hard points. Matt drags his hands down my chest to cup my breasts, teasing the sensitive nubs with his fingers. I'm squirming where I stand, rubbing my legs together to try to ease the ache there.

Matt nibbles his way across my jaw and whispers in my ear, "Stay still."

My legs still, earning a grin from my demanding man.

He gently trails his fingertips along the waist of my short denim skirt, unzips it and lets it fall around my ankles, leaving me standing before him completely nude.

He sucks in a breath as his eyes roam down my body, curses under his breath and then chuckles ruefully.

"I think I'm pissed at myself for allowing these men to see what's mine. I want to punch them all for the thoughts that I know are running through their perverted heads."

His words warm me, make me feel sexy and strong, and I grin back at him.

"You like that, don't you, little one?" He kisses my forehead, my nose, and then my lips. "There might be an exhibitionist in you yet."

I swallow and gape at him. Me? No way!

"I want you to sit with your legs bent and ankles together." He helps me to the floor and kneels before me, my toes tucked between his knees. He unzips his duffel and pulls out long lengths of red ropes.

"I like red on you," he murmurs as he begins to loop the rope around my ankles and feet. "You can touch me while I work."

I smile and push my fingers into his light brown hair as he bends his head over my feet, working intently.

"May I speak?" I ask softly so only he can hear me. The music is too loud for anyone else to hear us.

"Of course," he replies.

"This is sexy."

"You'll get no argument from me," he says. "I'll be checking in with you to make sure you're comfortable. Got it?"

"Got it," I reply. "I love how soft your hair is."

He snickers and continues to work, looping the cord between each of my toes and back up to my ankles. When each toe is done, he twines the rope around my ankles and halfway up my calf, and then takes my hands and helps me stand.

"Bend your knees again."

I comply, and Matt runs his hand up my inner thigh to cup my center in his hand. "Good, it's not too tight."

My hands are braced on his shoulders, but he grabs two loops that are hanging shoulder-width apart from the ceiling and pulls until they're at shoulder height.

"Hold on to these so you don't fall."

I grip on to the loops and watch him intently. He's begun to sweat, so he unbuttons his shirt and discards it without a thought, giving me a prime view of his gorgeous chest and abdomen.

I wish he'd turn around so I can see his firm ass in those pants.

But I know he won't.

He won't take his eyes off me, not while he's got me in his ropes.

He crisscrosses the ropes, tying intricate knots, over my belly and around my back. When he walks behind me, I close my eyes, soaking in the feel of his fingers on my skin, the sound of his breaths, tuning out the eyes watching around the room.

Only him and me.

From behind me, he lays kisses across my shoulders and down my spine to my ass, where he presses kisses above each cheek, making me shiver in pleasure.

God, I want him.

I want him to make me come right here, in this room, in front of all of these people.

I want him.

The ropes loop around my breasts and over my shoulders but not around my neck.

"How do you feel?" he whispers in my ear, pressing his body along my length.

"Turned on," I answer honestly.

"Good."

He circles me twice, checking over his work, and when he's satisfied that it's not too tight and the pattern is to his liking, he approaches me and again presses his body to mine, his naked torso against my own.

"I'm going to tie your hands now," he whispers against my lips. "If you start to lose balance, just say 'stop,' and I'll readjust. You won't fall."

I smile softly and press a kiss to his lips. "I won't fall."

"God, I love this with you," he whispers as he traces the ropes with his fingertips. "You're so fucking beautiful."

He raises my hands up over my head, and the loops I'm holding on to tighten, as though they're on a pulley. My hands are pulled over my head, but my feet are still comfortably flat on the ground, so I'm not suspended, I'm simply stretched long. When my wrists are touching, he takes one of the loops away and has me clasp my hands together, fingers laced, holding on to just one loop, and begins to thread the ropes around my arms and hands and wrists, making his knots, watching my face. My eyes are trained on his face, enjoying the way his breath has quickened, the slight sheen of sweat on his upper lip, the way he bites his lower lip when he's working a particularly difficult knot.

It's like I'm floating, watching him, enjoying his enjoyment of the moment. My body is humming in anticipation, but my spirit is calm. My heartbeat is thrumming, my blood thick in my veins, and my pussy is as wet as it's ever been, but my mind is content, and my heart is in love with this man before me.

I love him.

When the last knot is cinched, his hands slowly glide down my arms, my sides, up my belly to my breasts. He takes a step back and then kneels in front of me and presses a kiss to my navel piercing, which he's showcased in a circular series of beautiful red knots.

He grins and kisses it again, then presses a string of kisses down my abdomen, over my bare pubis, and slips his tongue over my clit.

I suck in a deep breath and watch helplessly as he does it again, his eyes on fire with lust and pride.

"Bend your knees," he commands and lifts me effortlessly, his hands planted on the globes of my bottom, pulling my core toward his face. My hands grip the loop, and I hold on as he tilts my pelvis up, rests my calves on his head and buries his face in my core, sending me straight into a high I've never experienced before.

I cry out as he laps and sucks on my pussy lips, presses his nose on my clit and buries his tongue deep inside me, sending me into the most amazing orgasm of my life.

Holy fucking hell!

I'm gasping and writhing as he sets my feet back on the floor and pulls himself up to stand before me. He grips the back of my hair and tilts my head back to devour my mouth with his. I can taste myself on him, and it only turns me on more.

"Do you know how amazing you are?" he asks, urgency lacing his voice. "Do you have any idea?"

I can't answer him. I'm a panting, quivering, sweaty mess.

With a whispered oath, he digs in his duffel and pulls out scissors and begins to cut the ropes, my hands first.

"You don't want to untie me?" I ask breathlessly.

"No time," he replies. His face is hard and dark and looks almost…*angry.*

"What's wrong?" I ask. "What did I do?"

He looks down in shock and visibly takes a long, deep breath, then wraps one arm around my waist and presses himself to me.

"Nothing, baby. You're amazing. I don't have time to untie you because if I don't get you out of here and home in the next ten minutes, I won't be responsible for my actions. I need to be inside you, I need to love you, and an hour in a private room isn't going to do it for me. I need to get you home so I can spend the night showing you what you mean to me."

I'm stunned. My mouth has dropped open, and I can only watch as he cuts through the ropes, tossing them aside impatiently. When I'm free, he accepts a blanket from the same dungeon master from earlier and wraps me in it, lifts me into his arms and carries me out of the room and down the stairs. I'm surprised to find that the majority of the people in the house have come upstairs to watch Matt work, but I'm filled with pride, too.

What he does with ropes is simply beautiful. He makes me *feel* beautiful.

I loop my arms around his neck and press kisses to his jaw before tucking my head under his chin, letting him carry me to the car.

"Thank you."

"For?"

"Tonight."

"We're just getting started, little one."

CHAPTER TEN

~Matt~

I can't get back to my place fast enough. The ten-minute drive feels like hours. My body is clenched, every muscle tight with lust.

Fuck me, I want her so bad my teeth ache.

Seeing her there, in my club, with my ropes wrapped around her, the trust and love coming from her green eyes as I took her body to the edge of sanity and back again, was more than I've ever experienced with a woman before.

My body is drawn to her. I *need* to feel her flesh against mine. There is no want about it.

She's as necessary to me now as breathing.

She's still wrapped in the blanket next to me, her clothes tossed carelessly into the back seat.

"I forgot my sandals," she exclaims as she sits up straight in the seat and turns her gaze to me.

"I'll fetch them for you sometime this week," I assure her as I pull into my parking garage. I walk around to her door and lift her easily out of the car, carrying her toward the elevator.

"Is there a camera in this elevator?" she asks casually.

"No," I reply.

"Will you please set me down?"

I narrow my eyes on her, but she just blinks innocently up at me. I know exactly what she wants to do.

"I want your mouth on my cock more than just about anything right now, baby, but…" The bell dings, and the doors open to my floor. "We're already here."

She grins and pushes her fingers into my hair, the way she's been doing all night long. "Killjoy."

"I think you'll change your mind," I whisper and carry her through my apartment to my bedroom.

"We've never spent the night here," she comments, looking around.

"I like your apartment," I reply with a grin.

She smiles, her eyes happy. "I like you."

"Happy to hear it." I chuckle and lower her onto my king-size bed. I reach up for the restraints, but she stops me with a hand on my chest.

"Wait." She bites her lip, as though she's thinking hard about her next words. "I don't want you to restrain me this time. I want to be able to touch you while you make love to me."

Her voice is soft, tender, and I couldn't deny her if I wanted to. I release the restraints and back away from the bed to shed my clothes quickly and join her.

She opens her arms in invitation, and I willingly go to her, climb over her small body, rest my pelvis and heavy cock against her core and my elbows on either side of her head.

"What do you need, sweetheart?" I whisper.

"You. Just you," she responds sweetly. She hikes her sexy-as-fuck legs up around my hips, opening herself more to me.

My cock slides through her slick heat, the tip bumping against her clit as I grind my hips against hers. I reach over for a condom, but she stops me again.

"I can't get pregnant, Matt."

I gaze down at her sober face and feel my gut tighten. I've never gone without suiting up in my life.

"Birth control?" I ask.

A shadow moves across her face, but then she nods and smiles. "Yeah, I'm on the pill."

"Are you sure you're okay with this, baby? I don't mind using them."

"I want to feel *you*," she whispers and bites her lip.

I kiss her forehead and grin down into her stunning face. "You feel so fucking good, Nic," I moan against her lips and then sink down into her, kissing her for all I'm worth. My hands cup her head as my mouth plunders. My body is on fire. Her hands travel lazily up and down my back, leaving trails of sparkling energy down to my ass, where she cups and kneads the muscles there, a low moan coming from her perfect, plump lips.

"I love your ass," she mutters before biting my lower lip.

Jesus, when was the last time a woman touched me while I fucked her?

When was the last time I *made love?* I can't remember. I don't mind being touched, but rendering a woman helpless while I bring her body to heights she didn't know she was capable of is the greatest high there is.

Until Nic. Every experience with her brings me to my knees. I love having her tied up in my ropes, but right now, with her remarkable hands gliding over my body, I'd swear this is the best I've ever had.

During the entire scene at the club and the drive home, all I could think of was getting her here and drilling into her, over and over until I made us both scream, and now that I have her here, I just want to take my time with her, explore her.

Make her moan and squirm and get lost in what I can do to her body.

I nuzzle her nose and pull it down her cheek to her ear. "I'm going to make love to you all night, Nicole."

"Promise?" she whispers with a grin.

"Absolutely," I reply as I brush light kisses down her neck to her shoulder, where I can trace the beautiful pink flowers inked on her skin as I pull free from her body and get ready to take us both to the edge of sanity.

I drift down to her breasts and settle in to feast on the hard nubs, scraping them with my teeth then soothing them with my tongue. Nic's hips twist and shift beneath me, pushing against my stomach. I drag my lips down her smooth, tight stomach to her sexy-as-hell piercing and farther still to her core.

I ate her out not an hour ago, and I can't wait to do it again.

When my lips wrap around her clit, her hips buck up, but I grip her with my hands and hold her down against the bed. Her fingers plunge into my hair, and she holds on tightly.

I hollow my cheeks and pull her pussy lips into my mouth, sucking in a pulsing motion. She digs her heels into my shoulders when I push two fingers inside her and cries out as an orgasm rips through her. Her juices flow around my fingers, and I lap them up like honey.

Fucking amazing.

I climb up her body, but before I can push inside her, she plants her hands on my chest and pushes.

"On your back, detective," she orders with a grin.

I smile down at her, kiss her cheek and do as she directs, dragging her with me. She rears up on her knees and pulls her hands—and nails—down my chest to my cock, circles both hands along the length and begins pumping up and down, milking me, watching my face as she drives me mad.

"Ah fuck, Nic," I mumble. "Baby, you're gonna make me…"

Before I can finish, she smiles smugly and lowers herself to pull the crown of my cock into her mouth and sinks down until I can feel the back of her throat.

"Holy mother of fuck!" I cry out.

She bobs up and down, those lips tightening around my dick as she pulls up and sucks, her hand following the motion while the other hand cups and fondles my balls.

I fall back onto the bed and swear my eyes are crossed. Sparks flare in my vision, the room is spinning and a warm warning sets up residence at the base of my spine.

Fuck!

"Nic, if you don't stop—ah God you're good at that—I'm going to come, baby."

She simply moans and continues until I grip her shoulders and pull her up the length of me, crush my mouth to hers and settle her knees on either side of my hips.

"You're going to be the death of me," I whisper against her.

She raises herself up, grips the base of my cock in her fist and sinks down onto me, slowly impaling herself inch by delicious inch until I can't tell where I end and she begins.

Her head falls back, eyes closed, as she begins to raise and lower herself on me, riding me slowly, clenching that incredible cunt around my cock.

My God, she's perfect for me in every way.

She opens her bright green eyes and smiles as she watches me, hums in happiness as I glide my hands up her thighs to her waist and guide her up and down.

Finally, I can't stand being this far from her another moment. I sit up and wrap my arms around her waist, pull her breast into my mouth and suck, sweeping my tongue over the tight nub. My hands find her ass, and I lower her on and off of me as she wraps her arms around my neck and holds on for dear life.

"Love this," she murmurs, rocking her hips against mine, as we find a perfect rhythm as old as time.

Love you, I think to myself. Instead of being completely freaked out and fighting the compulsion to run in the other direction, my heart calms. Now I understand what drives my brothers with their women.

I get it.

"Mine," I whisper.

"Yours," she answers and tips her forehead against mine.

I reach between us and tease her clit with my thumb, and her pussy clenches around me, convulsing and shuddering.

"Come again for me, baby. Let go," I murmur, crooning to her, watching her unravel around me.

Her eyes are pinned to mine as she bears down, grinds her clit against my thumb and comes apart, screaming my name and digging her nails into my shoulders.

The sweet pulses around my cock pull me in with her and over the edge, coming long and hard inside her, gripping her hips with all my strength.

She'll have handprints there later, and I can't bring myself to give a shit.

She's mine.

***

"I can't believe I let you undress me in a room full of people," Nic mutters against my chest.

We're lying on the bed, my hand drifting lazily up and down her back as her finger traces my abs and over the tattoo on my rib cage.

She claims to be an ass girl, but she sure has a thing for my stomach.

"I don't think we'll be repeating that," I respond casually, masking the ball of unease in the belly she's currently tracing.

"Okay," she replies and watches me with bright eyes and flushed cheeks.

"God, you're beautiful," I whisper and drag my fingers down her cheek.

"Talk to me."

I lift an eyebrow. "What would you like to talk about?"

"Tonight. Why won't we be repeating it?"

"Because I'm not comfortable with anyone else seeing your body."

"But undressing me was *your* idea," she reminds me, her voice exasperated.

"I know, but in hindsight, I'm not comfortable with other men seeing you."

"So no more club?" she asks with a frown.

I grin to myself. So she enjoyed the club.

"We can go again, if you like, but there won't be any more demonstrations."

"What if you're asked to demonstrate on someone else?" she asks, her body tight with worry as she waits for my response.

I tip her head back so I can look her in the eye. "I already told you, you're the only one I want to touch."

"But you're a master. Don't you teach?"

"Yes, but it's not necessary."

"Maybe you can demonstrate with me dressed sometimes," she suggests and shrugs like it's no big deal.

"You'd do that for me?" I ask, cupping her face in my hand.

"You enjoy it, Matt. The thought of you doing it with someone else brings out my catty side, so, yeah, I'd do it for you."

I don't know what to say. Has anyone who means this much to me ever supported me so completely?

Only Caleb, but even he can't understand it completely, as he's never been in the lifestyle.

In one quick motion I reverse our positions and tuck her under me, pull my hips back and slip inside her and set to work showing her what her trust and obvious love mean to me.

***

"I'm glad you're home, man." I clasp Caleb's hand and lean in for a man hug, excited to see my brother.

"It's only been two weeks, dude. Did Seattle fall apart while we were gone?"

"No, but it's much more boring without you and the girls."

"Uncle Matt! Mommy and Daddy are home," Josie informs me happily, hanging on to her mom with desperate arms like she fears her mom just might slip away again.

"I know, sweetheart. I'm happy to see them, too."

"Hey, Matt."

"Hey, doll." I lean in and kiss Bryn's cheek. She looks happy. Content. "How's the most beautiful girl in Seattle?"

"Get your own girl," Caleb snarls, then scoops Maddie up in his arms. "I missed you, buttercup."

"I missed you, too, Daddy." She laughs and kisses his cheek.

"Girls, come help me unpack. I think there might be some Italian souvenirs for you in our bags."

"Okay!" the girls exclaim and follow their mom up the stairs.

"How are you?" I ask Caleb soberly.

"Never better," he responds, and I know he speaks the truth.

He had a rough time of it a few months ago, afraid to love that sweet woman and her daughters, but with the help of a counselor and my fist to his face, he came around and finally married Brynna.

"You both look great. Italy must have agreed with you."

"Dominic has a helluva place." Caleb nods. "It's quiet and beautiful. Perfect if you want to romance a woman."

"I'm glad you both enjoyed it." I chuckle and watch my brother. His cheeks redden, and I tilt my head as my eyes narrow. "What's going on?"

"What are you talking about?"

"Something's up. You never blush."

"Fuck you, I'm not blushing."

"Just say it."

He sighs as his eyes turn to the top of the stairs. "We weren't going to say anything for a while yet because it's early, but Bryn's pregnant."

"That's fucking awesome, bro." I pull him in for a quick hug, truly happy for my younger brother. "How early?"

"Only a few weeks, but the sticks say she's pregnant, so she's going to go see a doctor next week. Don't mention it to the rest of the family."

"That's your story to tell," I reply and clap him on the shoulder. "Congratulations."

"Thanks," he replies and pulls two beers out of the fridge, pops the tops and hands one to me. "What's up with you?"

I shrug and take a long pull on the beer. "Work. Had dinner at Will's last week."

Been sleeping with the woman I'm in love with since you left.

"I heard. Will said you brought the baker with you."

"Will never could keep his damn mouth shut," I grumble.

"Ashamed of her?"

"Fuck no!" I shake my head adamantly. "No, I just would have rather you heard it from me."

"So what's going on with her?"

I sigh and lean back against the countertop, trying to figure out how to form the right words.

"I've been sleeping with her." But that doesn't sound right. I've been more than sleeping with her. I've been consumed by her, falling in love with her.

"Is she okay with what you're into?" he asks softly.

"Yeah. It's new to her, so I've been honest but taking it slow. Took her to the club last weekend." I smile as I recall her tied up in my red ropes, pulled up tall, panting and turned on. "She enjoyed herself."

"Good. She seems like a really sweet girl."

"She's the best, Caleb." My eyes find his. "She's smart, funny, loyal. So fucking sexy."

"You're in love with her."

"I am," I reply without hesitation.

"It's fast," Caleb remarks, rubbing his hand over the light stubble on his square jaw.

"I know," I reply honestly. "But it just feels right. I want to be her friend as much as I want to be her lover. She makes me laugh. I'm proud of her. She's accomplished a lot on her own, and she's so damn good at it." I shrug and laugh at my brother's stunned look. "What is that look for?"

"You're really fucking in love with her."

"I thought we just came to that conclusion."

"I'm just...wow. Okay, well, that's awesome. I want to spend some more time with her."

"You'll get to. I'm bringing her to Nat's birthday party tomorrow." I grin and take another drink of my beer. "Nic's bringing a new cupcake recipe. She made it up just for Nat."

"Cool." Caleb grins, and then his face sobers as he watches me. "Just be careful, man. You're the best person I know, and seeing you hurt is the last thing I want."

"I don't relish the thought of that myself." I chuckle and shake my head. "We're not throwing the *love* word around yet. We're learning each other and enjoying our time together."

"Good."

"Uncle Matt! Look at our T-shirts!"

The girls come bouncing down the stairs, their dark brown ponytails flying around their heads in their excitement to show off the souvenirs their parents brought home for them.

"And backpacks, too! For our coloring books!"

"This is all very cool," I reply. "Where is mine?"

"You don't want a backpack," Josie responds with a wrinkled nose.

"Why not?"

"Because you're a big boy," Maddie informs me. "But I'll share."

"I'm just teasing, darlin'." I pick her up and kiss her cheek loudly, then bury my face in her sweet little neck and blow raspberries, making her squeal in delight.

"I love you, Uncle Matt."

"I love you, too, baby girl."

CHAPTER ELEVEN

~Nic~

Today is the perfect day for a pool party. The warm Seattle sun is high in the cloudless, bright blue sky. Luke Williams'—*the* Luke Williams of the *Nightwalker* movies—and his wife Natalie's home is absolutely breathtaking. It's a large two-story stone home that sits near the jagged Washington coastline, just north of Seattle.

We are in the backyard next to a large pool. There's a large covered outdoor kitchen off the patio, and luxurious chaise lounges next to the pool with individual sun umbrellas to keep the hot rays off of delicate skin.

I opted to close the umbrella to get some sun on my white body, but suddenly a shadow falls over me.

I open my eyes to find Matt standing over me, clad only in black swimming trunks, opening the umbrella over me.

"Hey! You're blocking my sun."

"You've been in the sun long enough, little one. I don't want you to burn."

He picks me up, takes my seat on the lounge and settles me on his lap.

"This is better," he whispers in my ear as his hand glides down my naked side to my hip.

"Did you see the new dance instructor dance yesterday afternoon before the girls' class?" Stacy, Matt's sister-in-law, asks Brynna, who is sitting next to her.

"No, we didn't get there early enough. Is she good?" Brynna sits in Caleb's lap and wraps her arms around his neck.

Matt and I are sitting with Brynna, Stacy, Meg, Mark and Caleb. Natalie, Jules and Samantha are sitting on the stone edge of the pool, dangling their feet in the water, while Will, Leo, Luke, Isaac, Nate and Dominic play water volleyball.

I'm just exceedingly proud that I remember everyone's names. Matt's family is large, and friendly.

Except Jules. She's been friendly enough, but she keeps eyeing me, and I know she's dying to ask me questions.

Maybe I should approach her.

"Oh my Gosh, good doesn't begin to describe her!" Stacy replies to Brynna, pulling me out of my own thoughts. "She's freaking amazing. She used to tour with some of the most famous people out there, dancing for them."

"That's right." Brynna nods. "Didn't she tour with Beyoncé for a while?"

"That's what I heard," Stacy confirms.

"Wait. What is this dancer's name?" Samantha asks from her seat on the edge of the pool. Her gaze is on her brother, Mark, whose eyes are narrowed on her face.

"Meredith," Brynna replies.

Sam cocks an eyebrow. "Did you know that bitch is back in town?" she asks Mark as he stands and jumps in the pool, joining the guys in their game.

Everyone exchanges looks of confusion, but Mark just shrugs and tosses the volleyball in the air.

"Get over it, Sam." He serves the ball, and the other men begin to splash about, diving for the ball.

Good God, I'm surrounded by the hottest men in the world.

Luke Williams is just plain hot. I've known that for years. He was once named the Sexiest Man Alive in one of the most popular magazines in the country. But the other guys are just as beautiful.

Nate McKenna is as dark as Luke is fair. His long hair is pulled back with a leather strap at the nape of his neck. He has tribal tattoos that swirl down his arm and over one side of his chest. His gray eyes are intense, but when he looks at his Jules, his expression transforms into one of pure love.

Mark Williams is a mirror image of his older brother, if not even more good-looking, which I didn't know was possible. He's tall and fair and has startling blue eyes. He also seems to be carefree and fun.

The Montgomery brothers are all simply amazing specimens of male. Their hair ranges in shades of light brown to blond, but they all share those Montgomery blue eyes. Even Dominic, who is half-Italian and shares only a father with the other guys, has the ice-blue gaze like his half brothers.

And, of course, Leo Nash is the rock star of my fantasies.

And they're all shirtless, muscled and belong on the pages of a calendar.

But the women are just as beautiful and fun.

"I like your tattoos," Natalie says to me, pointing to my shoulder and side as she joins us, lowering herself onto an umbrella-covered chaise. She tugs at her black tankini with a frown. "I thought this damn thing would cover my belly."

"How are you feeling, little mama?" Matt asks softly and rests his hand on Nat's growing belly.

"I'm good," she confirms. "I've been having a little back pain, but I think it's just because this little guy is growing."

"She's being stubborn," Luke calls from the pool after volleying the ball over the net. "I keep telling her to go to the hospital, but she says no. I'm going to pick her up and take her, whether she wants to go or not."

"Maybe you should go," Matt agrees and frowns at her. His hand is still resting on her belly, and his blue eyes are soft.

He'd be an excellent daddy.

Panic takes hold of my heart and makes my mouth go dry. I can't give him this.

Good job, I fell in love with him and I can't give him everything he deserves to have in a woman.

"I'm fine," Nat insists. "It's growing pains, that's all. Trust me, I've done this before."

"Hey, ace, how about I jump in there and show you how it's done?" Jules calls out to Nate when he misses the ball.

"You're not playing, Julianne, and that's that," he replies.

"I can swim while pregnant," she reminds him with a pout. "We have a long road ahead of us, ace. Don't start putting limits on me now."

"You can swim," Isaac agrees. "But you can't play contact sports, brat."

"You could get hit with an elbow," Matt agrees. "We don't want you to get hurt, bean."

"Now you're all ganging up on me?" Jules asks incredulously. "C'mon, girls, help me out here."

"Sorry," Meg responds with a smile. "I agree."

"You all suck."

We all laugh at her, and I feel the panic from earlier start to recede. I just need to keep my eye on the ball. This is fun, nothing more.

Yeah, right.

"Back to your tats," Nat begins and takes a sip of water. "I like them."

"Thanks." I grin.

"You're pierced and tatted. You fit in well around here." Meg laughs. "I think it might be a prerequisite to be a part of this group."

"What are you talking about?" I ask with a laugh.

"Well, most of us have tats," Jules replies. "Meg's clit is pierced…"

"Hey!" Leo calls from the pool. "I thought we decided we weren't going to discuss my sister's privates anymore!"

"Yes, let's discuss all the girls' privates," Mark interrupts with a mischievous grin. "Except Sam."

"And Nate has a *very* interesting piercing," Sam adds, ignoring her brother and pointing to Nate's dick.

"Seriously." Nate scowls. "You all need to stop talking about the piercings."

"Dude." Dominic stares at Nate in shock. "Seriously?"

Nate shakes his head and sighs. "Just serve the ball, man."

"Well, my navel is as adventurous as I've been in the piercing arena." I eye Meg speculatively. "Does the clit piercing do fun things for you?"

"Oh, it's really the clitoral hood, and *yes.*" She grins widely.

"It's fucking awesome," Will agrees and gets slapped on the back of the head by Leo. "What the fuck?"

"Stop talking about Meg's junk," Leo demands.

"You're not piercing your clit," Matt whispers in my ear.

"Why?" I ask and look up into his eyes.

"Because then I wouldn't be able to touch it, and I can't go even one day without it," he whispers for only me to hear, making me blush. "And speaking of touching you"—his voice drops even lower—"do you know what I want to do with this string bikini you're wearing? I could have you tied up and be inside you in roughly thirty seconds."

Holy fucking hell, this man is hot.

"God, get a room." Jules smirks and sips on a bottle of water.

"I want another cupcake," Stacy announces and bounces out of her seat. "Can I get one for anyone else?"

"All the pregnant chicks need cupcakes," Jules confirms and sits in a chaise next to Natalie.

"I'll bring the whole box," Stacy decides and runs inside to fetch them.

"Will you please design and bake the wedding cake for my wedding?" Meg asks me with a wide smile.

My eyes widen in surprise. "Have you set a date?"

"No," she responds with a laugh. "But no matter when it is, we'll want you to do the cake. Seriously, you're the best."

Stacy makes a circle with the box, and most everyone takes one of the salted caramel treats with little cameras on top.

"These are the best gift ever," Natalie announces with a smile. "Thank you again."

"You're welcome."

"Right. Not that cupcakes aren't fantastic, but your husband got you a car for your birthday. *A freaking Porsche.*"

Nat smirks and gazes lovingly at her handsome husband. "He is good to me."

"I'd love to do your cake, Meg. We'll talk about the details later."

"*Yes!*" she exclaims. "Hey, babe, Nic's gonna make our wedding cake!" she calls to Will in the pool.

"Awesome! Do we need to do some taste testing?"

"Ignore him and his bottomless stomach." Meg shakes her head and bites into her cake.

"How do you stay so thin?" Jules asks me. "I swear, if I was around these every day, I'd be as big as a house."

"No, you wouldn't," Brynna replies with a roll of her eyes. "You have the best genes on the planet."

"I don't eat them," I reply with a shrug.

Everyone stops what they're doing and looks at me in surprise.

"Why not?" Dominic asks as he pulls himself out of the pool.

"It's a lot of sugar," I reply.

Meg tilts her head, watching me closely, but I shrug. "I just sample the ones that are new to make sure they're okay."

Matt's lips are planted on my temple. He pulls in a deep breath, kisses my cheek and then my shoulder.

God, I love it when his lips are on me.

"That's some fantastic willpower," Isaac murmurs as he also joins his wife from the pool.

"We're taking a break," Leo announces and sits next to Sam as Nate pulls Jules into his arms and kisses her sweetly.

"I'd better keep you with me," he murmurs to her. "Keep you out of trouble."

"You're all wet, ace."

"So?"

"So this is a new suit." She pouts prettily.

"Uh, swimsuits are designed to get wet, Julianne." Nate laughs and plants his lips on her shoulder.

"Speaking of willpower." Meg snickers at Will. "You guys should see this coworker of mine, Marla."

"Meg works at the Children's Hospital," Matt informs me.

"Yes, and Marla is a new nurse." Will scowls as he takes a bite of cupcake, making Meg laugh harder. "And, boy, does she have a thing for our Will."

"Most women do," Stacy responds, patting her own husband's back. "It's a Montgomery curse."

"Well, let's just say that Marla isn't coy about it."

"She's fucking embarrassing," Will agrees.

"I don't think I've seen Will embarrassed before," Luke adds and sits behind his wife, then pulls her back against him and rests his hands on her belly. "This is fun."

"She hits on him in front of everyone," Meg continues. "And if she wasn't such a…hmm…" She scrunches up her nose trying to come up with the right word.

"Persistent?" Jules offers.

"Well, let me put it this way. I wouldn't say she's a slut, but her favorite shade of lipstick is penis."

"Oh my God!" Brynna cries, busting up laughing with the rest of us.

These people are freaking hilarious!

"What's her number?" Mark asks with a wide, charming grin. "I'll take her off your hands, man."

"Trust me"—Meg shakes her head while laughing—"she's kind of psycho. Once she sinks her claws in, shaking her off is nearly impossible."

"Oh, yeah, you can keep her." Mark laughs and sips on a beer. "I don't want anyone permanent."

"You're disgusting." Sam scowls at her brother.

"Just honest."

"So what are you going to do about her?" Caleb asks. His hand is planted on Brynna's belly.

I glance up at Matt to find him watching his brother with happy eyes.

Could she be?

"Ignore her," Will mumbles. "And take security with me every time I go to the hospital."

"Are you okay?" Caleb asks Brynna.

"I'm fine, sailor. Stop worrying."

"What's going on with you two?" Dominic asks.

"Yeah, you've been doting on her all day," Natalie agrees. Luke leans in and whispers in Nat's ear then nibbles on her neck, and her eyes go wide. "No way."

"Dude, is she pregnant or something?" Mark demands.

Brynna blushes bright red, and Caleb sighs deeply.

"She is!" Jules cries.

"You didn't tell me!" Stacy accuses her with angry eyes. "Oh God, you're going to have a baby!"

"We weren't going to say anything," Brynna begins, but her eyes fill with tears. "It's super early. I haven't even been to the doctor yet."

"When did you find out?" Natalie asks.

"On our last day in Tuscany," Caleb replies. "The stick says I knocked her up."

"You're so classy." Jules rolls her eyes and looks over at Matt. "You knew!"

"I was sworn to secrecy," he replies calmly.

I take a deep breath and realize that I'm a bit shaky. I didn't eat much this morning and barely picked at the food at lunch because my nerves got the better of me, being around Matt's family for the first time.

Stupid!

I know better. The conversation continues around me, but I no longer really hear what they're saying.

How am I going to get through this without drawing attention to myself?

My breathing and heart rate have increased, and I'm starting to feel woozy.

This one has come on fast.

"Hey, are you okay, baby?" Matt asks and tilts my face back to meet his gaze. He frowns down at me. "You don't look so good."

"I think I just need to eat something," I reply and pull myself out of his arms, but as soon as I stand, I have to grip the back of the chair so I don't fall. My head is spinning.

My sugars have crashed.

Fuck.

"Hey, hey, hey, baby." Matt stands and helps me down into a chair.

I push my head down between my knees and focus on my breathing.

"What's wrong? You're scaring me, Nic."

"For fuck's sake, is she preggo, too?" Mark demands. "What is it with this family?"

"I don't think that's it," Meg replies and kneels next to me. "Nic, are you diabetic?"

"Yeah," I whisper. "I don't think I ate enough today."

"Someone run inside and grab her a sandwich and a glass of orange juice," Meg orders sternly.

"On it," Dominic announces and breaks into a run to the house.

"When was the last time you checked your sugars?" Meg asks and caresses my back in long, slow strokes.

"This morning. Every morning," I reply and focus on breathing. The shaking is worse now.

"Maybe we should take her to the hospital," Matt announces. His voice is as hard as steel.

He's angry.

"She'll be okay in a few minutes," Meg assures him as Dominic returns and passes me the juice. "Slow sips. We don't want you to spike."

I take a bite of the sandwich first and then sip the juice, feeling foolish.

"I'm okay," I assure everyone. "Really."

"You almost passed out, sweetheart," Will responds. "We'll feel better if you just sit here for a few and eat."

"Why didn't you eat earlier?" Jules asks, concerned as she looks between me and Matt.

"Nerves." I shrug. "New people. I'm shy."

"Jesus," Matt whispers and paces away from me.

"Are you on meds?" Meg asks and checks my pulse.

"No." I shake my head. "I manage it with diet and exercise."

"That's why you don't eat your cupcakes," Leo says, his eyes also worried.

I stop sipping the juice to look around. All of these beautiful people are gathered around me, worried, watching me as though they might have to save my life any second.

They care about me.

"Like I said, too much sugar," I reply and take another bite of the turkey sandwich Dominic delivered. "I haven't had an episode like this in years. Honest." I look up at Matt, but his face is hard, and his eyes are angry. "I take very good care of myself."

The shaking has stopped, and my heart rate has returned to normal as I finish the sandwich.

"I'm sorry I worried everyone."

"Do you need to lie down?" Luke asks.

"No." I shake my head again and smile at the handsome former actor. "I'm really fine."

"You're not fine," Matt responds in a cold voice.

"Matt…" Isaac begins, but Matt cuts him off with a harsh look.

"You should have told me."

I look around again and firm my chin, raising it and squaring my shoulders. He will not shame me in front of these people.

"You never asked," I reply just as coldly. "I'm fine, Matt."

"I think she could use another sandwich," Meg suggests with a knowing look at Matt.

"I think so, too. Come with me."

He pulls me out of the lounge and into his arms and carries me toward the house.

"We need to talk."

CHAPTER TWELVE

~Matt~

I'm going to paddle her ass.

I stomp across Luke's yard toward the house. Jesus, she took five years off my life back there. I haven't been that scared in a long time, and I'm a fucking cop.

"I can walk," she mutters with a pout, but I ignore her. "Did you hear me?"

"I heard."

"Put me down," she tries again, but I tighten my hold as I push open the sliding glass door and carry her into the formal dining room just off the kitchen and private from prying eyes outside. I set her down on the table and cage her in with my hands on either side of her hips.

"I thought you trusted me," I begin, my voice low and hard.

Her green eyes widen before she frowns. "I do."

"If you trust me, why didn't I know before you almost passed out that you're diabetic?"

"Because it isn't a big deal!" she cries with an exasperated sigh.

"It is a big deal, Nicole, and let me tell you why." I settle in closer to her so she has to look me in the eye. "It's my job to take care of you. How can I do that if I don't know what you need?"

"My diabetes is controlled very well, Matt." She lays her hand on my arm reassuringly. "I'm very strict about what I eat. That's why I don't drink more than two alcoholic drinks at a time. No cupcakes or other sweets. I never want to be on meds ever again."

"You were medicated?" I ask.

She nods. "In my early twenties, I was about fifty pounds overweight and didn't care what I ate. Lots of sugar. I was on meds, and I finally decided that I didn't want to live the next fifty years of my life that way. My ex-boyfriend, Ben, was a personal trainer, and he helped me."

I stiffen at the mention of another man in her life, even if it was years ago. I don't give a shit that it's irrational. My emotions are all over the place right now.

I take a deep breath to reel myself back in and study her face.

"That's when you got your navel pierced."

She nods again. "It was a reward, like I told you."

"Why did you never say anything, Nic? We've eaten together many times. I've asked you why you don't eat your cupcakes more than once."

"It's nothing to be dramatic about." She shrugs, and I see red.

"Your health is nothing to be dramatic about?" I push my hands in my hair and pace away from her, leaving her on the table. "I fucking *scened* with you at the club, Nicole. What if you'd had a diabetic episode while you were in my ropes?" Just the mere thought almost brings me to my knees. I wipe my hand over my mouth and turn back to her. "This could change everything about our sex life."

"No!" she cries, her eyes wide in horror. "Matt, today is not the norm for me. I'm not fragile."

"You're everything!" I yell back. I lean back into her. Her head is tilted back, and she's watching me with wide, emerald-green eyes. "Haven't you figured that out? You're everything. I'm in love with you. If anything happened to you, it would destroy me."

I cup her face in my trembling hands. "You scared the fuck out of me out there, Nic. I didn't know what was wrong. If I'd already known about the diabetes,

I would have been able to *do* something, but you had my hands figuratively tied by not telling me. Yes, you're strong and you have your life handled, but who the fuck takes care of *you?*"

She swallows hard and continues to watch my face.

"This is my fault," I continue. "I never asked you if you had any medical conditions, and I should have. You've just had me so off balance since the moment I met you. You're all I think about."

"I'm sorry…"

"I'm not complaining, little one." I swallow and lean my forehead against hers. "Being with you is exactly where I need to be, but it's my job to make sure that your every need is met. I can't do that if I'm out of the loop."

"Matt." She sighs and cups my face in her hands, strokes her fingers down my face, soothing me. "I wasn't keeping it a secret. It's something I've lived with for years, and I don't usually have any problems. I didn't tell you, not because I don't trust you, but because I don't want to be treated differently. I wasn't thinking today, and I was stupid. I'm so sorry that I scared you."

"You are different, baby. You're so different for me that you've changed my life. What do you need? How do I help?"

"I don't need anything." She shakes her head and offers me a soft smile. "Really. Maybe another sandwich."

"I can get you that." I wrap my arms around her shoulders and hold her to me. "Is there anything else I need to know about your health?"

She stills, and I pull back, watching her face. "Tell me."

"I have polycystic ovary syndrome," she replies softly. "That's why I'm on the pill."

I don't know what that means. "So the pill regulates that?"

She nods soberly. "Anything else?"

"There's nothing else."

"Nicole."

"There's nothing else," she repeats firmly. "I'm not fragile, Matt. But if I'm ever not feeling well, I'll tell you."

"Is this why you had the headache last weekend?"

"No, I really did just have a headache."

I sigh and rest my lips on her forehead, breathing her in. She's so precious to me.

"How are you feeling now?"

"Better, but I'll eat another sandwich and maybe drink another juice, and I'll be just fine."

"Okay." I step back and help her off the table and lead her into the kitchen to grab a sandwich and some juice. "Do you want to go home?"

"No, there's a party going on outside." She grins at me. "A fun party with hot guys."

"Really."

She snickers, enjoying teasing me, and I maintain a sober face, letting her have her fun.

"Yeah, there's a rock star and a hot football player here."

I tilt my head to the side, curl my lips up in a half smile and step toward her. "Is that right?"

"Mmm hmm."

"Are you trying to make me jealous, little one?"

She bites her lip, and the pulse in her neck speeds up with excitement.

"I'm just telling you who's here."

"I see." I lean into her and rest my lips next to her ear. "If any of them—brothers or not—so much as touches you, I will break their fucking fingers. You're mine."

She sucks in a breath in surprise and holds it, waiting for my next words.

"Mine," I repeat. "I don't share, remember?"

"Possessive much?" she asks breathlessly.

"Oh, fuck yeah, I am. You might want to remember that." I grin down at her as I take her hand and lead her outside, back to the group, who quiets as we return.

"Everything okay?" Jules asks.

"I'm much better. Turkey does wonders," Nic replies with a wink as I pull her into my lap and wrap my arms around her waist.

"Good." Natalie smiles warmly and catches my gaze. "How about you, detective?"

"Never better," I respond.

"We are talking about Meg and Will's engagement party," Jules fills us in.

"Engagement party?" I ask, surprised. "I didn't think you were going to have one."

"We weren't." Meg shrugs and rolls her eyes at Jules. "But Jules thinks it's necessary."

"Jules wants to have an excuse to buy a new pair of shoes," Nate adds, earning himself a poke in the ribs by his wife. He lays his hand gently over her belly and nuzzles her ear. "I'll buy you all the shoes you want, baby."

"We can have it down at the vineyard and keep it pretty private," Dom suggests.

"Alecia could totally pull it together quickly," Jules adds and claps her hands.

I catch Dom's scowl but choose not to comment.

"We should do it before summer training starts," Will agrees.

"And before Leo leaves on tour again," Meg adds.

"Hell, there's not much to plan for just the family," Isaac points out. "If Dom is gonna host it, and we're going to have it catered, we could do it next weekend."

"I'll check the calendar, but that should work," Dominic agrees.

"Fun!" Stacy says and kisses her husband's cheek.

"Do I have to dress up?" Mark asks with a frown.

"No, come as you are," Meg replies. "Will and I aren't fancy."

"Thank God." Mark sighs. "Will there be single chicks there?"

"No!" Everyone yells in unison and then dissolves in laughter.

***

I'm still out of sorts about her diabetic episode when we arrive back at her apartment for the night. It's been a hell of a roller coaster of a day. I've been semihard just because she's been in that tiny string bikini all day, her skin against mine in the warm sunshine, and if my family hadn't been around, I would have had her naked and under me in roughly three seconds.

But then to watch her episode, the sheer fear of not knowing what was happening to her, has had me in knots the rest of the afternoon.

"You're quiet," she murmurs after I close the door behind us. "What are you thinking?"

"I'm thinking," I reply and take her hand in mine, leading her to her bedroom, "about how I'm going to punish you for keeping such a big secret from me and scaring ten years off my life today."

Her eyes go wide, and every muscle in her tiny body tightens.

"If you think you're going to spank me like that poor girl at the club, you can just think again," she replies. Her cheeks have gone pink, and her breathing has increased.

I pull her tank over her head and tug on the strings of her bikini, letting it drop into my hands.

"I'm not going to spank you," I reply and kiss her forehead.

"What are you going to do?" she asks breathlessly.

"You'll see. Sit in the chair by the window."

She complies and watches me as I kneel before her, grip her shorts and pull them over her hips and down her legs, then tug the strings on the bikini bottom, pulling it out from under her.

Her vanity sits on one side of the chair, and the bed frame is on the other. I guide her legs up, spread them wide and rest her knees over the armrests of the overstuffed chair, then take the top of her bikini, loop it under one knee and tie it to the vanity. Then I do the same on the other side, securing it to the bed frame. She's spread wide for me now, and she can't move.

And she's fucking gorgeous.

"You're already wet," I murmur and glide one fingertip down through her slick folds.

"I like it when you tie me up," she reminds me breathlessly. "If this is my punishment, you're doing a really bad job of it, babe."

I grin humorlessly and settle in to prove her wrong.

I press open-mouthed kisses down her thighs then lick the crease between her leg and her center, making her moan and bury those amazing hands of hers in my hair. Her skin is so soft and smells like coconut and sunshine from her day in the sun.

I lick at her pussy, pushing my tongue up through her lips to her clit and back down again, and she lets out a long moan.

"You like that, don't you."

"You know I do." Her hips pulse a bit, but she can't move far with her legs secured.

"Do you like keeping secrets from me, too?" I ask and then pull her clit into my mouth, sucking firmly.

"No," she breathes and tosses her head back and forth on the chair. She grips my hair again when I push two fingers inside her.

Just when I feel her begin to contract around my fingers, I pull out and duck out of her reach, not touching her at all.

"What the…?"

"It's going to be awhile before I let you come, baby."

Her eyes narrow on my face as she pants and glares daggers at me. Her lips are swollen from her own teeth biting on them, and her core is sopping wet, from my mouth and her own juices.

She's fucking delicious.

She reaches down to touch herself, but I grip her wrist in my hand, kiss her palm and place her hand over her head.

"If you try to finish the job yourself again, I *will* spank you."

I lean down and press a kiss to her freshly shaved pubis, then nibble my way up to her sexy-as-hell piercing, all the while barely touching her wet pussy with my fingertips.

"You're killing me," she murmurs.

"Not yet," I reply softly and kiss my way up to her breasts, pulling on them with my teeth.

She's squirming under me. Her hands are in my hair then gripping my shoulders. I sink two fingers inside her again and begin to fuck her hard, and just when her legs begin to shake, I stop and back away.

"Matt!"

"You see, Nic, this is how frustrated I am when you don't talk to me and tell me everything I need to know." I circle her hard clit with my thumb, that being the only place I'm touching her. "Just when I think I know everything I need to, I discover something new that you should have told me before."

"Getting to know each other is a process for any couple," she reminds me breathlessly.

I kiss down her body and then raise my head to look her in the eye. "You're right. I'll eventually learn what your favorite song is, what you wore to your senior prom and how old you were when you got your driver's license." I sink my fingers into her again and lick her clit. "But this was a biggie, little one. And you scared the fuck out of me."

Her eyes are glassy with lust as she bites her lip again, watching me fuck her with my mouth and my fingers. Her nipples are standing at attention and wet from my mouth.

God, she's the most beautiful thing I've ever seen.

And the most precious.

"You have to learn that there are no secrets between us." I grip the cheeks of her ass in my hands and lift her off the chair and push my face right into the core of her, lapping and sucking and kissing until she's screaming and begging for me to let her come, but I stop and set her back down.

"Please!" she cries. "I can't stand it."

Tears are running down her face, her arms thrown over her head and gripping the back of the chair. I would normally drag this out, make her beg for the chance to come, but her tears are my undoing. The point has been made, and I just need to give her what she wants and what I need more than breathing.

I push my shorts down my hips, tug my shirt over my head and fling it aside, then push inside her, hard, buried balls-deep. I cover her with my body, gripping the chair for leverage, and fuck her in long, slow strokes.

"I was so frustrated with you today," I murmur and kiss her cheek. "You deserved this, to feel this frustration. If I ever find out that you've kept something like this from me again, it'll be the same punishment."

She wraps her arms around me and holds me close, buries her face in my neck.

"Please," she whispers. "Oh God, Matt."

I pull up off of her so I can watch us, my cock moving in and out of her wet heat, her lips swollen and pink around my dick and our bodies sweaty.

She's gripping me like a vice, and I feel the tension begin low in my belly, and I know I'm about to come. I cover her clit with my thumb and watch as she comes apart, legs shaking, muscles pulled tight, and squeezing me with all she's worth.

I cry out her name as I come with her, pushed to the hilt and grinding against her core, giving her everything I've got.

I collapse onto her torso for several minutes, concentrating on breathing in and out. Her fingers in my hair remind me that I need to untie her. I undo the knots and massage her knees and hips, then lift her in my arms and settle us both in her soft bed.

"I'm sorry for today, and that I didn't tell you before," she finally whispers against my chest.

I glide my fingertips down her back, deep in thought. I love her so much. If anything were to happen to her, it would destroy me.

"No more secrets," I whisper.

"No more secrets."

***

"You don't have to come to work with me today," Nic assures me for the third time while she pulls freshly baked cupcakes out of the oven.

"Watch out, I'll think you're trying to get rid of me."

"You know that's not true." She shakes her head at me as she sets the hot cakes on a wire rack to cool. "But it's your last day off, and you should enjoy it. I only have to work until one. It's Sunday."

"And you're here alone."

"Trust me, I worked many Sundays alone before you came along, Detective Montgomery."

"Yes, but now you don't have to," I remind her softly and pull her into my arms to kiss her silly.

She melts against me and wraps her arms around my neck, clinging to me, her mouth pliant and more than willing.

"Do I have to put you on the payroll?" she asks breathlessly when I let her up.

"Hmm." I shift my head from side to side as though I'm giving it a great deal of thought. "I guess you can pay me in sexual favors."

"Oh really." She laughs and begins frosting another batch of cakes.

"Or just go with me to Will and Meg's party next weekend."

"You don't have to do me favors to get me to hang out with you and your family."

"Okay, sexual favors then."

She laughs, a full-out belly laugh, and my gut clenches. I love the sound of her laughter and the way her eyes shine with happiness.

"You're gorgeous," I whisper.

Her smile fades slowly, replaced by pure lust.

"I'm glad you think so." Her voice is soft and a bit shaky. I love catching her unaware and tilting her off balance.

"What can I do to help?"

"Here, frost these." She shows me how to apply the frosting in a swirly fashion on top of the cake and leaves me to my task.

"These smell great," I murmur. "What kind are they?"

"White chocolate raspberry."

"Can I order a dozen of these for tomorrow?" She glances at me in surprise. "I'll take them in to work."

"Sure." She smiles widely and then turns back to the job at hand.

"So did you have fun yesterday?"

"I did. Your family is hilarious."

"They do keep things interesting," I agree proudly. "We're close."

"I can tell. You all care deeply for one another."

"Yes," I reply simply.

"It was fun. They're nice people."

"You fit in well," I comment casually.

She pauses and then carries on as though men tell her every day that they enjoy seeing her with those they love the most.

"I'm glad you think so."

"Is something wrong?" I ask.

"Nope," she replies with a fake smile. "As soon as you're done there, we'll open."

"Talk to me."

"I'm fine," she insists. "I'm going to go unlock the door."

She hurries out, leaving me dumbfounded. What did I say?

Women and their hormones.

***

A few hours, and several dozen customers, later, the bell dings above the door as Caleb saunters into Succulent Sweets, carrying a brown paper sack.

"Caleb!" Nic grins widely, happy to see my brother.

"Hey, pretty lady." He leans his elbow on the counter and winks at her. "How you doin'?"

Nic laughs and shakes her head at Caleb. "I'm fine. Are all the Montgomerys charming?"

"Nope, just me." Caleb winks again and sets the bag on the countertop. "This is for you."

"What is it?"

"I ordered you lunch," I reply.

"But I'm working."

"I can handle this. You need to eat."

She stares at me in surprise, looks between Caleb and I and then kisses my cheek before taking the bag into the back.

"I won't be long!" she calls out.

"Take your time," I reply. "Thanks, man."

"No worries. How is she today?"

"She's fine."

"Scared us all yesterday." Caleb peruses the glass case full of goodies. "Hand me a carrot cake."

I pass him the pastry and hold my hand out for money. "She doesn't work for free, asshole."

"Jesus, I brought food. A man can't get paid in cupcakes?"

"No."

He hands me a five, and I don't give him his change.

"Bastard." Caleb laughs.

CHAPTER THIRTEEN

~Nic~

A lot has happened in the past twenty-four hours.

Okay, that might be the understatement of the freaking year.

I focus on eating the sandwich Caleb brought me and sipping the juice I poured, eager to get right back to work.

Yesterday *was* fun. Matt's family is huge and a bit overwhelming. They're all beautiful and successful and so fun. Hilarious.

Loving.

I don't know what it is to have a family like that, and a large piece of me longed to settle in and belong there for a long, long time.

Jesus, you're pathetic.

I take the last bite and walk back out of the kitchen.

"We want you both to come," Caleb says. "Oh good, you're back."

"Caleb just invited us to dinner with him and Bryn tonight."

"Oh," I reply and frown in thought.

"It's not a requirement, but your reaction isn't great for my ego, sweetheart."

I laugh and shake my head. "Thank you for inviting me." I turn to Matt. "I have a standing date with Bailey every Sunday afternoon. We walk down to Vintage for a glass of wine and appetizers."

"That's cool." Matt shrugs, as though it doesn't bother him in the least. "You should go hang out with Bailey."

"Really?" I ask skeptically.

"I don't need to monopolize all of your time, sweetheart. Just most of it." He smiles wolfishly and kisses me square on the mouth. "Why don't you meet me at Caleb's later?"

"That will work. Matt will give you our address." Caleb boosts himself up on the counter so he can lean across it and plant a kiss on my cheek, earning a low growl from Matt, which only makes Caleb laugh. "See you both later."

He waves and walks out just as Bailey walks in, checking out Caleb's ass as he leaves.

"Holy shit, did you see that?"

"That was my brother," Matt confirms with a grin.

"And you must be Matt," Bailey guesses with a flirty grin and holds her hand out to shake. "We've crossed paths now and again but have never really met. I'm Bailey. The best friend."

"Pleasure," Matt responds with a charming smile. "I've seen you around."

"And as the best friend…" Bailey begins.

"Bailey," I warn her, but she doesn't even acknowledge me as she continues.

"I can say if you hurt her, I'll make your life a living hell. I don't give a shit if you are a cop and a Dom. You don't scare me."

Matt's eyebrows climb, and then he walks around the glass case and pulls Bailey in for a big hug, much to her surprise.

"You're supposed to be wary of me, not hug me. I threatened you."

"Thank you for loving her so much," he murmurs in her ear. He kisses her cheek and pulls back then circles back around to my side. "Do you have it handled from here, little one?"

"Um…" I have to clear my throat past the knot that's formed there. Bailey also looks shell-shocked. "Yeah, I'm good."

He tilts my chin back with his finger and lowers his lips to mine, gently nibbling, sweeping his own soft lips across mine, then sinks in and slips his tongue between my lips, kissing the breath right out of me. When he pulls away, he has to hold my shoulders firmly until I regain my balance.

"Wow," Bailey mutters with a chuckle.

"I'll see you tonight." He drags his knuckles down my cheek and then turns to walk out through the kitchen. "See you soon, Bailey."

"See you!" She watches him leave with shining eyes.

I walk to the front door and lock it and then begin the process of cleaning up so I can leave for the day.

"I'll be ready to go in about twenty minutes," I inform her, as though the hottest man on earth didn't just kiss me senseless.

"He's hot," she says casually.

"You knew that already."

"His brother is hot, too."

"And married."

"All the good ones are." Bailey pouts. "What are you guys doing tonight?"

"Can we talk about this over wine?" I ask with a sigh. "There's a lot to tell."

"Oh God, please hurry. The suspense is now killing me."

She helps me clean up and get organized for tomorrow, dancing in place as if she has to pee, making me giggle.

"You're crazy," I inform her.

"I'm impatient," she corrects me. "Let's go. Hot waiter Dan is waiting for us."

I toss my apron in the hamper, fetch my wallet and lock the back door behind us. Bailey links her arm through mine as we walk down to Vintage.

"It's gorgeous today." I pull in a deep breath of summer air. I can smell the salt from the Puget Sound just a few blocks away. Families are out, pushing strollers and carrying toddlers, enjoying Seattle on this sunny Sunday.

"We are having a great summer," Bailey agrees with a smile. She leads me into Vintage and offers Damn Hot Dan a flirty grin. "Hey, handsome."

"Hello, ladies." He nods at the hostess and seats us himself. "Your usual?"

"Yes, please," we say in unison.

"Coming right up." He winks at Bailey and walks to the bar.

"He likes you."

"He's adorable." Bailey sighs. "And painfully young."

"Dude, he's probably in his mid-twenties."

"Too young. I need someone with more life experience for what I'm looking for." She waves me off, sits back when Dan delivers our drinks and takes our appetizer order, then eyes me over the rim of her glass. "Talk to me."

"I really need you to help me get my head back on straight. Talk some sense into me."

"Okay." She nods.

"I can't fall in love with him."

"Right." She wrinkles her forehead in confusion. "Wait. Why not?"

"Because, we're just having fun together, remember?"

She nods slowly and then shakes her head. "When did we say that?"

"He took me to meet his family," I begin. "And they're great. Did you know his brother-in-law is Luke Williams? Like, *the* Luke Williams. The one whose poster was on my wall when I was a teenager."

"Wow."

"And Luke's sister is with Leo freaking Nash, Bailey. Not to mention, his brother is Will Montgomery, the football player. So, I was at this pool party with celebrities and beautiful people, and they're all really, really nice. And so damn funny."

"That's cool. Can I get an invite next time?"

"It's not funny, though. My sugars crashed because I was stupid and didn't eat enough yesterday, so Matt found out about the diabetes..."

"You hadn't told him?" she asks with a deep frown.

"And then he was mad at me because I hadn't told him."

"He's a Dom, Nic. Of course he was pissed." She takes a sip of her drink and digs in to the food when Dan delivers it.

"And then he let it slip that he's in love with me."

She slowly lowers a chip to her plate and stares at me in shock. "What did you say?" she asks with a squeak.

"Nothing."

"*Nothing.*"

"It was in the heat of the moment. I'm not even sure he realized he said it. It was when he was mad about the medical stuff." I wave that off, unable to think about it because it makes me a quivering mess all over again. "But I'm becoming too attached to him, Bailey."

"Why?" she asks, completely confused.

"He should have kids," I whisper softly. "You and I both know I can't give him that."

"You are so ridiculous." Bailey groans. "You don't know that."

"I'm pretty sure. I can't fall in love with him. I'm not the girl for him."

"Right, so, he has an amazing family, a good job…" She's ticking his attributes off on her fingers. "He's not a freeloader or a loser, he's loyal and good with kids, and he's fucking amazing in the bedroom. That bastard!"

"Ha ha."

"So, you went from not wanting him because he's a Dom to not wanting him because he might want kids one day?"

"You make it sound so dumb." I laugh. "I'm trying to guard my own heart here, Bailey. I'm not trying to hurt him. Or me."

"You're such a worrier. Just keep doing what you were doing in the beginning. Enjoy him and cross the kids issue if and when he proposes."

I choke on my drink at the mention of proposing, my eyes watering as I cough and sputter.

"Okay, so the idea of marriage scares you," she mumbles. "I was kind of joking, Nic."

"Don't even say that!"

"Honey, I just witnessed you two together. That was a smitten man."

I start to reply, but she holds her hand up, stopping me. "And you were just as smitten. I know it's early days, but Matt isn't going anywhere. Just enjoy him."

"He is amazing in bed," I concede.

"Oh sure, rub it in. You're cruel. I stuck up for you back there and threatened a man of the law, and all you can do to pay me back is remind me that you're getting laid and I'm not?"

I giggle and pop a chip in my mouth. "It's really, really good sex."

"I hate you."

***

"You made it!" Brynna exclaims as she opens the door to me.

"I almost didn't find you," I admit with a rueful smile. "You're kind of tucked away here."

That's an understatement. Caleb and Brynna live in a beautiful house in the Alki Beach neighborhood of Seattle. This is one of my favorite parts of the city, especially in summer. There are shops to browse, excellent restaurants, including my favorite pub, The Celtic Swell, and miles of paths to walk and admire the Seattle skyline.

"Well, I'm glad you did find us." She pulls me in for a hug, and I have to stand on my toes to reach her.

Brynna is tall, with long dark hair and gorgeous dark eyes.

"The guys are out back with the girls, who are currently trying to talk us into a later bedtime."

"It's summer." I shrug like this is a normal thing. "How are the girls?"

"Great. Let's go see them."

She leads me through the house and out back, where a one-eyed dog is barking happily and Caleb and Matt are both doing pull-ups on a metal bar.

"Holy crap," I mutter and stop in my tracks, watching as both men steadily raise and lower themselves on the bar. They've both taken off their shirts, and their backs and arms are riots of pure muscle. Caleb has a tattoo on his shoulder, but I can't read it from here. They're both covered with a light sheen of sweat, and they're calling out taunts to each other.

"Uncle Matt is at twenty!" Josie calls out.

"Daddy has nineteen!" Maddie adds.

"I'm going to beat you, little brother."

"Bullshit," Caleb replies.

"Daddy has to put money in the Swear Jar!" Josie announces.

"Seems they distracted the men with pull-ups to get out of going up for bed," Brynna says and crosses her arms over her chest, watching her man. "They make quite the pair, don't they?"

"Good God, it should be illegal to look like that," I agree. "How do you keep your composure at family events, Bryn? Seriously, I thought I was going to have a heart attack yesterday."

She laughs and drapes her arm around my shoulders, hugging me to her side. "It is a bit intimidating in the beginning, but they're all just normal people, Nic. Will farts like crazy and blames it on Meg. Jules' hormones are so crazy right now, she snips at everyone and then cries and begs for forgiveness. It's the usual sibling stuff."

"Huh." I tilt my head and watch the men both drop to the ground.

"Do you have siblings?" Brynna asks.

"I have a sister, Savannah, but she and I aren't terribly close."

"I don't have any siblings. Stacy and I are cousins, but we were raised more like sisters."

She grins as Caleb scoops Josie in his arms and spins her about the yard. Matt and Maddie are petting the dog, who is on his back and in doggie heaven while the two scratch his belly. "Okay, girls, bedtime!"

"But, Mom, Nic just got here!" Maddie comes running over to me and wraps her arms around my legs. "I missed you!"

I giggle and squat next to the sweet girl. "You have only seen me in my bakery when your mama came to see me about her cupcakes, silly. How could you miss me?"

"I like your bakery," she replies and shrugs, like that explains everything.

"Well, thanks."

"Are you Uncle Matt's girlfriend?" Josie asks. She has her hand tucked in Matt's and is watching me with wary eyes.

Protective little thing, isn't she?

"I am," I respond, *for now,* and smile at Josie. "How are you, Josie?"

"Fine." She buries her face in Matt's hip as he pulls his T-shirt over his head. He laughs, scoops her into his arms and brushes her long dark hair away from her face.

"Why are you so shy?" he asks her.

She shrugs and lays her head on his shoulder.

"She's silly," Maddie informs me. "This is our dog, Bix. He's very brave."

"And handsome," I agree.

The dog lifts his paw as if in greeting, and I reach over to shake it.

"You girls need to go to bed. It's already past your bedtime," Brynna informs them.

Caleb takes Maddie's hand, who has now decided to pout, and signals for Bix to follow them.

"Can you read to us?" Josie asks Matt.

"Sure." He turns to me and kisses my cheek. "Hey, baby. I'm glad you're here. Mind if I go read to the girls?"

"Of course not," I reply with a smile and push my fingers through his soft dark blond hair. "I'll help down here."

"I'll get the grill going," Caleb announces and passes Maddie off to Matt, who takes the two girls and their dog into the house.

"What can I do to help?" I ask Brynna.

"You can help by sitting with me on the deck. Caleb is going to grill burgers, and everything else is done." She sits in a blue chair, and I take a matching love seat next to her.

"Did you have fun with Bailey?" Caleb asks me as he fires up the grill.

"I always have fun with Bailey," I reply with a laugh.

"Caleb said you guys like to go to Vintage." Brynna pours us both a glass of sun tea from a frosty pitcher. "It's a fun place."

"I love it," I agree. "We've been going there every Sunday for a couple years now."

Caleb drops four burger patties on the grill, and the sizzle and smell of the grill fills the air.

"You have a beautiful home," I comment and sip my tea.

"Thank you. It's actually Natalie's place. She let the girls and me move in here after Jules moved in with Nate." Brynna smiles and picks up a celery stick from a veggie tray and nibbles.

"That was really nice of her," I reply.

"Nat's the best. She's supersweet and loyal almost to a fault," Brynna says. "But I think Caleb and I are going to start looking for a bigger place, since we have a new one on the way. We'll need the space."

"I'm telling you, Isaac should build us a place," Caleb tells his wife.

"Oh goodie, we can argue about toilets and floor plans." Brynna rolls her eyes.

"What did I miss?" Matt asks as he joins us. He takes a seat next to me, wraps his arm around me and pulls me against his side.

"Nothing much. Did the girls go down okay?"

"I read two stories. But I'll place bets that someone will need a drink of water before the hour is out." He kisses my temple and drags his fingertips up and down my arm, over the ink on my shoulder, sending goose bumps across my skin.

"There's a lot of activity going on down here that they might miss out on," Brynna agrees wryly.

"Is tonight a special occasion?" I ask and lean my head on Matt's shoulder.

"Kind of, but we didn't want to make a big deal out of it." Caleb flips the burgers, closes the lid and joins us. "The wedding was where we did our adoption ceremony, but we just got the paperwork today that says the adoption is final."

"That's wonderful!" I exclaim. "They are lucky to have you both."

"Congrats, man." Matt fist-bumps his brother. "But they've been yours for a long while."

"True." Caleb nods. "How do you want your burger cooked?"

"Medium well," I answer. "Seriously, can't I help with something?"

"You worked all day. Relax," Matt whispers in my ear. "We got this."

"I didn't work all day." I laugh but relax further into the cushion and sip my tea. "But I'll let you guys handle the cooking."

"You look beautiful," Matt murmurs.

I wrinkle my nose at him, making him laugh.

"I love the tattoo on your shoulder," Brynna comments and tilts her head in thought. "Maybe I should do something like that."

"You can't get tattoos when you're pregnant, legs," Caleb reminds her.

"I know. Later."

"I can recommend a guy. I'm thinking about getting another one."

Matt's hand stills on my arm, and he pulls back to look down at my face. "What are you thinking of getting?"

"I haven't decided. I just have the itch to get something new," I respond with a shrug. His eyes flare, and it's obvious that the idea turns him on.

He likes body art.

"Burgers are ready," Caleb announces.

"So, I think I need to hear some good stories about Matt as a kid," I remark as I squirt ketchup on my bun.

"I have a million. What do you want to know?" Caleb asks while Matt glares at him.

"Everything," I reply with a laugh. "But start with the embarrassing stuff."

"He had a blankie until he was nine," Caleb begins.

"I suggest you shut it," Matt growls, making me giggle.

"He was always the most sensitive of the group," Caleb continues.

"I have stories, too, you know, *little brother,*" Matt reminds him.

"I want to hear some, too!" Brynna claps her hands and bounces in her seat. "This is fun."

"Matt was always a Batman fan. He liked to wear the bath towels as capes and run through the house, saving Gotham City from evil."

"Caleb was always the evil one," Matt adds, his eyes narrowed. "Stop talking. I'm warning you."

"I think Mom has photos of Matt in the fifth grade, when he let Jules, who was five, cut his hair."

"Caleb wet the bed until he was six," Matt murmurs deceptively softly and raises a brow at his brother. "And you never could tell Jules no either, so don't give me that shit."

"Was Matt quiet as a kid?" I ask, enjoying the men's banter immensely.

"Yeah." Caleb nods. "He's always been quiet. Somber."

"I was making up for Will's crazy ass."

"What about Caleb?" Brynna asks Matt. "Was he always the strong silent type?"

"No," Matt replies, watching his brother thoughtfully. "That happened after the first year or so with the SEALs."

"You were a SEAL?" I ask, my eyes wide. Holy shit, that explains his hot body.

"Yeah." Caleb concentrates on his beer bottle.

"Thank you for your service," I reply softly and smile when his eyes find mine. "My dad was Army. He was in Viet Nam."

Caleb nods and meets Matt's gaze. Something unsaid passes between them, and then Matt's phone rings.

"Fuck, it's Asher." He puts the phone to his ear. "Yeah."

"I hope he doesn't have to leave," Brynna murmurs.

"This can't wait until tomorrow morning? He's not going anywhere," Matt mutters and then curses and pushes his hand through his hair, a sure sign of frustration. "Okay, I'll be there in a bit."

He clicks off and shoves his phone in his pocket, then looks at me apologetically. "I guess it's good we brought separate cars. I have to go in to work."

"Okay." I lift a shoulder, as though it's no big deal and try not to be disappointed. This is his job.

"I'm sorry."

"It's your job, Matt. It's fine."

"Give us a moment," Matt murmurs to Caleb and Bryn, kissing Bryn's cheek before he takes my hand, leading me into the house. "Thanks for dinner. I'll call you tomorrow, man."

Once in the kitchen, Matt pulls me into his arms and kisses me senseless. His fingers dive into my hair, and he holds on almost desperately as he devours my mouth, as though he's branding me.

Finally, he pulls away, breathless. His blue eyes are bright with lust.

"This is not how I planned to spend the night," he informs me. "I was very much looking forward to taking you home and losing myself in you for a few hours."

I swallow hard and then smile bravely. "Rain check."

"I'm sorry," he repeats.

"Matt, this is just how it is. You're a cop. I'm proud of you. Go do your job."

He sighs and hugs me close, rocking back and forth for a moment before planting his lips on my forehead and taking a deep breath.

"I'll call you later," he murmurs.

"Sounds good."

He kisses me once more and then heads out to his car.

"I should probably go, too," I announce when I walk back out onto the deck.

"Can I have a word with you before you go?" Brynna asks.

"Of course," I reply and reclaim my chair.

"Do you mind if I stay?" Caleb asks.

I look between their faces, both sober and serious, and I start to feel very nervous. This is where they tell me I'm not good enough for him.

"I don't mind," I reply softly.

"I just have to offer you a little advice," Brynna informs me. "I was married to a cop. The twins' biological dad," she adds at my look of surprise. "It's not easy, Nic. Don't ask him to choose between you and his job. Neither choice would make him happy."

"I would never do that," I reply with a scowl. "And the fact that you'd say that says that you don't think very highly of me."

"That's not true," Brynna disagrees with a shake of her head. "I'm just warning you that cops aren't easy to be involved with. And, honestly, I'm not trying to sound like a bitch, which I just realized, I kind of am. Matt is one of the best men I've ever known. He's done a lot for my family, Nic. Including knocking some sense into this one." She points at Caleb with her thumb and offers me a small smile. "I love him. I just don't want him to get hurt."

"He'll never make you think that you take a back seat to the job," Caleb adds.

"I have no complaints about Matt's job," I reply honestly. "I'm proud of him. He's a good cop. I know it's demanding, and I'm sure there will be times that it's damn inconvenient, but it is what it is."

I shrug, and both Brynna and Caleb seem to visibly relax.

"I like you," Caleb comments. "I think you're very good for my brother."

"Thank you," I whisper. "I hope you're right."

***

I can't stop thinking about him. I lay my e-reader on the end table and rub my eyes with the pads of my fingers.

I have no idea how long I've been staring at the same paragraph, thinking about Matt. I haven't heard from him yet, but that doesn't surprise me. If he got called in, he's busy.

How is it that I miss having him here in my bed with me and we've only been seeing each other for such a short time? Maybe he'd read to me, or watch a movie.

Or make love.

My body flares at the thought, and I shift my hips, rubbing my legs together, trying to ease the ache between them.

I want him.

Finally, I pick up my phone and send him a text.

Please get out of my head. I'm trying to sleep.

I watch the phone intently for several minutes, and finally he responds.

You're always in my head. Are you okay?

I grin and begin to type.

Yes, I'm fine. Miss u. Wish u were here. I'm naked.

I giggle and roll onto my belly, waiting impatiently for his response.

Killing me. Are you wet?

Been thinking of u, so YES!

I bite my lip, watching my phone. After a few minutes, it rings.
"Hello?"
"You're killing me, baby."
"I thought we were going to have fun text sex," I reply with a giggle.
"I needed to hear your voice." He sounds tired. Frustrated.
"Tough night?"
"Yeah, and it's going to be a long one. Asher and I will be working through the day tomorrow, too."
"Do you still want the cupcakes you mentioned this morning?" I ask and roll back over, staring at the ceiling.
"Definitely. That might be the only time I get to see you tomorrow."
"I'll have them ready for you," I promise him.
"Back to the subject at hand."
I hear his grin, and I can't help but smile back and clutch the phone a little tighter.

"You say you're wet?"

"And horny as hell," I reply.

"What are you doing about that?" His voice has gone soft as velvet, but it's also taken on that edge it gets when he slips into his bedroom Dom mode, and heat immediately floods my body.

"I wasn't doing anything about it yet," I reply, my voice harsh now.

"I want you to spread those soft thighs of yours and plunge two fingers inside yourself. Now."

I follow his direction and groan at the erotic feeling of having his voice in my ear and my own fingers deep inside me.

"Matt," I groan.

"Now rub the ball of your hand over your clit. Hard, baby."

I moan and rub my clit vigorously as I move my fingers in and out of me quickly. Fuck me, just the sound of his voice sends me out of my mind.

"Babe, I'm gonna come," I moan.

"I need you to come fast for me, little one, and I'll finish the job myself tomorrow night. That's a promise."

"Oh God."

"I'm going to tie you up and lick you from head to toe, Nic. Would you like that?"

"Holy shit," I moan and come apart at the seams, thrashing, my legs rubbing against each other, draining every ounce of pleasure from my clit I possibly can.

"That's my girl," he croons in my ear. "Good girl."

"I miss you," I choke out. *I love you!*

"Tomorrow night, I promise."

"Okay." I take a deep breath and then laugh. "That was fun."

"For you. I'm going to have to take a minute before I go back into the office so Asher doesn't get a look at the wood I'm sporting."

I giggle and roll onto my side. "If I was there, I could take care of that for you."

"God, stop talking like that, baby."

"Are you alone?"

"Yes."

"Does the door lock?"

"Are you suggesting I jack off in a storage closet?" he asks in surprise.

"I would love to hear you come," I whisper.

"I'll come for you all night tomorrow night, sweetheart."

I grin. "I can't wait."

"Good night, love."

"Good night." *Love.*

CHAPTER FOURTEEN

"There's someone at the door," Anastasia announces as she walks into the kitchen. "We still have twenty minutes before we open, but he says he knows you and to check your phone."

I pull my phone out of my pocket and see two texts.

Asher and I will be at the shop in 30.

We are at the front door. Your faithful employee doesn't trust that I know you.

I run out to unlock the door for them, grinning when I see Matt leaning his ass on the glass, dressed in jeans and a blue button-down that I know matches his eyes.

His ass looks amazing in jeans.

He turns and smiles at me as I unlock the door, step back to let him and Asher in, and then lock the deadbolt again.

"Sorry we're early," Asher says as he saunters over to the glass case to ogle the treats inside.

"You're fine," I reply. "Anastasia, this is Matt and Asher."

"Sorry." She blushes and shrugs. "I just don't feel comfortable opening the door early to people I don't recognize."

"You did the right thing," Asher assures her.

"How are you?" Matt asks softly and cups my cheek in his hand.

"Happy to see you," I reply and turn my face to press a kiss to his warm palm. God, I'm so mushy.

His eyes flare with happiness, then darken when I skim my teeth over the base of his thumb.

"Keep that up and I'll have you tied up in that apron and against the wall of your kitchen in one minute," he whispers into my ear before kissing my cheek and pulling back, grinning wolfishly.

"Promises, promises," I tease. "I have your cupcakes ready to go." Keeping his hand in mine, I lead him to the kitchen, where his boxes are waiting for him. "I hope everyone likes them."

"They'll love them. The guys are becoming addicted to these. You just might put the doughnut industry out of business yet." He winks, and I glow under his praise.

"From your lips to God's ears." I nod. "Leo's article will hopefully draw more people in, too."

"Leo's article?" he asks with a raised brow.

"Yeah, he said that he mentioned my shop in an interview. Shocked the hell out of me."

"Huh." Matt nods approvingly. "That's cool."

"You look tired." I push my fingers through his soft hair and rub the muscles at the base of his neck. "Did you catch any sleep?"

"Not really." He sighs and rubs his hand over his face and then studies me for a moment. "I'm sorry about last night."

"Stop apologizing. Seriously, it's okay, babe. I missed you, but you have a kick-ass job where you fight crime and defend the American dream." I grin up at him as he smirks.

"Uh, something like that." He pulls me into his arms for a big hug.

There's nothing sexual about this, aside from the sparks of awareness that shoot through me whenever he touches me. Instead, he seems to be soothing both of us. His hands glide down my back and rest at my waist, holding me tightly against him. He buries his nose in my neck and breathes deep. "I'd like to come to your place when I'm done tonight."

"I'd like that, too," I agree without hesitation. "I'll make you dinner and everything."

He chuckles and kisses the top of my head. "That's the best offer I've had in months. Thank you."

"Don't thank me until you've had my mediocre cooking," I warn him. "I can bake like a champ, but cooking isn't really my strong suit."

"I can cook." Matt shrugs, but I shake my head adamantly no.

"No way, detective. You'll have worked a twenty-four-hour shift. I'll feed you."

I pass his boxes to him and lead him out of the kitchen just as Asher hangs up his phone with a curse.

"Abby canceled on me for today. What the fuck?"

"Who's Abby?" I ask, looking between both men in confusion.

"My babysitter," Asher replies and swears again, combing through his phone. "She has a family emergency and can't watch Casey today."

I frown at Matt, but he shakes his head discreetly, as though he'll fill me in later.

"You don't have anyone else to watch him?" I ask.

"Her," Asher corrects me absentmindedly. "Casey is my daughter. And no, I don't have anyone else."

"I can watch her," I offer.

"You're working," Asher replies, frowning as his head whips up.

"Well, the last time I checked, I own the joint, so I can invite anyone I wish." I offer him a big smile and wink at Anastasia, who nods in agreement. "How old is Casey?"

"Nine," he replies. "She's a good kid. She'll probably just bury her nose in her iPod and stay out of your hair."

"We'd love to have her. Can Abby drop her off here?"

Matt grins and leans his hip against my counter, crosses his arms, watching us both.

"I'll text and ask her," Asher replies, relieved. "Are you sure about this?"

"Of course." I wave him off and walk to the door to unlock it. It's time to open for the day. "She'll be fine here."

"Abby says she'll have her here in about ten minutes. Thanks, Nic. Really."

"My pleasure. I could use the extra help." I chuckle and am shocked to find myself caught up in a bear hug from a very strong, handsome Asher. "Whoa!"

"Watch your hands, partner," Matt warns him.

"You're the best." Asher sets me back on my feet and kisses my cheek. "Dump that asshole and marry me."

Matt's eyes narrow and darken and his lips firm, but he stays where he is, watching.

"Sorry, handsome." I pat his cheek and back out of his embrace. "I'm content with what I have."

"Damn." He smiles ruefully.

***

"You'll love the strawberry ones," Casey assures a customer, carefully placing four of the cupcakes in a white box, her tongue held between her pink lips in concentration. Casey is adorable. Where her father has dark hair and eyes, Casey has long, curly red hair, green eyes and freckles all over her perky little nose. Her skin is perfect, soft and pink.

She looks like a porcelain doll and is going to give the boys a run for their money one day.

"Thank you, young lady," the elderly customer says with a grin and then takes his treats to Anastasia to pay.

"You're welcome," she replies politely.

"You're a natural at this," I inform her. "Want a job?"

She giggles and pats her white apron that is roughly four sizes too big for her small body. "I'm too young to work."

"I guess so," I agree with an exaggerated sigh. "But one day, you'll be great at this."

She smiles widely, showing off a missing tooth. "I'm glad I got to come here today instead of staying with Abby."

"You don't like Abby?" I ask as I rearrange the almost-empty glass case.

"I love her, but sometimes it's boring." She pouts a bit and then jumps in, helping me.

I smile to myself and step slightly to my right, making room for her.

"We just hang out at her house and watch TV all day. Summer is boring."

"Does your dad do stuff with you on his day off?" I ask. I wonder where her mom is!

"Yeah, Dad's days off are the best. But he works a lot." She shrugs and eyes the strawberry cupcakes. She's already had two today.

"You can take all of the strawberry ones that are left home with you today," I say, earning a big smile. "We'll consider it your pay for all of your help."

"Wow! Thank you!" She hugs my waist tightly. "They are my favorite."

"I'm going to lock the door, Nic," Anastasia says.

"Sounds good, thanks."

"We're closing already?" Casey asks with a frown.

"Yep, it's closing time. But I have to mix some frosting for tomorrow morning. Do you want to help?"

"Yes!" She races into the kitchen, eager to help.

"I think you have a new best friend." Anastasia laughs. "I'll handle the cleanup out here so you can get prepped for tomorrow."

"Thanks. Just let me know if you need me."

I walk into the kitchen to find Casey waiting for me by my large stainless steel work station.

The same one that Matt made love to me on just a few weeks ago.

"Okay, let's get to work."

I hand her ingredients and bowls, and she and I work together, measuring and mixing. She's funny and sharp as a tack, catching on quickly.

"Justin Bieber is so not cool anymore," she says with an eye roll. "Austin Mahone is hot."

"He's *hot?*" I ask with a laugh. "Aren't you too young to think that anyone is *hot?*"

"Yes, definitely," Asher replies as he and Matt walk into the kitchen.

"Daddy!" She thrusts the bowl she's holding into my hands and runs to her father, jumping into his arms. "I'm a worker bee now!"

"You are?" he asks with a laugh.

"That's what Nic said. Right, Nic?"

"You're an excellent worker bee," I agree, nodding my head.

"Were you a good girl?" Asher asks her.

"I helped all day! Nic let me serve customers and make frosting and I met Leo Nash!"

"Leo stopped in this morning," I add, laughing. "She thought that was pretty cool."

Casey smiles and nods and hugs her dad, then squirms out of his arms and hugs Matt around the waist. "Hi, Uncle Matt."

"Hi, munchkin." He squats next to her and tweaks her nose. "I'm glad you had fun today."

"Can I come back tomorrow?" she asks as she throws her arms around Matt's neck, hugging him tightly.

"No, you'll be back with Abby tomorrow," Asher replies.

"Oh." Casey pulls out of Matt's arms and looks at me with longing.

I'm such a sucker.

"Maybe, if your dad says it's okay, you can come here once a week, as a treat."

"Can I, Daddy?" She clasps her hands together over her chest and bounces on the balls of her feet. "Please?"

"Nic, you don't have to…"

"I wouldn't offer if I didn't like having her here," I reply honestly. "She's a joy, Asher. I would love to spend a day with her each week, at least until summer is over."

Asher looks at Matt, who just smiles and shrugs, staying out of it.

"Please, Daddy?"

"If you really don't mind, Casey would love it," Asher begins hesitantly. "But I don't want to impose."

"Nonsense." I turn back to my frosting, bag it up and put it in the fridge. "She's a big help. The customers love her. And"—I hand Casey her box full of leftover strawberry cupcakes—"she works for cupcakes. We all win here."

"Well, then, I think you two have a standing date."

"Thank you!" Casey hands her father her box, and I barely have time to stoop to catch her as she throws herself into my arms. She's so slender, so sweet. She smells like vanilla and shampoo, and I hug her tightly for just a moment.

"You're welcome, sweetie. I'll see you next week, okay?"

"Okay!"

"Let's go, bubba." Asher takes Casey's hand and waves to us. "I'll see you on Thursday, Matt."

"Get some sleep," Matt calls out, his gaze still pinned on mine.

His eyes are hot and full of lust and something else that sends tingles through me and makes ravenous butterflies set up camp in my belly.

"How are you?" I ask.

"Hungry," he replies and slowly moves toward me.

"Nic, I'm leaving, too! See you tomorrow!" Anastasia calls out.

"Thank you, Anastasia!" I pull my apron off and toss it in the hamper. "I have dinner going upstairs."

"You do?" he asks softly and reaches out to brush his knuckles down my cheek. "That's not all I'm hungry for, you know."

"Well, it's a good place to start," I reply shakily. "Then we can work our way to other things."

"Bossy little thing, aren't you?" He chuckles.

"It was just a suggestion." I lift one shoulder in a shrug, watching his mouth as he licks his bottom lip.

"Are you finished here?" he asks.

"Yes."

"Good. Let's go home." He takes my hand in his and lifts it to his lips, kissing each knuckle softly. "I want to spend some time with you. Enjoy you." He leans in and kisses the apple of my cheek, then pulls his lips down to my ear. "Then lose myself in you until we both pass out."

I nod and pull in a deep breath, relishing the smell of him. He smells musky, like pure unadulterated *male*, and it makes every instinct in me sit up and beg.

"Which part are you agreeing to?" he asks as he drags his nose along my jawline.

"All of it," I whisper.

He grins, kisses me chastely and then pulls back, leaving me already missing his warmth and impatient to get upstairs with him.

"Let's go."

✳✳✳

"You are not a bad cook," Matt informs me with a grin as he stacks our plates in the dishwasher. "You had me worried."

"The slow cooker is easy." I laugh. "It's hard to screw anything up in there."

The whir of the air-conditioning kicks on, battling the hot Seattle summer heat.

"Doesn't heat the place up like the oven does either," Matt agrees. "I'm surprised you have AC in here. This is an old building."

"I had it installed. My ovens downstairs make it necessary to cool the rest of the building, especially in the summer."

He nods, locks the dishwasher and sets it.

"You shouldn't be doing this," I insist for the third time. "You worked hard today."

"So did you."

"Not for almost twenty-four hours," I remind him.

"My job isn't any more important than yours, little one. We both worked today, we'll both clean up from dinner."

"That's very diplomatic for a Dom." I cross my arms over my chest and lean my hips against the counter.

"I told you from the beginning, I'm not interested in a slave. That's not who I am."

"That's convenient for me, because if you were, you wouldn't be here."

"I know." He exhales and walks toward me, his face sober now. "What's going on in that beautiful head of yours?" He pushes his fingers through my short hair and cups my neck in his palm.

"What do you mean?"

"The Dom thing still makes you nervous, doesn't it?"

"Sometimes," I confirm. "I'm just still getting used to it."

He frowns but nods, his eyes darkening in concern. "Just talk to me when you get nervous, Nic."

"I do," I assure him and push my hands up his chest, over the hard muscles of his pectorals. "You feel good."

"Is that so?" His eyebrow quirks up, and his lips tip up into a half smile. "I have a plan."

He leads me into the bedroom, and when we're by the bed, he kisses my knuckles again and grins at me. "Trust me?"

"Of course," I reply instantly, making him inhale sharply.

"I love that you answer without any hesitation," he murmurs as he pulls my T-shirt over my head, unties the red ribbon from my hair and tosses it on the beside table, and unclasps my bra, exposing my breasts to him. "Trust is the most important thing in this relationship, Nic."

"I know," I whisper. I can't look away from his face as he watches his own hands, exploring my torso. "I want to touch you."

"I'm right here, baby."

I unbutton his shirt and slide it off his shoulders, letting it fall to the ground, as he opens my black capris, pushes his hands inside against my hips and guides them down my legs along with my panties.

He's standing before me in just his faded blue jeans, the elastic of his blue boxer-briefs peaking out of the waistband. I slip my finger inside, beneath the elastic, and pull him toward me.

"I want you naked," I murmur.

"Yes, that would be ideal," he agrees.

"I love your body," I continue, tracing his muscles with my fingertips, up his torso, down his arms and back again. "Your skin is smooth, but your muscles are hard. I especially love this," I murmur as I trace the V at either side of his hips.

"What else do you like?" he asks and leans his forehead against mine. He's panting now, and there is a hard ridge to the front left of his jeans.

"I like these." I gather his hands in mine and bring them up to my lips to kiss both palms, then place them on the small of my back and push his jeans down his hips to gather at his feet.

I slip my hands beneath the elastic of his underwear again and this time lower them, cupping his ass firmly.

"I really love this," I murmur and smile against his lips so close to mine.

He grins in return and glides his own hands down to cup my rear. "That feeling is completely reciprocated, baby."

He sucks in a breath when I clench my fist around his hard cock and pull all the way to the tip, then down again, holding him at the base.

"This does amazing things to me," I say.

"You're amazing," he replies. "God, Nic, I don't even remember what my life was like before you."

My heart stills for a moment and then picks up double time. I bite my lip and frown. I just don't know what to say.

How do I respond to that, when I've never felt like this either and it scares the living shit out of me?

He kisses my forehead and lifts me in his arms, then lays me on the bed.

"Is this the restraining portion of the evening?" I ask with a grin.

He smirks and pulls his ropes down from the railing of my four-poster and begins twining them around my wrists.

"How did you guess?"

"I just had a feeling," I reply and lift my head to kiss his arm as he works, threading and knotting his ropes around my hands.

When he's finished, he rests my arms comfortably over my head and kisses my lips slowly.

"Comfortable?" he asks.

"Yes."

He reaches over to the bag he brought with him and pulls out a bottle of lubricant and tosses it on the bed at my hip.

I cock an eyebrow in question.

"You'll see. Be patient."

"I don't typically have a lube issue," I remind him.

He kisses my shoulder, over the pink flowers there, and down to my chest.

"Just trust me. You'll see. First, I want to kiss your beautiful body." His lips trail down to nibble and pull on my left nipple, then beneath my breast to my bra line and over to the other.

Dear God, that's sensitive.

"Is that more sensitive than your nipple?" he asks in surprise.

"I guess so," I murmur and shimmy my hips in anticipation. "Who knew?"

"Well, now we do," he replies and drags his nose around my breast in a wide circle, nibbling the underside of each mound, making me moan. "Oh, I'm going to enjoy this."

He grins up at me and continues on his journey lower, to my piercing and lower still, but instead of burying his face in my pussy when he spreads my legs, his lips trail over my hip and down my thigh to my knee. His tongue circles the kneecap, and then he plants firm, wet kisses down the rest of my leg to my foot.

He's kneeling between my legs and brings my foot up to his mouth, pressing a kiss to the arch.

"Oh my," I breathe.

"Another spot, huh?"

"Oh yeah."

"So noted." He bites the arch gently, kisses it again and then moves to the other foot, paying it the same attention.

My hips are moving, and I'm squirming beneath him. White-hot heat has pooled in my belly, making me long for him to be inside me.

"Matt," I groan.

"Yes, my love," he replies, making me still and find his eyes with my wide ones. He tilts his head, watching my reaction, then kisses his way back up my leg, over my hip and up my side. When he's covering me with his body, he's careful to hold his hips away from mine, not touching me with his cock at all, and whispers against my lips, "What were you going to say?"

"I need you," I breathe.

He grins and licks my bottom lip. "You'll have me, little one. I'm going to flip you over. You'll rest on your elbows."

"But I want—"

"I didn't ask, Nicole," he interrupts, making my heart skip a beat. His eyes narrow in on my neck. "You like it when I dominate you like this, don't you, baby?"

I nod wordlessly, panting, a big quivering mess.

Fuck yes, and I had no idea it's something I *could* like!

He grins against my lips and then suddenly sits back and flips me effortlessly onto my stomach, hooks one arm under my hips, boosting me up on my knees, resting forward on my elbows.

My hands are still tied and useless, and if I thought I felt vulnerable before, it was nothing compared to this.

Nothing.

I can't see him. I can only feel him, hear him.

His hands pull firmly down my back to my ass, kneading my muscles, making me groan. "I love your body, too, Nicole. Your body is firm and small, but your ass is round and fits my hands perfectly." He cups the globes in his hands and spreads the cheeks, exposing my core. "Your pussy is gorgeous. Pink."

His breath is right there, at my opening, and I just know he's going to lick me, suck my lips until I can't stand it anymore, and I'm not disappointed.

He licks me in one long, fluid motion from clit to anus and back down again, then back up to run that talented tongue around my labia. I can feel myself swell under his touch. I grip the sheets in my hands and push back, not shy about asking for more of him.

"Do you know how much I thought of you last night, baby?" he asks as he inserts two fingers into my pussy and lazily circles them, brushing over my sweet spot. "I thought of doing this to you last night, tied up and begging me for more."

God, I love his dirty mouth!

"I love how your cunt clenches around my fingers." He kisses my right ass cheek. "My tongue." Kisses my left cheek. "My cock."

He sucks on my clit for just a millisecond, and when I cry out, begging him for more, he just continues to circle those fingers in my pussy.

"I don't want you to come yet. I have more planned for you."

He's going to fucking kill me.

He plants his lips over my clit again, making me crazy, then pulls away right before I'm about to come.

"Matt!"

"Patience," he croons.

"I want you!"

"I know, and I love it." He kisses my ass again, then the small of my back, and begins to kiss up my spine, between my shoulders, my neck and then covers me with his body, one hand still planted with his fingers inside me, and rests his lips next to my ear. "Do you remember when we read your book, about two men fucking one woman?"

"Yes."

"And you said that you'd like to know what it feels like?"

I nod my head, but he bites my earlobe and growls, "Words."

"Yes, I remember."

"You are mine. This"—he wiggles his fingers inside me, making me bite my lip—"is mine. But I'm going to show you what having both of your holes fucked at the same time feels like. Are you ready?"

"God, yes," I reply immediately.

He chuckles and kisses his way down my back. I hear him uncap the lube and suddenly feel cold liquid pouring down my asshole.

"It's cold." I chuckle, but somehow, even that is hot as hell.

"I'll warm you up," he replies and pulls his fingers from my pussy up to my slippery ass, just playing with the very outside. "How does that feel?"

"Weird, but good," I reply. I lean down, resting my cheek on the bed, pushing my ass higher in the air, ready for whatever he's about to give me.

He guides his cock into my pussy, sliding easily inside me, burying himself balls-deep with a low growl. "God, Nic, you're so fucking tight."

I clench around him, hard, unable to stop my muscles from hugging him, pulling him even deeper. His fingers are still circling my ass, rubbing, until he slips one inside, knuckle-deep and stills.

"That's just one, baby."

"Oh God, Matt!" It feels so full, so…*amazing.*

He begins to move, slowly pumping his rock-hard dick in and out of me, dragging the head over my sweet spot, helping me climb higher and higher.

"Tell me when you're getting close. I don't want you to go over yet."

"Matt!" I cry again.

"Tell me."

"I'm going to…"

He stills, breathing hard.

Sweat has broken out over my body, and I can barely catch my breath, but I don't even care. If he doesn't start to move, I'm going to maim him.

He pulls out halfway, and another finger joins the first, then he slams home again, stretching me even further.

"Holy fuck!" I cry out.

"You're doing so great, baby." He leans down and kisses my back, and then begins to move again, fucking me in long, measured strokes.

It's bloody amazing.

And then he begins to move his hand opposite of his dick, filling and emptying me in tandem, until I'm screaming and begging, for what I have no idea.

I'm not even sure I'm speaking English.

"Now, baby. Now you can come."

I rock my hips back, and when his free arm circles my waist and his fingers brush over my clit, I'm lost. I cry out, my body exploding in white heat, bearing down on him and calling out his name.

Both of his hands are gliding up and down my back now. He's buried balls-deep and unmoving, letting me ride out the rest of my orgasm. Finally, he *pulls* out of me and turns me to my back and quickly unties my hands.

"I need your hands on me," he pants, untying his knots as quickly as possible.

"Need to touch you," I agree, and when I'm freed, I cup his face and kiss him deeply.

He plunges inside me and braces himself on his elbows, wrapping himself around me as if he just can't get close enough.

"I love you, little one," he whispers against my lips.

I still and snap my eyes open, staring into his deep-blue ones. My heart thumps against his chest as he pulls his hips back, sliding out of me almost completely, then pushing back inside me again. I bite my lip and feel tears form in the corners of my eyes.

"Give in to this, Nic. Let me prove to you that I will be one of the best decisions you ever make."

He brushes his lips over my cheeks, wiping away the tears that are falling as I watch this amazing man above me.

But what if I can't give him everything he deserves?

"I love you, too," I whisper and wrap my arms around his neck, clinging to him.

He buries his face in my neck and quickens his pace, chanting my name, and words of love, as he finally lets go, succumbing to his own orgasm.

He pulls out, kisses me one last time before sauntering into the bathroom, where water starts to run. A few moments later, he returns with a warm washcloth. After he cleans me, he hugs me to him. I'm resting on his chest, and he brushes my hair with his fingers, kissing my forehead.

"How do you feel?" he whispers.

Wrecked. Emotionally wrung dry. Physically consumed.

"I don't know if I have the words," I reply.

"Give them to me anyway."

I bury my nose in his chest, then look up into his face and brace my head on my hands, watching him. "I feel good."

He nods and then chuckles. "Not really the reaction I was going for, but okay."

I climb up him and cup his face in my hands, looking him in the eyes, needing to give him the words, and suddenly determined to do my best to give him what he needs.

"I feel full, Matt. Physically and mentally. I feel like we've turned a corner that we can never turn back from, and I'm terrified and excited at the same time. I'm just trying to come to terms with it all in my head, but I want you to know that you have me."

His face softens, and he nuzzles my nose with his. "And you have me, baby."

CHAPTER FIFTEEN

~Matt~

"Take it back off. Now." I stare at her eyes in the reflection of the mirror and have to physically hold myself back from stalking to her, pulling her out of that dress and fucking her against the mirror.

Hmm…fucking her against the mirror.

"We have to be there in an hour." She laughs and shakes her head. "And I had to actually work to look like this, so you don't get to mess it up until we get home later."

I cock my head and smile.

Challenge accepted.

I'm going to give Bailey a big fat kiss when I see her next. She and Nic went shopping for this masterpiece yesterday, and according to Nic, Bailey had to talk her into it.

Thank Christ she did.

The dress is sage green and gray, strapless, showing off her insanely sexy tattoo. There is beaded fringe at the bottom, like an old-fashioned clapper dress from the forties, which is the only thing about it that makes it decent, because the hemline is a bit shorter than I'm comfortable with.

I'm going to fuck her in that dress.

With her panties tied around her wrists behind her back.

I adjust myself, not trying to be discreet, and watch as Nic applies her lipstick, hooks silver hoops into her ears, and then turns to get my approval.

Dear God, she's fucking gorgeous.

"Do I look okay?" she asks with a smile.

"It's not fair to be more beautiful than the bride-to-be," I tell her with a sober expression.

"That's an old line if ever I heard one." She laughs and retrieves her small purse, tosses her phone, wallet and lipstick inside and shrugs. "I'm ready."

"It wasn't a line," I say. "You are stunning. And I'll have to murder my brothers just for looking at you tonight."

"Trust me." She laughs. "Your brothers are completely happy with the women they have."

I lean in and kiss her neck gently, enjoying the shiver that moves through her.

"I love it when you wear blue," she murmurs, sliding her hand down my button-down shirt.

"You do?"

"It makes your eyes look even more blue, if that's possible."

"Let's go before I—" My phone interrupts me.

"I hope that's not your job," she says. "Not today."

"It's not. It's Jules. What's up, bean?"

"We're at the hospital," she begins, her voice heavy with tears.

"Are you hurt?" I ask, narrowing my eyes. My gut clenches in fear.

"No, it's not me." She sniffs. I can hear a baby crying in the background. "It's Nat."

"What happened?" Nic frowns, looping her arm around my waist, listening and worried, and I wrap my arm around her shoulders, soaking up her support and love.

"Natalie is bleeding, Matt. She could lose the baby."

"Fuck."

"Everyone's on the way here. The party is canceled."

"We'll be there in fifteen. Are you at Harborview?"

"Yes." She sniffs again and then sobs. "Oh, Matty, what if she loses the baby?"

"Is Nate with you?"

There's a shifting, and Nate's voice comes through the receiver. "I'm here. I have Julianne. Stacy and Bryn's parents took all the kids home except Livie. Luke's parents and yours are on the way."

"Nic and I are on the way, too. We'll be there in a few."

"Drive safe."

He clicks off the line, and I shove my phone in my pocket and pull Nic into my arms, holding her tight. "It's Nat."

"I heard. You should go."

I frown down at her and cup her face in my hands. "You're coming."

"It's a family emergency, Matt…"

"You're coming," I repeat. "I need you there."

She nods, and I take her hand, guiding her out of the apartment and down to my car. The five-minute drive to the hospital is one of the longest of my life, comparable only to when Brynna and the girls were in their accident several months ago.

Nic reaches over and takes my hand in hers, laces our fingers and squeezes reassuringly.

Fuck, I love her.

"I'm glad you're here," I murmur and kiss the back of her hand.

"Nat's going to be okay," she states firmly. "And the baby, too."

I smile and nod and silently pray that she's right.

When I pull up to the hospital, I park my car at the curb by the emergency room and lead Nic from the car.

"We can't leave the car here."

"Yes, we can. I work with this hospital regularly. They won't tow me."

"Okay." She shrugs.

I glance down at her and grin. Her legs look amazing in those heels.

"I'm looking for Natalie Williams," I inform the registrar, who meets us in the ambulance bay.

"I don't think we have a Natalie Williams in the ER, detective." She says. "Is an ambulance on the way?"

"She's probably on the floor," he informs her. "Can you find her?"

"Oh, sure, let me check." She types on her keyboard and bites her lip then smiles. "There she is. Room 402. Do you know how to get up there?"

"I do. Thanks," I reply and walk through the ER, through the back hallway to the elevator.

"Geez, you just walk through here like you own the place," Nic comments with a laugh.

"Asher and I are here on cases quite a bit." I smile down at her as we wait for the elevator.

"Where is Asher's wife?" she asks softly.

"She passed away about three years ago." My gut clenches as I think back to that dark time for my partner. "She was in an accident."

"Oh, I'm so sorry." She blinks quickly, and I can see that she truly means the words. "Poor Casey."

"It was rough on both of them," I agree. "They're doing better now, but it hasn't been an easy road."

"Does he have family here?"

The elevator doors open, and we climb aboard.

"No, his family is in New York. He's been talking about going back home to be near his family, for help with Casey."

"That would be a tough decision to make."

The thought of losing my partner is as appealing as the thought of losing my right arm.

We can hear Livie wailing as we leave the elevator and walk toward the waiting room. Jules is holding the fussy toddler, bouncing and crooning to her, but Livie won't be placated.

The room is full of family all dressed for a formal party, some sitting, some standing, all pretty much quiet.

Will and Meg are talking with Mark, Sam and Leo in one corner. Isaac and Stacy are standing with Caleb and Brynna while Nate and Dominic both try to help Jules quiet Liv.

"Matty!" Jules cries and walks to me immediately, leaning into me, cradling Livie to her. "Oh my God, it was so terrifying!"

"Okay, shush now, bean." I take Olivia from her, hold her to my chest, and she rests her head on my shoulder, takes a long, shuddering breath and sighs.

"Why wouldn't she do that for me? She loves me," Jules sobs.

"She knows you're worried and upset, Jules. It makes her upset, too. Now take a deep breath and fill me in."

"We were driving to the vineyard," she begins. "We were maybe five minutes out of the city, and suddenly Nat said that she had to go potty, and we all know how it can be when you're pregnant. When you have to pee, you have to *pee*." She swallows and wipes her tears from her cheeks.

Nic takes Jules' hand in hers, and if I wasn't already in love with her, it would have happened right then.

"We pulled over so she could use the restroom," Nate says. "And she came out saying she was bleeding. So we turned right around and came straight here. They started some tests in the ER but brought her up to this floor because, regardless of the results, they'll want to keep her at least one night."

"Any idea at all what's going on?" I ask and pat Liv's back. She's fallen asleep on me now, making little sucking motions with her heart-shaped lips.

She might be the most beautiful baby I've ever seen.

"We're waiting to hear from Luke," Dom replies. "He's in with her."

"Where is my baby?" my mom calls out as she and Dad come off the elevator.

Jules hugs Mom and kisses her cheek. "She's being seen by the doctor."

"Why can't we get back there? Is it worse than they're saying?" Samantha demands. "If it's just a little blood and they're monitoring, we should be able to take turns sitting and waiting with her."

"I think it's a combination of the pain she's been having over the past few weeks, along with the bleeding," Meg replies. "If she goes into labor, they won't want us in there. They're triaging her."

"Neil," my dad says as he shakes Luke's dad's hand. "Where's Lucy?"

"She's back there with them. The doctor said they could take one person, and Lucy went back first."

"I want to go back next," Jules insists.

"Here, will you take Livie?" I ask Nic. "I'm going to go talk to the nurse."

Her eyes go wide, but she takes the baby from me, settles Liv on her shoulder and sways back and forth, kissing her head.

Jesus, she looks good with a baby on her.

I shake that thought off and march over to the nurse at the nurse's station.

"I'm Detective Montgomery," I begin. "I'm Natalie Williams' brother. Can you give me any information?"

"I'm sorry, detective, I don't have any information for you. The doctor is with her. I'm sure her husband or mother-in-law will come brief you all soon." She leans in and lowers her voice. "Is that Will Montgomery, the football player? And Leo Nash?"

I stare at her hard, clenching my jaw, until she looks down in embarrassment. "I hope my family doesn't have to worry about the press hearing about our emergency." The threat is veiled, but it's plain as day: Don't fuck with my family.

"Of course not. I'm sorry. It shouldn't be long until you hear something."

I nod and walk back to Nic, Jules and Nate.

"Want me to take her?" I ask, gesturing to the sleeping baby.

"No, I have her," Nic replies with a soft smile. "She's asleep. We won't move her."

"My mom's coming back to get her," Stacy says. "They didn't have enough car-seat space in the van for all the kids."

I nod and shove my hands in my pockets and sigh in exasperation. Waiting is the worst. There's absolutely nothing we can do, and I can tell by the looks on all my brothers' faces that it's making us all nuts. I glance down at Nic and see that she's eyeing my mom nervously, and I realize what an asshole I am.

"I'm so sorry, Mom and Dad, I just realized that you haven't met Nic yet." I cringe and pull Nic to my side. "This is Nicole Dalton. Nic, these are my parents, Gail and Steven Montgomery."

"So nice to meet you," Nic replies and shakes both of their hands.

"Oh, no, it's our pleasure." Mom's eyes are wide in surprise when they meet mine and then she smiles broadly at Nic before looking up to me with a million questions in her eyes. I know I'll be getting the third degree later.

"This fucking blows." Will sighs and rubs his hands over his face.

"I want to see my girl," Mom whispers and brushes a tear from her eye.

I rub my hand up and down Mom's back, soothing her, and glance over to see Nic with her lips resting on Livie's head. She's whispering to her and rocking her back and forth, and I suddenly feel like I've been punched in the face.

I see the whole package when I look at this woman. Marriage and babies and houses and bills. Fights and laughter.

Everything.

"Any news?" Stacy's mom asks an hour later as she hurries out of the elevator and hugs Mom close.

"Not yet," I reply.

"Well, keep us updated. I'm going to take Liv with me. I want to get back quickly to make sure the other kids haven't killed the adults and taken over the world."

"Thank you," I reply. "She'll probably sleep for a while. She tuckered herself out with all those tears."

Nic gingerly hands the baby over to the other woman, runs her hand over Liv's dark curls and smiles as they walk away.

"You baked Brynna and Caleb's cake," Mom says to Nic, making conversation.

"I did." Nic nods. "I own Succulent Sweets in the city."

"How lovely," Mom replies and loops her arm through Nic's, dragging her away to have a chat.

Nic glances back at me over her shoulder, and I just smile and shrug.

"Your mom will be gentle," Dad assures me and then claps me on the shoulder. "She's a looker, that one."

"She is," I agree.

"Owns a business, so she's smart, too."

"Very smart."

"Must be special. You don't typically bring girls around."

I nod and then look my dad in the eye. "She's the one, Dad."

He firms his lips and watches me for a moment, glances over to where Nic and Mom are chatting with Jules, Meg and Sam. Finally, he turns his gaze back to me and nods. "I look forward to getting to know her."

"You'll love her."

He nods again and then we all turn our attention to Luke, who is walking toward us. His face is pale, his eyes look scared, and his hair is messier than usual.

"What's going on?" Mom asks, dashing to his side.

Luke wraps his arm around Mom's shoulders and kisses her head.

"She's going to be okay. The baby is fine, too."

We all breathe a huge sigh of relief.

"But they're keeping her for a while."

"Why?" Meg demands.

"She has kidney stones, which is where the bleeding was coming from when she went to the bathroom," Luke replies. "The 'growing pains' she says she's been having have actually been kidney pain." He shakes his head and swears under his breath. "I knew I should have made her go to the doctor."

"You couldn't have known," Mom assures him and pats his chest.

"So if it's just stones, why can't she go home?" Mark asks with a frown.

"They want her to pass it here, and monitor the baby until she's out of the woods."

"I'll stay, too," Jules volunteers.

"You'll come home after you look in on her," Nate corrects her. "You're pregnant, too."

"She's my best friend."

Nate pulls Jules back into his arms and whispers in her ear. Finally, she smiles and leans away, nodding up at him. "Okay. You're right."

"So, everyone can see her," Luke continues, "but maybe a few at a time, because that room isn't very big."

Mom, Dad, Luke's dad, Neil, and Jules go in first, leaving Luke with us.

"Scared the fuck out of me," he whispers and hugs Meg to him. "When she said she was bleeding, I panicked. My life doesn't work without her in it." He swallows and shakes his head, then plows his fingers through his hair.

"Scared the fuck out of all of us," I reply.

"Did you get to see the baby?" Meg asks.

"Yeah, they did an ultrasound," Luke replies and grins. "His little heart is strong, and he's kicking away. The doc said he's healthy. But there's still a chance she could have him early, so she has to take it easy."

"Having babies early is not the end of the world," Brynna reminds him and hugs him tight. "Mine were early, and look at them now. But our girl is strong, and both she and the baby are going to be just fine."

"Thank you," Luke replies, his voice hoarse. "Thanks, everyone. It's always moments like this that our family amazes me."

"Don't get mushy, bro." Mark smirks. "I'm going to go in next and kiss my sister-in-law."

"Don't get your lips anywhere near my wife," Luke growls at his brother, and we all laugh.

"Just a little peck," Mark continues with an easy smile.

"I'll fucking punch you."

"No, you won't," Mark replies and saunters toward Nat's room with a swagger in his step.

I glance down at Nic and frown when I see her face has gone pale, and she's frowning. "What's wrong?" I whisper into her ear.

She shakes her head and smiles up at me, the fakest damn smile I've ever seen. "Nothing. I'm just worried about Nat and the baby. I'm glad she'll be okay."

"How are *you* feeling?" I ask.

"I'm fine." She waves me off.

I will get to the bottom of this soon.

"I'm sorry we ruined your engagement party," Luke says to Meg with a rueful smile.

"Nah, don't be. I didn't really want one anyway, and Jules got her new shoes…"

"And a new dress," Nate adds with a chuckle.

"So we all win," Meg finishes, making us all laugh.

I glance around the room and sigh, relieved that everyone is safe and healthy. Leo is holding Sam in his lap, whispering in her ear soothingly as she leans on him. Will, Meg, Isaac and Stacy all make their way into Nat's room, anxious to see Natalie for themselves. Nate and Dominic are chatting with Luke, and I have the woman of my dreams by my side.

Speaking of, I'm ready to check with Nat myself so I can get my girl home and take advantage of her in that hot dress.

"Why don't we just go out to dinner together after we've all seen Nat before we all head home?" Will asks.

So much for taking Nic right home.

I glance down at her, and she just nods with a half smile.

"We're in," I confirm.

Finally, it's our turn to see Natalie, and I guide her into my arms, holding her tightly to me for a long minute. Nat takes a deep breath, clinging to my shirt and then pulls away.

"Scared me," I murmur down to her.

"Me, too," she replies with a smile. "I'm sorry."

I shake my head and back away so Nic can get close.

"Matt was right. Things are never boring with this family," Nic says with a wink. "But maybe from now on, we'll keep things less exciting."

"I'm in favor of that," Natalie agrees with a smile. She rubs her hand over her belly and gazes over at her husband, who has also joined us.

"I think a bunch of us are going to go get dinner. Do you want one of us to bring you guys back anything?" Nic asks, and I smile at her.

"No, thanks," Luke replies. "Nat has to eat what they give her, and I'll grab something from the cafeteria. The food's not too bad."

"Yuck," Nic replies, sticking her tongue out.

"Bring him back a burger," Nat adds and shakes her head at Luke. "No cafeteria food, baby."

"We can do that," I reply. "Call me if you need me."

"I will."

"I love you, sweet girl." I kiss her cheek and push her hair back behind her ear. "Take care of them," I say to Luke and wave as we leave Nat's room and join the others, ready to go out for dinner.

CHAPTER SIXTEEN

~Nic~

"I wasn't listening to a thing anyone was saying all the way through dinner," Matt informs me as he unlocks his apartment door and ushers me inside. "All I could think about was getting you home."

"And naked?" I ask with a raised brow.

"Not exactly," he replies with a wolfish smile.

He tosses his keys in a glass bowl by the door and advances on me. He backs me farther into the living room, sits on his couch and pulls me onto him to straddle his lap. I have to shimmy my dress up around my hips to spread my thighs wide enough to comfortably sit on him. His eyes flare and darken as he glides his big hands up my bare thighs to cup my ass. "You looked amazing today."

"Thank you," I reply and offer him a small smile. I won't let him see that my whole world has been turned upside down in the span of mere hours.

He and I aren't going to work. I've known it from the beginning, but this afternoon at the hospital cemented it for me.

But I'm too fucking selfish to let go of him without saying goodbye, even if it's only with my heart.

"You looked hot yourself," I murmur. "Of course, you look hot in most anything."

"I don't think that's true," he disagrees with a grin.

"It is." I lean in and nuzzle his nose with mine then kiss his cheek and down to his neck where I breathe him in.

I'm going to miss the smell of him.

"The green in this dress makes your eyes shine," he whispers and licks my chest across the top of my dress. "Watching you move in it is every man's fucking fantasy."

"*Every* man's?" I ask skeptically.

"This man's," he replies and nips my chin before claiming my mouth with his. His hands plunge under my hemline, grip the black thong I bought specifically for this dress, and rip it on each side, sliding it off me.

"That was new," I murmur breathlessly.

"I'll buy you another one," he replies. "Put your hands behind your back."

I scowl down into his face. I don't want him to tie me up. Not this time. This is the last time we'll make love, and I want to touch him, feel every glorious muscle under my hands as he moves inside me, but he doesn't know yet, and I can't argue.

I pull my arms behind me, and he quickly ties me with my own underwear then pushes me back on his knees so he can look his fill.

"Beautiful," he whispers. He unfastens his pants and pushes them down his thighs far enough to unleash his cock.

"Please take your shirt off, too," I whisper, keeping his gaze locked in my own.

He tilts his head but does as I ask, unbuttoning just two buttons on his shirt and pulling it over his head, tossing it aside. He reaches for my hips, and I raise up on my knees as he pulls me close to him and sink down on him, seating myself perfectly on top of him.

"Fuck, you're already so wet," he growls and plants wet kisses on my neck.

I begin to rise and fall on him, squeezing my muscles with every pull up.

He bites his lip and looks down where we're joined, watching with hot eyes.

He reaches around me and grabs my hands in his, holding me prisoner as his hips piston up and down beneath me, fucking me hard.

"Holy fuck," he grinds out, his eyes gliding up and down my body, over the curves in the tight dress, down to where we're joined and back up again to look me in the eye. "Love being inside you, little one."

I bite my lip, afraid I'm going to cry. I love it, too!

"Please untie my hands."

"Are you hurting?" He stills, his face sober. He cups my cheek in one palm and watches me closely.

"No." *Yes!* More than I ever have. "My hands don't hurt, but I really want to touch you. Please."

He frowns but reaches behind me and unties my hands.

I immediately wrap my arms around his neck and bury my face against his throat. I begin to move my hips, riding him hard and fast.

"Ah fuck, Nic," he growls and once again grips my hips, guiding me as I ride him.

I keep my face planted in his neck so he can't see the tears that fall silently as I make love to him, showing him with my body how much I love him.

"Baby, I'm going to come. If you don't slow down, I'm going to come."

I speed up. The tears stop, and I focus all of my energy, everything I am, on Matt.

Suddenly, he stands and reverses our position, laying me flat on the couch, all without falling out of me.

"I have to..." he mutters and begins to fuck me with long, hard thrusts, pounding into me unlike he ever has before, until he finally reaches between us and plants his thumb on my clit, making me fall over the edge into oblivion with him.

Before we can catch our breath, he pulls me back up into his arms and carries me, with my legs wrapped around his waist and arms around his neck, to the bedroom. He lays me gently on the bed, covering me with his body, brushing the backs of his fingers over my face.

"Matt," I begin and have to clear my throat, praying I don't start crying again.

"Yes, little one."

I open my mouth to reply but have to close it again and try to get my thoughts in order.

"Hey." He frowns and continues to caress my face, my hair. "Talk to me, baby. You've been acting strange since we were at the hospital."

"I just…" I try to look away, but he grabs my chin and holds me in his gaze. "I love you," I tell him simply.

And it's true.

But I'm not right for you. I can't make the words come. I'm such a fucking wimp. But I know him, and he'll try to fix it, to tell me that everything will be fine, and I don't think they will.

Seeing him with his family, worried over that unborn baby, soothing Olivia and holding her safely on his shoulder, showed me that I can't fit in with his family.

I can't *give* him a family.

And of anyone I've ever met in my life, Matt deserves that. I love him too much to ask him to do without it.

His face softens, and he kisses me tenderly before pulling away and lying next to me. He pulls me to him and nuzzles my nose with his. "I love you, too."

His eyes are heavy, and soon he's fallen asleep, breathing deeply.

I stay, watching him for a long time. I have no idea how much time passes as I listen to his even breaths, comb my fingers through his soft hair and take in every scent, every inch of his face and body, memorizing him.

Finally, when dawn is just beginning to come through the window, casting the room in a gray glow, I rise carefully, pull my dress down, retrieve my shoes and bag from the living room and let myself out of Matt's home.

And his life.

CHAPTER SEVENTEEN

~Matt~

I frown as I begin to surface from sleep and realize that Nic isn't pressed up against me like she usually is in the morning. I open my eyes and glance around, but she's not in the bed. The sheets are cool where she should be.

I lie and listen for a moment, hoping to hear movement in the kitchen. Maybe she decided to get up and make breakfast?

But there is no sound anywhere. Not in the kitchen. Not in the bathroom.

The apartment is still.

Where the fuck is she?

I push out of bed and walk through the apartment, just to be sure she isn't curled up somewhere quietly reading, and when my suspicions are confirmed that she's gone, I'm stumped.

What the fuck?

I pull my phone out of my jeans that were laying on the floor by the bed and call her, but she doesn't answer, so I tap out a quick text.

Hey, baby. Where did you go? Please tell me you're out getting breakfast.

I use the bathroom, splash water on my face and pull on some clothes. When she doesn't respond to my text, I call her again, only to be sent to voice mail.

Did something happen to her? Did she get a call about her family, or the bakery?

Maybe she left a note?

I search the apartment again but come up empty. No note. No message.

She's just gone.

Cold, hard fear grips my gut as I grab my keys and slam out of my apartment to go search for her. Anything could have happened to her. What if she'd gone out to get coffee and was mugged? Raped?

Jesus, should I call the hospitals?

I find parking in front of the bakery and knock on the front door, praying she's here. She isn't open yet.

Tess answers with a confused frown. "Hi, Matt."

"Is Nic here?"

"No, this is her Sunday off. I haven't heard from her."

I nod and back away from the door. "Thanks."

I jog upstairs to her apartment and bang on her door, but there's no answer, and no movement inside.

Just as panic is about to set in and I reach for my phone to call Asher and Caleb for help in finding her, I hear footsteps on the steps behind me. I whip around to see Nic, sweaty in her workout clothes, loud music plugged in her ears. She's watching her feet and hasn't seen me yet.

My breath leaves me in a loud sigh. Thank God she's okay.

She raises her eyes and startles when she sees me at the top of the stairs. Her eyes are read and puffy from crying.

"God, baby, what's wrong?" I ask as she pulls the earbuds out of her ears. "What's going on?"

She shakes her head and finishes climbing the stairs, unlocks her door, and leads me inside.

"What is going on, little one?" I soften my voice as I walk into her apartment and shut the door behind me. "Why didn't you tell me you were leaving?"

"Because you would have tried to make me stay," she replies and marches into her bedroom.

I follow closely behind and watch from the doorway as she tosses her phone and earbuds on the bed and toes off her shoes.

"Of course I would have tried to make you stay. I love being with you."

"I couldn't stay." She shakes her head and paces out into the living room, where I again follow her.

She's not making any damn sense.

"Nic. Stop."

She stops cold and looks at me with those wide green eyes, and my skin prickles the way it does when a case is about to go very bad.

I don't want to hear what she's about to say.

"We're not going to work out, Matt." She swallows and takes a deep breath.

"Why?" I fold my arms over my chest and lean against the wall, watching her. If she's going to dump me, I'm not going to make it easy for her.

"You should have kids."

I blink at her, sure I've misheard her. "Okay."

"You have a big beautiful family, and you should have kids, too. Healthy kids. Lots of them."

"Why do I feel like I've come in on the middle of a conversation?" I ask in frustration. "You're not making any sense."

"Do you want kids?" she asks desperately.

"Sure. Eventually."

"See?" She throws her arms in a wide circle and begins to pace around the room again. "I mean, I know that talking about kids now would have most men already through the door and running down the block, but you see what I mean."

"No, honestly, I don't see anything at all. I have no idea what in the bloody fuck you're talking about."

She sighs and scrubs her hands over her face then looks me in the eye just as a tear slips down her cheek, almost sending me to my knees.

"Baby…" I begin, but she quickly backs away with her hands up in front of her.

"Don't."

"You have got to talk to me, Nicole."

"I know I just…" She combs her fingers through her sweat-dampened hair and paces around her living room, then stops and props her hands on her hips. "I can't be with you anymore."

"Why?"

"Because I can't."

"You can do better," I growl and narrow my eyes.

"I am not what you need or want."

I raise my eyebrows in surprise and then let out a laugh. "Have you been hanging out with me lately, Nic? 'Cause I beg to differ."

"I need to be in control. I don't have a rich family to fall back on if this bakery doesn't work out. I don't have people around me to pick up the pieces if my health fails."

"You could."

She stops cold and stares at me, her mouth opening and closing, and then she just gets even angrier. "Oh, so now you're proposing? What the fuck?"

"Nic, I need you to be very specific here. Are you saying you don't feel anything for me?" Because if she is, she's a motherfucking liar.

"I feel too fucking much!" she explodes. "I feel everything! And I'm not talking about the palm of your hand on my ass!"

"So you don't want a kinky relationship? Is that what has you running? I felt your hesitation when I tied your hands last night."

"No!" She drops down into her chair and hangs her head in her hands in defeat. "That's not what I'm saying."

"I'm so lost, I don't know what the fuck is happening, Nic. Work with me here."

"I can't give you a family, Matt. Ever."

I frown and watch her as she raises her defeated eyes to mine. "I don't understand."

"I told you about my health issues."

I nod, still trying to connect the dots.

"I can't have babies."

"Diabetics have healthy babies every day, Nicole."

She shakes her head and laughs humorlessly. "I also have the PCOS."

"The reason you're on the pill." I nod, remembering.

"I don't need the pill for birth control, Matt. The PCOS *is* my birth control. With that combined with the diabetes, a pregnancy is not a good idea for me. *If I happened to get pregnant by some miracle, the pregnancy would be high-risk and difficult.*"

"Okay." I shrug. "What does this have to do with us?"

"Have you not been listening?" She looks at me like I'm an idiot, and I scowl back at her.

"You can't have children. Although, I think there might be ways around that, with as far as medical science has come, but even if that's true, why can't we be together?"

"Because I can't give you what you deserve!"

"What I deserve?" My blood is heating now. "What, exactly, do you think I deserve, Nicole?"

"A nice, submissive woman who can give you lots of babies and live happily ever after," she whispers, not meeting my gaze.

I sit in the chair opposite her and stare at her for a long minute.

"Are you fucking kidding me?"

"No." She shakes her head and clasps her hands together. "I love you enough to let you go and to find that person who can give you those things."

"You know what, Nic? No one likes a fucking martyr."

Her gaze whips up in shock. "Excuse me?"

"You heard me. Who the fuck are you to decide what I need and want?"

She stands to get in my face. "Well, isn't that just fucking hypocritical?"

I stand and clench my fists at my sides, glaring at her, trying to ignore the gaping hole in my chest where my heart once was.

"I've always been one thousand percent honest with you, Nic. While you've only shared what was convenient or I ripped out of you. I told you from the beginning, trust is imperative in this relationship."

I advance on her, not touching her, and push my face within inches of hers. "It's my fucking *job* to keep you safe, and knowing what you need and want is a part of that. I'm in love with you. You need time to get your head on straight? Fine. I'll leave you alone for now, but I'm telling you right now, you are *mine*. Nothing will ever change that."

"I'm saying *red*," she whispers.

I stare at her in shock for several seconds without blinking.

"You said at the club that all I have to say is 'red,' and it all stops."

She's using a fucking *safe word?*

I pull her against me and kiss the breath out of her, putting all the anger and frustration I'm feeling into this kiss, then I pull away and brush my thumbs down her cheeks, wiping her tears away.

"I don't know how you got it in your head that you can't give me what I deserve when I'm looking at everything I've ever wanted in a woman. *You* are what I need and deserve, Nicole. When you figure out that your medical issues are a fucking excuse to push me away, you come find me. In the meantime, you're right. 'Red' is a term I understand perfectly."

With that I turn away and walk out of her apartment without looking back.

***

I drive straight to the hospital. I need to see Natalie, and not worry about my own issues for a while.

Everything that Nic said in her apartment is rolling around in my head in a big, fucked-up, jumbled mess.

Jesus, how did we get here?

I walk into Natalie's room with a bouquet of flowers that I spent way too much money on in the gift shop.

"Hey." She grins and holds her arms open for a hug, which I happily oblige.

"Hey, sweet girl. How are you feeling?"

"Better today," she replies.

"She passed the stone during the night," Luke says as he shakes my hand. "We'll be heading home tomorrow."

"Thank goodness." Nat sighs. "I miss my baby girl."

"Don't worry about Liv, just worry about you," Luke instructs her and then laughs when Nat sticks her tongue out at him.

"She always was a handful," I remark with a smirk. "I'm happy to see things haven't changed."

"Why did you come here? Just to be mean to me?" she asks and narrows her eyes on me.

"I came to check on you."

"What's wrong with you?"

"Nothing."

"You look pouty." She smirks.

"I do not." I scowl and reach out to pull on a strand of her long dark hair. "I don't pout."

"You totally pout. Did Nic smack you around this morning?"

You have no idea.

"I'm not pouting."

"Okay." She grins. "I'll call Jules, and she and I will just gang up on you."

"I will tell the doctor to keep you here another day."

"You're mean!" she exclaims.

I laugh and lean in to kiss her cheek. "Don't forget it."

She cups my face in her hand and says quietly, "I love you, and I'm a good listener if you need one."

I smile gently and kiss her cheek one more time before pulling away. "I love you, too. Thank you. You just work on feeling well and cooking that boy in there, and I'll be happy."

"He's cooking," she replies and rubs her hands over her belly.

"How are you, man?" I ask Luke. He looks tired, sitting with his laptop on his lap, keeping an eye on his wife.

"Better now that she's on the mend and the baby is safe," he replies. "I think we're both looking forward to going home."

"He's going to make me rest." Nat pouts. "And no more photography until after the baby's born."

"You Nazi," I exclaim in outrage, making Natalie laugh. "How dare you take proper care of your wife?"

"I know, I'm evil."

I laugh as I back toward the door. "I love you. *Rest.*" I give her the stink eye. "I'll look in on you in a couple days."

"Yes, detective." She waves and giggles as I leave and almost bump right into my mother.

"Hi, Mom." I give her a big hug.

"Hi, darling." She pulls back and smiles up at me and then sobers. "Oh, we need to talk." She turns and walks with me down the hallway to the waiting room.

"I thought you were here to see Nat."

"I'll see her after you and I talk."

"What are we talking about?"

"Don't be a shit," she scolds me and sits in one of the plastic chairs, motioning for me to sit opposite her. "Now, tell me what happened."

I frown at her and then laugh, looking up at the ceiling. "Am I seriously having this conversation with my mom?"

"You are," she confirms. "Come on, I know something is up. Of all of my children, you've always been the hardest to read." She rests her chin on her hand and watches me for a moment. "So sober. So serious. But it's when your eyes look sad that give you away. You had that look when Asher's wife died. When Brynna and the girls were hurt. Let me help."

I clear my throat and am shocked when the whole story begins to flow, minus the Shibari, of course.

"So, she's decided that because she can't have kids, and she thinks that I *deserve* to have kids, that she's not the right person for me."

"Did you point out to her that there are several different ways to add children to your family?" Mom asks, tapping her chin with her finger, deep in thought.

"No, I was too surprised, and admittedly pissed, to bring that up."

Mom nods and sits back in her seat with a sigh. "I'm sorry about her health concerns."

"She manages them well." I shrug. "She's not on medication, and she takes good care of herself. She's actually quite healthy."

"Good." Mom grins, her eyes shining. "And you love her."

"Against my better judgment today, yes." I laugh again and rub my hands together. "She challenges me. She's funny and smart, and it's easy to be with her. She knows things about me that no one else in the world knows and…"

"And she loves you anyway," Mom finishes softly.

"Yeah."

"It sounds to me like she's a bit scared, son. It sounds like this relationship is still young, and happened quickly. Falling hard and fast is exhilarating and scary all at the same time."

I nod again, and then she hits me with, "Do you think *Nicole* wants children?"

I think back to how great she was with Casey, with Maddie and Josie, and how naturally she snuggled Olivia in her arms and rocked her back and forth.

"She'd be an awesome mom," I respond softly.

"You know, it can't be easy for a woman who believes she's infertile to spend a lot of time around pregnant women and couples with children. I'm not saying she doesn't enjoy being around the whole gang, but it might have played with her emotions a bit, too. Each time she sees Nat, Jules and Brynna and their men hovering over them, it's a reminder that she might never have that." She leans in closer and takes my hand. "And it's a reminder that she might not be able to give that to *you*."

"Shit," I whisper.

"Indeed." Mom kisses my cheek and stands. "She'll come around."

"I hope you're right, because the thought of being without her leaves me hollow."

"Oh, darling, that's wonderful." She laughs when I frown at her in frustration. "It means it's real."

"Oh, it's real all right."

"Give her a little time to talk to her friends and miss you a bit."

"Thanks, Mom."

"That's what I'm here for, dear." She winks and leaves me to go check in on Natalie, the daughter who didn't come from her body but couldn't be more hers if they shared the same bloodline.

Chapter Eighteen

Two weeks later

~Nic~

"Thanks for your help today, Tess." I grin at the young woman as she gathers her purse to leave for the day.

"My pleasure, as always, boss," she replies with a happy smile. "No wine with Bailey today?"

I shrug and shake my head as though it's no big deal. I just can't face her, or anyone really, right now.

"All you've done for the past two weeks is hole up in this shop and then sit at home," Tess points out with a frown. "You're starting to wig me out."

"I'm fine," I reply, irritated. "Have a good evening."

"You, too." She sighs dejectedly.

I follow her to the front door to lock it behind her, but just as Tess leaves, Gail Montgomery approaches, smiling warmly, dressed in casual denim capris and an orange T-shirt.

"Hi, Mrs. Montgomery." Good God, what is she doing here?

"Hello, dear. I know you're about to close. I was hoping for a moment of your time. Privately."

"Of course." I raise a brow and motion for her to come inside and lock the door behind her. "Have a seat."

"Thank you." She sits at one of my small round pub tables and smiles as I sit opposite her. "How are you, Nic?"

"I'm fine."

Her eyes narrow as she watches me, an expression I'm all too familiar with on her son. "That's good."

"What can I do for you?" I ask. "Would you like a cupcake? Cup of coffee?"

"Oh, not right now, although I might take a few home to Steven." She leans an elbow on the table and looks about my shop. "This is a beautiful bakery."

"Thank you."

"Have you spoken to my son?" she asks bluntly.

"Not in a few weeks," I reply softly and feel the stab to my heart. God, I miss him so much it hurts.

"I see." She frowns and links her hands, resting them in her lap. "May I ask why?"

I clear my throat and frown. Geez, how much do I tell his mom? "Honestly, it feels like a betrayal to him to talk about our relationship with you without him here."

She smiles widely and reaches across the table to lay her hand on my arm. "I like you, Nic. It's only because I like you that I'm here. I spoke with Matt the morning that you had your fight."

My eyes widen in surprise.

"That startles you," she guesses correctly.

"Matt's not really the kind of person to seek someone out to talk to," I reply honestly.

"He didn't seek me out. He ran into me at the hospital."

"Oh, how is Natalie?" I ask, genuinely concerned. Another difficult part of losing Matt was losing the fragile friendships that I'd just started to form with his family.

"She's very well, thank you." Gail shifts in her seat and considers her next words carefully. "Nic, Matt confided in me about your medical troubles."

Well, she just keeps shocking the hell out of me.

"I'm actually quite healthy," I reply.

"He said that, too, but he said that the main reason you believe you can't pursue your relationship with him is because you may not be able to give him children."

Tears prick my eyes as I stare down at the tabletop. I can only nod in response.

"And that you think that Matt should have a large family."

"I've seen him with the kids, with his pregnant sisters, Mrs. Montgomery. He'd be an excellent father, and he should have that."

"I agree, but Nic, why do you feel that you can't eventually have that with him? Aside from the fact that your relationship is new, and marriage and children are still in the distant future, why do you not think that you could be the woman to eventually share those things with him? You're obviously very much in love with each other."

"Because I can't have children, ma'am. Sure, I may be able to get pregnant through the miracles of modern medicine, but the PCOS is so bad that I've been advised that I *shouldn't* have children."

"And why is it necessary for the children you may have to be biologically yours?"

I sit in stunned silence and stare at the older woman, then crease my brow in confusion. "Isn't that usually how it works? Matt should have his own biological children."

Gail's eyes flare in irritation, and she crosses her arms over her chest, and I have a bad feeling that I've just pissed off the mama bear.

Shit.

"Because you're new to our fold, let me explain something to you about our family, Nic. The saying 'blood is thicker than water' is bullshit. My Natalie first came into our family when she was in college with Jules. They became fast best friends, and Nat came home with Jules during holidays and such. And when her parents died, leaving her orphaned, we are the ones who stood by her, helped her through that difficult time, and continue to love her. Natalie is as much my daughter as Jules is, but she isn't my biological daughter." Gail smiles softly.

"Caleb," she continues, "just adopted Maddie and Josie and couldn't love them more than the baby he's conceived with Brynna. Those girls are *his*. In every way, Nic."

I remember the girls with Caleb when I was invited to dinner and smile as I nod in agreement.

"Another example is Meg and Leo. They both came from some of the most difficult of circumstances, but found each other and have claimed each other as brother and sister since Meg was a preteen. But they don't share parents, Nic. They just love each other so much that they made a family together.

"The Williams family, all of my sons and daughters-in-law, have become as much my family as those I gave birth to."

God, I'm such a moron. All this time, I thought it would be important to Matt to have children of his own, but it never occurred to me that he would welcome children who might come to us through other means.

"And Dominic," Gail continues, much to my surprise. "Did Matt tell you that story?"

"Just that Dominic is his half brother."

"I'm surprised he worded it that way," Gail murmurs. "My husband and I had a rough time of it right after Caleb was born. We split for a few months, and during that time, Steven slept with a woman while on a business trip, resulting in Dominic."

My mouth drops as I stare at her, shocked.

"We didn't know about the baby until early this year when Dominic hired a private investigator to find his biological father. It shocked Steven, but between you and me, it turned my world upside down. Nic"—she leans in and lays her hands on the table—"my husband had a child with another woman. I knew about the sex more than thirty years ago, right after it happened, but now there was a man in front of me, claiming to be my husband's *son*. His mother died last year, and he was curious. What was I supposed to do? Throw him away and pretend he never existed?"

"What did you do?" I ask, enthralled.

"I welcomed that man into our family. I'd forgiven Steven a lifetime ago, and Dom is his child. He's come to fit in very well with our family, and my other children love him, too."

"You are an extraordinary family, ma'am. Families like yours don't happen every day."

"Oh, darling, we are not perfect, that's for sure. But my point is, whether it's through blood or pure love, family is family. I dare you to tell me that the twins, Olivia and the new baby about to come aren't my grandchildren."

"Of course they are," I reply immediately.

"And any children that you and Matt are blessed with, whether they come from your womb or through adoption, or even surrogacy, would be loved just the same, Nic. That's what a family is."

The tears are flowing freely now.

Gail scoots her chair around to mine and rubs my back soothingly.

"I'm so ridiculous," I choke out.

"You love him, sweet girl. You thought you were doing what was right for him."

"I love him so much it hurts to breathe."

Tears fill Gail's own eyes as she nods. "Only a woman in love would be so stupid. I'm sure it didn't help being around the pregnant girls and the kids."

I shrug and then nod, chuckling through my tears. "I feel so silly because I really like Nat, Jules and Brynna, and I'm happy for them all. I would never begrudge them the children they're having."

"Well, you're not a monster, Nic. But it's a hard thing to see their men hold their bellies."

"I…" I begin and then just sigh, hanging my head in my hands. "Yes. It's hard."

"It's easier when you have people around you who love you and understand."

"I don't want anyone's pity. I have so much to be thankful for, and I don't want anyone to feel sorry for me."

"There's a big difference between support and pity, Nicole, and you know it."

I bite my lip and nod reluctantly. "I made a mess."

"You can clean it up."

"You think?" I ask hopefully. "Matt and I haven't been seeing each other long, so to bring up kids now was relationship suicide."

Gail laughs and pats my shoulder. "It might have been early, yes, but I don't think Matt's thoughts were far from yours. One thing you have to understand about my Matthew: Honesty is paramount to him. Maybe it's the cop in him, but he will respect you going to him and being honest. Then you two can take it from there."

"Why did you choose today to come see me?" I ask, curious.

"Because Matt is a grouchy ass, and after two weeks, I figured you needed a nudge."

I giggle and nod. "I have some thinking to do, but I'll go talk to him soon."

"Good. Now, about those cupcakes."

"Here, let me box some up for you."

***

"Thank you, dear. Good luck."

Gail nods and walks down the block, carrying her box of cupcakes.

I take a deep breath and lock the door, then set about cleaning up for the day, letting my mind wander.

She's right. I don't have to give birth to children for them to be mine. Why hadn't I ever thought of it before?

And then I remember.

Because my whole life, it was drilled into me by my parents and doctors: You'll never have children.

But maybe, just maybe, someday, I might.

I grin and jump when my phone vibrates in my pocket.

"Hello?"

"Hey, gorgeous."

"Ben!" I grin and climb the stairs to my apartment, happy to hear from my old friend. "How are you?"

"I'm great. I'm in Seattle for the week. Have dinner with me tonight." His voice is warm and familiar, and I realize I've missed him like crazy.

"I would love that. What time?"

"I can head your way now."

"I'll be ready."

Ben was my boyfriend in my early twenties when I still lived back home. I was overweight and not taking care of myself, and the handsome personal trainer had loved me anyway, and helped me get healthy.

Not because he didn't like me the way I was, but because he wanted me to be healthy and whole, and I'd loved him for that.

Ben was my first love.

And now he's one of my best friends.

I fix my hair and makeup and change into a lacy pink tank top with a flowy white skirt and sandals, and when I pull the door open for him, he scoops me into his arms and turns a circle in my living room.

"You look wonderful!" I exclaim and kiss his cheek as he sets me back on my feet.

"You look...hungry." He laughs. "And beautiful, as always."

"I am hungry. Feed me, please."

"My pleasure. Mexican?"

"Mmm...yes." We jog down my steps and walk up the block to one of our favorite Mexican places in Seattle. "What are you in town for?"

"A job interview."

"You're moving here?" I ask excitedly.

"Hoping to, yes. I'm never going to do more with my career back home. We both know that."

"You should have warned me that you were coming." I smack his arm playfully as the hostess seats us in a booth against the wall. Someone else drops off chips, salsa and water, and I greedily dig in.

"You haven't lost your appetite," he observes drily.

"Never," I agree and grin. "Seriously, why didn't you give me a heads-up?"

"I thought I'd surprise you." His hazel eyes are happy as he smiles at me. "How have you been?"

"Meh," I reply and shrug, feeling much better now that I've had the encouraging talk with Gail and am now having dinner with my dear friend.

"Explain the *meh*."

"Oh, it's a long, drama-filled story."

"The best kind." Ben winks and pops a chip in his mouth.

I tilt my head and watch him. He's not just handsome, although with his muscles for days, light hazel eyes and square jaw, he's certainly one hot number. Ben is a beautiful man, inside and out.

"You're a good person, Benjamin."

"Uh, don't say that, Nic. That only leads to 'but,' and we broke up a long time ago."

I toss my head back and laugh hard, then throw a chip at him. "Don't be a douche. I was paying you a compliment."

"I see that you've kept up with your workouts. You look great." He tilts his head, watching me closely. "But I know you, and you have circles under your eyes, so spill it."

I sigh and lean my chin in my hand. "I'm an idiot."

"Agreed."

"You're a jerk."

"Typically, yes."

I laugh again and shake my head. "Stop it. You are not. There is a guy."

"Do I want to know this?" His handsome face cringes. "I mean, I know we're just good friends, but I don't think you're supposed to know who your ex-girlfriend is sleeping with. It's weird."

"How do you know I'm sleeping with him?"

"Are you?"

"Yeah."

"Now I know."

"Jealous?" I ask with a raised brow.

He sits back and actually thinks about it, surprising me. I expected a witty comeback, but instead he just answers honestly.

"Not jealous in the way I would have been five years ago, but worried because you mean a lot to me and I don't want to have to kill him for hurting you."

"I hurt him, Ben." I sigh and push my fingers through my short hair.

"I like the haircut, by the way."

"Oh, thanks. It was time for a change." I take another bite of chip. "Anyway, I fell hard and fast for him. He's a great guy. A cop." I tell him all about Matt and his family, how we met, *everything*. And it feels good because I haven't been able to tell anyone everything about my relationship with Matt, and I know that Ben won't judge me.

"So, aside from the kinky sex, which sounds like a lot of fun to me, but makes me very uncomfortable in relation to *you*"—he cringes again—"he sounds like a solid guy."

"He is."

"So what's the issue?"

"I broke up with him."

"Why?"

I bite my lip and stare at the half-eaten basket of chips.

"Nicole…" Ben lowers his head to catch my gaze. "Why?"

"I thought he deserved better than me," I whisper. "With my medical stuff and everything."

Ben's brow creases in surprise. "Nic, I've been around the block a time or two, and I'm telling you right now, there are few better than you."

My jaw drops in surprise. "If you propose right now, I'm going to throw this margarita in your face."

He laughs and shakes his head. "My girlfriend might have an issue with that."

"Girlfriend!" I squeak. "You haven't told me about a girlfriend! Is she here or in Wyoming?"

"She's in Wyoming, but if I get the job here, I'm hoping she'll move out here with me."

"Who is she? Do I know her?"

"We'll get to her later." He waves it aside and reaches across the table to take my hand in his large one. "Do you love him?"

"Yeah. But to be honest, his family, although they're great, they are damn intimidating. Half of them are celebrities, Ben. There's money, and they're all beautiful and just...I *read* about these kinds of people."

"Are they assholes?"

"No." I shake my head emphatically. "They're really nice. I mean, they're protective of each other, and there were some curious looks and questions, but they were great about making me feel welcome."

"Good." He nods. "Not all families are like yours."

"My family isn't that bad," I reply softly. "They just don't pay much attention to each other."

"So being around a family that *does* pay attention is new." Ben chuckles and shakes his head. "I always wondered why you weren't one of those girls who calls or texts all the time, always in my way. For a while, I thought you just weren't interested."

"No, I guess it's just not in my nature to have to always be in someone's back pocket." I smile and squeeze his hand. "You know I was interested."

"Yeah, and then you decided to go to culinary school and break my heart."

"I'm sorry," I murmur. "I didn't want to hurt you."

"We got over it," Ben replies with a shrug. "So you know you're going to have to apologize to the guy for being a dumb-ass."

"Yeah." I laugh. "There will most likely be groveling involved."

"Nah, don't stoop to groveling, babe." He winks and takes a sip of water. "So what are you going to do about it?"

"I'm going to talk to him. Probably tomorrow."

Ben nods and then looks up at someone who's approached the table.

I glance up, expecting to see the waiter, but instead, my eyes collide with a very angry blue gaze.

"Matt." Holy shit. I pull my hand out of Ben's, but Matt's gaze follows my hand, not missing it.

Not missing a thing, I'm sure.

"Nicole," he returns, coldly but softly. "I'd like to have a word with you privately, please." He glances down at Ben, who grins and offers his right hand to shake.

"Hi, I'm Ben."

He doesn't clarify exactly *who* he is, which exasperates me and seems to amuse the hell out of Ben.

"I'm Matt." He shakes Ben's hand, out of manners hammered home by Gail more than anything, I'm sure, and pins me in his hard stare.

"Now."

CHAPTER NINETEEN

Matt leads me behind him, through the restaurant and down a short hallway to the restrooms. He opens the men's room door and when he sees that no one is inside, he pulls me in with him and flips the deadbolt.

"Matt…"

"Two weeks." He cages me in, my back against the door and his hands planted on either side of my head. "We haven't spoken in two weeks, and now you're out with some new guy?"

"It's not what it looks like…"

"What it looks like"—he lowers his face closer to mine. His eyes are feral, angrier than I've ever seen them, and he's panting—"is the love of my life allowing another man to hold her hand over dinner and flirt with her. What the fucking hell, Nic?"

"He's just a friend," I insist and glare at him, but my stomach quivers at the feel of him so close to me. "He's a very good friend."

He growls and plants his mouth on mine, not gently, not carefully, but with hunger and lust, as though he's been without water for days and I'm a mirage in the desert. He cups my face in his hands and plunders my mouth, his tongue seeking my own. He bites my lower lip and then plunders again as his hands glide down my sides to my hips and thighs, where he gathers the soft material in his fists, yanking it up around my waist before ripping my panties in two, throwing them over his shoulder.

"You are *mine*. I stayed away like I promised I would, but I'm done, Nic." His voice has softened, but it's still intense. His hand glides up the inside of my thigh as he leans his forehead on my own, his eyes clenched closed. His hand drifts higher until his fingers graze my lips and circle my clit gently.

"I can feel how fucking wet you are, little one, but apparently I need to remind you who you belong to."

He boosts me up against the wall and presses his denim-covered cock against my core, rocking against me, making me gasp and groan. Hell yes, I'm his! And suddenly, he can't get inside me fast enough. I don't care that we're in the restroom of a restaurant. I need him. Now.

He leans back to unfasten his jeans, unleashes his cock and very gently rubs the head of his hard dick over my clit and through my folds, until he slips inside me, burying himself as deep as he can go. He pulls both my hands over my head and pins them with one of his hands, supports my ass with the other and proceeds to fuck me hard and fast, panting and growling. He bites my neck, leaving a mark, I'm sure, then kisses me again, until we both have to break away to breathe.

"I told you before, I'll never share you, sweetheart, and I meant it." He releases my hands to cup my face in his palm, brushing the apple of my cheek with his thumb.

God, he's consuming me. I can feel the frustration rolling off him in waves, and while his movements are urgent, he's still gentle, careful not to hurt me.

He'd never hurt me.

He leans his forehead against mine and in a low voice commands, "Come."

And I can't help it, I do. Having him touch me, inside me, is my undoing, and I come hard, bucking my hips and clenching around him.

"There is nothing sexier than watching you come," he groans and explodes inside me.

We're both panting, and I'm quivering from the aftershocks of both of our orgasms. Before pulling out of me or even setting me back on the floor, he grips my chin in his hand and keeps my gaze pinned to his.

"You have five minutes to get rid of the asshole and get in my car. You are already spending the night tied to my bed, but you take even a second longer and you'll be blindfolded as well."

I gape at him as he pulls out of me, tucks himself away and sets his watch. He turns to the sink, wets a paper towel and returns to me, kneeling at my feet, cleaning the insides of my thighs where his semen has streamed out of me. He straightens my skirt, tosses the towel away, stands and kisses me thoroughly and completely, then takes my hand in his and leads me out of the bathroom back to my table.

When we arrive, Ben is grinning wider than I've ever seen him.

Matt leans in and kisses my cheek, then whispers in my ear, "The clock is ticking. I'll see you outside," and then he's gone.

"So, are things resolved?" Ben asks, watching Matt walk away.

"Uh, I think the groveling is about to come sooner than I expected," I reply in embarrassment. "I'm sorry, Ben, but…"

"No, don't be sorry. I'll be here all week. We'll catch up another day."

I lean in and kiss his cheek. "Thank you."

I grab my purse and hurry out of the restaurant to find Matt parked in front of the entrance, the engine running, and waiting for me.

I climb into the passenger seat and watch him warily. "I'm here."

"That's a good start," he replies and pulls away from the restaurant toward his own apartment.

"Where are we going?"

"Home."

"Why?"

The look he sends me is hurt and angry, making me sink back into the seat. "You and I have some things to work out. The first of which being you don't go out on dates with anyone but me."

"We broke up, Matt. I can see whomever I choose."

"Bullshit." His voice is low and hard, and the usual calm that Matt exudes has settled back around him.

"Excuse me?"

"You heard me."

He parks in his space and pulls himself out of the car and around to my side, opens the door and waits for me to climb out of the car.

I hold my hand out for his. He takes it, raises it to his lips and kisses my knuckles tenderly before leading me into the elevator. He's quiet as the elevator climbs to his floor, then he leads me down the hall to his door.

Once inside, I'm at a loss. I'm not sure where to take it from here.

Do I just blurt out *I'm sorry?*

"Let's start with who was he," Matt begins and sits on the edge of a chair in his living room. He gestures to the couch opposite him, and I sit, remembering our last night together here on this sofa.

"Ben," I begin and clear my throat, "he's a good friend."

Matt raises an eyebrow, waiting for more of an explanation.

"He's from my hometown, and he was my boyfriend until I moved here to go to culinary school."

Matt's eyes darken, and his hands clench into fists.

"There's been nothing sexual happening with him in years, and frankly, right before you walked up and interrupted, we were talking about *you*." I raise an eyebrow and then keep talking, "And how I was going to clean up this mess I caused."

"Dating other men isn't the answer," Matt mutters.

"He's in town for the week and invited me to dinner and wanted to know why I look sad." The last few words are a whisper as I look down at my feet.

"Why are you sad, little one?"

I feel tears gather, so I cover my face with my hands and take a deep breath. "Because I miss you," I murmur. "Matt, I owe you a big apology."

"Lower your hands and look me in the eye."

I comply and am shocked to see tears in his eyes when my gaze finds his. "I'm so sorry, for not being more open with you, for assuming instead of discussing. Hell, for just being an idiot in general."

"You're not an idiot, but I accept the apology for the rest of it." He wipes his hand over his mouth, watching me. God, he looks amazing. His hair is a riotous mess, and his eyes look tired, but the T-shirt he's wearing molds to his upper body, showing off every line of every muscle, and his jeans are just delicious.

I can't stop looking at him, soaking in the sight of him.

Oh, how I've missed him.

"I can't stand this." Matt stands and pulls me to my feet then lifts me into his arms, sits on the couch and settles me in his lap. "This is better."

I loop my arms around his neck and cling, just hugging him tightly, breathing him in.

"Talk to me, baby."

I lean back to look into his face, gliding my fingertips down his cheeks. "I'm afraid."

"Of what?"

I swallow and let a tear fall on my cheek.

"Ah, baby, don't cry. It kills me."

"I'm sorry," I whisper. "I'm afraid that one day you'll decide that I'm not really what you need."

"Why would I ever decide that?" He frowns at me in confusion.

"I know it's early, and we have a lot of time ahead of us, but when I saw you with your pregnant sisters, and all the kids in your family, it occurred to me that if we continue on the path we're on, I'd have to admit to you sooner or later that I can't give you those things. I don't want you to make the decision to be with me now and then a couple years from now regret it because you want to start a family."

"I'm not going to lie, baby. I do want a family someday. But there are other ways of having children. I would never want you to put your body through something that it's not capable of. At the heart of it, we are you and me. This"—he wags his index finger back and forth, pointing to both of us—"doesn't work without you. So, when we come to a place where we're ready to add more people to this life, we'll work together to decide how that's going to work."

"I know that now," I admit shyly.

"What changed your mind?" he asks.

"Your mom came to see me today."

"Oh God," he groans and then chuckles. "What did she say?"

"She reminded me that family is about love, and the rest is details. She's a smart woman."

"Yes, she is."

"I don't want to lose you," I whisper. "I love that you're so supportive and proud of me. You encourage me to be better, and you don't try to control every aspect of my life.

"But I also love when you go all bossy and controlling in the bedroom, and I can give that part of myself over to you and trust you to know what I need and what makes me feel good. It's nice to have a place where I don't have to worry."

"Ah, baby." He leans in and kisses my forehead tenderly. "You finally figured it out."

"Yeah." I nod and shrug and then bite my lip, afraid of the next question.

"What is it?"

"Can we try this again?"

"I never gave up in the first place," he reminds me. "I have been waiting for you. And then I walk into that restaurant to pick up dinner, and I see you there with another man, and for the first time in my life, I had murderous thoughts."

"Killing him wouldn't have solved anything."

"Who said I wanted to kill *him?*" he asks with a raised brow.

"Killing me wouldn't solve it either."

"I never want to feel that way again," he whispers and hugs me closer. "I'm not typically a jealous man, Nicole, but when I saw him holding your hand, I almost lost my mind."

"I get it," I assure him. "If the tables were reversed, I'd cut a bitch."

He laughs and stands with me in his arms and marches back to his bedroom.

"Are you really going to tie me to the bed?"

"Are you going to skip out on me in the morning?"

"No," I reply as he sets me on my feet. I reach for his shirt, helping him peel it over his head. "God, you look amazing in this shirt."

"You're good for my ego, little one." He smirks. "I think I'll tie you up later. First, I want your hands on me."

"Thank God," I mutter and unfasten his jeans, watching him spring free. "We should have a shower."

"We will."

"We should have one first."

"Remember a few minutes ago when you said that you like it that you can let go and let me handle this part of things?" His eyes are sparkling with humor as he undresses me, pulling my tank top over my head and yanking my skirt down my hips, leaving me in just my bra.

"Yes."

"Stop trying to top me, stubborn woman, and enjoy."

I giggle as he boosts me up onto the bed and covers me with his body, resting his hips against my pelvis, nestling his cock in my folds.

He buries his fingers in my hair and brushes his nose across my own then sinks in and kisses me deeply, licking across my lips and inside, then nibbling the corners of my mouth and down my jawline to my neck. "Your skin is so fucking soft."

I hitch my legs up around his hips and pull my hands down his back to his ass.

"Matt," I whisper as hot need sets up camp between my legs. The gentle brush of the head of his cock against my clit just isn't enough.

"Yes, baby."

"Oh, God, please," I growl as he circles his hips, sliding his cock through my wet lips.

"You're always so ready for me, little one." He pulls his hips back and then slowly pushes inside me. "God, so tight."

Tears gather and fall into my hairline.

Matt scowls down at me, kisses my mouth gently, caressing my hair and my cheeks. "What is it?"

"I didn't think we'd ever be here again," I whisper. "I love you so much."

He closes his eyes and rests his forehead against mine as he sinks into me and rests there.

"I know," he answers. "I don't ever want to lose you, Nic. You put your arms around me, and I'm home. I'm permanently in love with you. Don't ever forget that."

EPILOGUE

Two months later

-Matt-

"I can't believe you talked me into letting you drive my car." I smirk and shake my head then glance over to see that she's driving at least ten miles per hour over the speed limit. "Slow down, Nicole."

"I love to drive, and I never get to anymore."

"I'll buy you a car," I remind her and hold my breath as she takes a curve a bit too fast. "And for the love of Jesus, slow down!"

"Oh, don't be a killjoy." She rolls her eyes and then shrieks when there are red and blue flashing lights and a siren behind us. "Oh shit."

"I tried to warn you," I mutter at her.

"It's okay, I got this."

I raise my brow and then watch with absolute amusement when she rolls down the window and wipes frantically at her nose.

"I'm so sorry, officer!"

"Hello. Did you realize you were going nine miles an hour over the speed limit?"

"No! I didn't. I'm sorry. I was having a sneezing fit."

I sit back and cross my arms over my chest, watching with amazement as my little spitfire of a girlfriend tries to get out of this ticket.

"A sneezing fit?" the officer asks.

"Yes, you know when you suddenly have to sneeze and you do it like eight or nine times in a row?"

"Oh, yeah, I've done that before."

"I couldn't stop it, and I guess I must have accidentally sped up." She sniffs again and then to my utter amazement, the cop shrugs and nods.

Shrugs and nods!

"Well, let me have your license anyway so I can make sure everything is in order, and then you can be on your way."

"Thank you so much," she gushes and hands over her license then grins smugly at me when the cop walks back to his cruiser.

"Are you fucking kidding me?"

"What?" she asks innocently with wide eyes and then laughs her ass off. After a few moments, the cop returns with her license.

"Well, it seems it's your lucky day, Ms. Dalton. My computer is down, so I can't even issue you a warning."

"Oh!"

"A sneezing fit, huh?" He shakes his head and laughs, taps the hood of the car. "That's a new one. Be safe."

And with that he walks back to his car and pulls away.

"I told you I had it covered," she says with a smile. "Works way better than crying."

"Are you pulled over often?" Geez, maybe I should pull her record to see what's on it.

"No." She shakes her head and then laughs. "Well, maybe."

"Slow the fuck down and you won't get pulled over."

She parks the car in front of the park where we're going to have our picnic and drops my keys in my palm when I hold my hand out.

"That was fun." She grins.

"I'll drive us home," I reply and climb out of the car, pull the picnic basket from the trunk and lead her to a tree off the beaten path.

She spreads the red and blue quilt on the ground, kicks off her flip-flops and sits down.

"I'm starving."

"Are you okay?" I ask. I still worry about her diabetes, but she is always on top of it.

"Oh, I'm fine. I'm always hungry."

"Before we dig in," I begin and rub my suddenly sweaty palms down my blue jeans, "I have something for you."

"You do?"

"Yes."

"Oh dear God." Her face pales, making me laugh and shake my head.

"Not that something. And I can see by your reaction that you're definitely not ready for that yet."

"Oh." She frowns for a second, almost in disappointment, making me grin again. Maybe she'll be ready sooner than I thought.

But not today.

"We're going to the club tonight," I remind her.

She grins and nods, blushing beautifully.

"We don't go very often," she replies. "It'll be fun."

I nod and pull a small square blue box with a white bow out of the picnic basket and watch her eyes widen.

"You have good taste," she whispers.

"I chose you." I shrug and push my fingers through my hair, trying to decide what to say. "Have you noticed at the club that some of the submissives wear collars?"

"Yes," she replies and frowns.

"In some cases, those collars mean as much if not more than a wedding ring between the Dom and his sub. It's not just a symbol of ownership, but of companionship as well. For me, I'm not interested in seeing you wear a true collar, but…"

I hand her the box and watch as she tugs the lid off and gasps at the platinum chain inside. She pulls it out of the box and holds it up, examining the simple pendant of two linked hearts.

"I would like for you to wear this, as a symbol of being mine. I want you to be tied with me in every way, just as I'm tied to you." I take the chain from her and clasp it around her neck and brush my finger over the two delicate hearts. "I want everyone to know that you're mine, little one."

"I am yours, babe." She looks down at the hearts and back up into my eyes, smiling happily. "And I'll wear it proudly. Thank you."

She launches herself at me, pushing me onto my back on the hard ground and kisses me soundly. "It's beautiful."

"You're beautiful," I reply and brush my thumb over her lower lip.

"I'm hungry," she reminds me and rolls onto her back, still admiring the hearts.

I'm so relived that she loves it. I sit up and pull our meal out of the basket, and when I glance back down at her, she's staring at me with so much love and trust it steals my breath.

"Keep looking at me like that and it'll be awhile before we get around to lunch, and there are children not far away."

She grins and sits up next to me, kisses my shoulder and then my cheek. "I love you."

"I love you back."

The With Me In Seattle series continues in book seven.
Don't miss Mark and Meredith's story in
Breathe With Me
Coming in summer 2014.

Want more steamy romance in the Montana mountains?

Turn the page to read on for a sneak peek of Kristen Proby's

Seducing Lauren
Book Two in the Love Under the Big Sky Series

Coming soon from Pocket Books

SEDUCING LAUREN

Book Two in the Love Under the Big Sky Series

"Hey, Lauren."

"Hi, Jacob, what can I do for you?" I ask with a smile, opening my front door wider for the friendly county sheriff deputy.

"Well, I'm serving you." He offers me an embarrassed smile and hands me a large envelope, then backs away. "Have a good day."

Without moving back inside or shutting the door, I stare down at the envelope in surprise.

Served?

I rip open the envelope and see bright, flaming, inferno red as I read the court document.

"The fucker is *suing me?*" I exclaim to an empty room and read the letter clutched in my now trembling hands for the third time. "Hell no!"

I grab my handbag and slide my feet into flip-flops, barely managing not to fall down the porch steps as I tear out of my house to my Mercedes and pull out of my circular driveway.

I live at the edge of Cunningham Falls, Montana. The small town was named after my great-grandfather, Albert Cunningham. Ours is a tourist town that boasts a five-star ski resort and a plethora of outdoor activities for any season. Thankfully, summer tourist season is over and ski season is still a few months away, so traffic into town is light.

I zoom past the post office and into the heart of downtown, where my lawyer's office is. Without paying any attention to the yellow curb, I park quickly and march into the old building.

The receptionist's head jerks up in surprise as I approach her and slam the letter still clutched in my hand on her desk.

"*This,*" I say between clenched teeth, "isn't going to happen."

"Ms. Cunningham, do you have an appointment with Mr. Turner?"

"No, I don't have an appointment, but someone in this firm had better find time to see me." I am seething, my breath coming in harsh pants.

"Lauren." My head whips up at the sound of my name and I see Ty Sullivan frowning at me from his office doorway. "I can see you. Come in."

I turn my narrowed eyes on Ty and follow him into his office. I am too agitated to sit while I wait for him to shut the door and walk behind his desk.

"What's going on?"

"I need a new lawyer."

"What's going on?" He asks again and leans back against the windowsill behind his desk. He crosses his arms over his chest. The sleeves of his white button-down are rolled up, giving me a great view of the sleeve tattoo on his right arm.

"This is what's going on." I walk to his desk and thrust the letter at him. "Jack is trying to sue me for half of a trust fund that he has no right to."

Ty's handsome face frowns as he skims the letter. "You came into the trust while you were still married?"

"Yes," I confirm warily.

"And you didn't tell him about it?" he asks with raised brows.

"I didn't even know the damn thing existed until after my parents died, Ty. Until *after* I kicked Jack out." I pace furious circles in front of his desk, breathing deeply, trying to calm down. "He doesn't deserve a dime of my inheritance. This isn't about money, it's about principle."

"I agree." Ty shrugs. "Have you talked with Cary?"

"I was just served with the letter," I mumble and sink into the leather chair in defeat. "Cary's a nice guy, but I just don't think he's the right lawyer for this job." I glance up at Ty and my heart skips a beat as I take him in now that I'm calming down. He's tall—much taller than me, which is saying something given that I stand higher than five foot eight. He has broad shoulders and lean hips, and holy hell, the things this man does to a suit should be illegal in all fifty states.

But more than that, he's kind and funny, and has a bit of a bad boy side to him too—hence the tattoos.

He's been front and center in my fantasies for most of my life.

I bite my lips and glance down as his eyes narrow on my face.

"Why do you say that?" he asks calmly.

"It took two freaking years for the divorce to be final, Ty. I don't want Cary to drag this out too."

"It wasn't necessarily Cary's fault that the divorce took so long, Lauren. Jack had a good lawyer and your divorce was a mess."

That's the fucking understatement of the year.

"Will you take my case?" I ask.

"No," he replies quickly.

"What?" I ask, my dazed eyes returning to his. "Why?"

He shakes his head and sighs as he takes a seat behind his desk. "I have a full load as it is, Lo."

"You're more aggressive than Cary," I begin to say but halt when he scowls.

"I really don't think I can help you."

Stunned, I sit back and stare at him. "You mean you won't." I hate the hurt I hear in my voice, but I can't hide it. I know Ty and I aren't super close, but I considered him a friend. I can't believe he's shooting me down.

He folds the letter and hands it back to me, his mouth set in a firm line and his gray eyes sober. "No, I won't. Make an appointment with Cary and talk it over with him."

My hand automatically reaches out and takes the letter from Ty, and I'm suddenly just embarrassed.

"Of course," I whisper and rise quickly, ready to escape this office. "I'm sorry for intruding."

"Lo . . ."

"No, you're right. It was unprofessional for me to just show up like this. I apologize." I clear my throat and offer him a bright, fake smile, then beeline it for the door. "Thanks anyway."

"Did you want to make an appointment, Lauren?" Sylvia the receptionist asks as I hurry past her desk.

"No, I'll call. Thanks."

I can't get to my car fast enough. Why did I think Ty would help me? *No one will help me!*

All the connections I have in this town, all the money I have, and that asshole is still making my life a living hell.

I drive home in a daze, and when I pull up behind a shiny black Jaguar, my heart sinks further.

Today fucking sucks.

Prepared to call for help if need be, I pull my cell phone out of my bag and climb out of my car. I walk

briskly past him and up the steps to the front door.

"Hey, gorgeous."

"I told you not to come here, Jack. I don't want to see you."

"Aw, don't be like that, baby. You're making this so much harder than it needs to be."

Shocked and pissed all over again, I round on him.

"I'm the one making this hard?" I shake my head and laugh at the lunacy of this situation. "I don't want you here. The divorce has been final for weeks now, and you have no business being here. And now you're trying to fucking *sue me?*"

He loses his smug smile and his mouth tightens as his brown eyes narrow. "No, I'll tell you what will make it easy, Lauren. You paying me what's rightfully mine is what will make it easy. You hid that money from me, and I'm entitled to half."

"I'll never pay you off, you son of a bitch." I'm panting and glaring, so fucking angry.

"Oh, honey, I think you will." He moves in close and drags his knuckles down my cheek. I jerk my head away, but he grabs my chin in his hand, squeezing until there's just a bit of pain. "Or maybe I'll just come back here and claim what's mine. You are still mine, you know."

My stomach rolls as he runs his nose up my neck and sniffs deeply. Every part of me stills. *What the fuck is this?*

"A man has the right to fuck his wife whenever he pleases."

"I'm not your wife," I grind out, glaring at him as he pulls back and stares me in the face.

He flashes an evil grin and presses harder against me. "You'll always be mine. No piece of paper can change that."

I don't answer, but instead just continue to glare at him in hatred.

"Maybe you should just go ahead and write that check."

He pushes away from me and backs down the stairs toward his flashy car, a car he bought with my parents' money, and snickers as he looks me up and down. "You've kept that hot body of yours in shape, Lo. Maybe I'll come back sometime and take a sample. Remind you of how much you loved it when I fucked your brains out."

I swear I'm going to throw up.

I can't answer him. I can only stand here and glower, shaking in rage and fear, as he winks again and hops in his Jag and drives away.

Jesus Christ, he just threatened to rape me.

I let myself into the house and reset the alarm with shaking fingers. I take off in a sprint to the back of the house and heave into the toilet, over and over again until there's nothing left and my body shivers and jerks in revulsion.

How can someone who once claimed to love me be so damn evil?

When the vomiting has passed, I rinse my mouth and head over to the indoor pool that my parents had built when I was on the swim team in high school. I shuck my clothes, but before I pull my swim cap on, I dial a familiar number on my phone and wait for an answer.

"Hull," he answers. Brad is a police detective in town, and someone I trust implicitly.

"It's Lauren."

"Hey, sugar, what's up?"

"Jack just left."

"What did that son of a bitch want?" His voice is steel.

"He threatened me." My voice is shaky and I hate myself for sounding so vulnerable. "I want it documented that he was here."

"Did you record it, Lo?"

"No. I wasn't expecting it. He's been an asshole in the past, but this is the first time he's come out and threatened me since he . . ." I pace beside the pool, unable to finish the sentence.

"That's because I put the fear of God and jail time in him." He's quiet for a moment. "Is there anything you need?"

I laugh humorlessly and shake my head. "Yeah, I need my asshole ex to go away. But for now I'll settle for a swim."

"Keep your alarm on. Call me if you need me."

"I will. Thanks, Brad."

"Anytime, sugar."

We hang up and I tuck my long auburn hair into my swim cap and then dive into the Olympic-size pool. The warm water glides over my naked skin and I begin the first of countless laps, back and forth across the pool.

Swimming is one of two things in this world I do really well, and it clears my head.

I do some of my best thinking in the pool.

Is all of this worth it? I ask myself. When I married Jack almost five years ago, I was convinced that he was in love with me and that we'd be together forever. He'd been on my swim team in college. He was handsome and charming.

And unbeknownst to me, he'd been after my money all along.

My parents were still alive then, and even they had fallen for his charm. My father had been a brilliant businessman, and had done all he could to convince me to have Jack sign a prenuptial agreement so Jack couldn't stake any claim to my inheritance.

But blind with love and promises of forever, I had stood my ground and insisted that a prenup was unnecessary.

My dad would lose his mind if he knew what was happening now. If only I'd listened to him!

I tuck and roll, then push off the wall, turning into a backstroke.

The small amount of money that Jack is trying to lay claim to is nothing compared to the money I have that Jack knows nothing about. Since our legal separation, I've become very successful in my career as an author, but I wasn't lying when I told Ty that it's not about the money.

This is my heritage. My family worked hard for this land, for the wealth they amassed, and Jack doesn't deserve a fucking dime of it. That's why the divorce took so long. I fought him with everything in me to ensure that he didn't get his greedy hands on my family's money.

In the end he won a small settlement that all of the lawyers talked me into.

Jack wasn't happy.

I push off the edge of the pool and glide underwater until I reach the surface and then move into a front crawl.

After my parents died in a car accident just over two years ago, Jack made it clear that he didn't love me, had been sleeping around since we were dating, but expected me to keep him in his comfortable lifestyle.

And when I threw a fit and kicked him out, he slammed me against the wall and landed a punch to my stomach, certain to avoid bruising me, before he left.

Thanks to threats from Brad, and Jack knowing how well-known I am in this town, he hadn't bothered me since.

And now he's threatening to rape me.

Rape me!

It's not worth it. Living in constant fear and embarrassment of seeing Jack around town. Seeing the pity in the eyes of people I've known my whole life when I see them on the street.

And now coming home to an ambush because he's feeling desperate.

I'm done.

Exhausted and panting, I pull myself out of the water and resign to go see Cary in the morning to agree to a settlement.

It's time to move on.

It's early when I leave the house and drive to the lawyer's office. I don't have an appointment, and I don't even know for sure if anyone is there yet, but I couldn't sleep last night. I couldn't lose myself in work.

I need to get this over with.

When I stride to the front door, I'm surprised to find it unlocked. Sylvia isn't in yet, but I hear voices back in Cary's office.

I stride through his door like I belong there, and both Cary's and Ty's faces register surprise when they see me in the doorway.

"You know, Lo, we have these things called phones. You use them to call and make what's known as an appointment."

Ty's gray eyes are narrowed, but his lips are quirked in a smile. He's in a power suit today, which makes my mouth water immediately. His shoulders look even broader in the black jacket, and the blue tie makes his eyes shine.

"Ha-ha," I respond and sit heavily in the seat before Cary's desk. "I'm sick of this shit."

"Ty told me you came by yesterday," Cary informs me as he leans back in his chair.

"I was fucking served papers," I mutter and push my hands though my hair. "But I think I want to settle."

Ty raises his eyebrows. "I'll leave you two alone."

"You can stay," I mutter. "I could use both of your opinions. I'll pay double for the hour."

"That's not necessary." Ty's voice is clipped and he frowns as he gazes at me. "Why the change of heart?"

I lean back in the chair, tilt my head, and look at the tin tiles on the ceiling.

"Because Jack's an asshole. Because now he's decided to threaten me." I shake my head and look Cary in the eye. "But no payments. It's going to be in one lump sum and he needs to sign a contract stating that he'll never ask for another dime."

"Wait, back up." Ty pushes away from the desk and glowers down at me. "What do you mean he threatened you?"

"It doesn't matter."

"Lauren," Cary interrupts, "it does matter. What the hell happened?"

"When I returned home, Jack was at the house."

"Does he still have a key?" Ty asks.

"No." I shake my head adamantly. "I changed all the locks and installed a new alarm system the day he left."

"So he was waiting outside," Cary clarifies.

"Yes. I told him to leave, that I didn't want to see him and he isn't welcome at the house. He said I was making things harder than they need to be." I laugh humorlessly as Cary's eyebrows climb toward his blond hairline.

"I reminded him that there's nothing difficult about this at all. We're divorced. It's over, and he can just go away." I shrug and look away, not wanting to continue.

"What did he threaten you with?" Ty asks softly.

I raise my eyes to his and suddenly my stomach rolls. "I'm going to be sick." I bolt from the room and run to the restroom in the hallway, barely making it in time to lose the half-gallon of coffee I consumed this morning. When the dry-heaving stops, I rinse my mouth and open the door to find Ty on the other side.

"Are you okay?" he asks quietly.

I nod, embarrassed. He reaches up and gently tucks a stray piece of my hair behind my ear.

"What did he threaten you with?" He asks as he leads me back to Cary's office.

I swallow and cross my arms over my chest. I don't want to say it aloud. "He just threatened to be a dick."

"Bullshit," Cary responds, leaning forward in his chair. "Lo, the man wasn't afraid to put his hands on you when you told him to leave . . ."

"What?" Ty exclaims, but Cary continues.

"So you need to tell me what he threatened to do to you if you don't give him what he wants."

I shake my head and close my eyes, remembering the feel of Jack's nose pressed to my neck and the crazy look in his eyes when he wasn't getting what he wanted.

"Excuse us for a minute, Cary."

Ty takes my hand in his and leads me toward the door.

"Uh, my client, Ty, remember?"

"We'll be right back," Ty assures him and leads me into his office and shuts the door behind us.

"What did the asshole threaten to do to you, Lauren?"

"You said no yesterday, Ty. This isn't your case."

He shrugs, as if what I just said is of no consequence.

"Answer me."

I simply shake my head. "It doesn't matter. Cary and I will figure it out. You don't have to stay in there with us."

I try to walk past him but he catches my hand in his, keeping me in place.

"Lauren . . ."

"Stop, Ty. You don't want me—I get it."

"Are you fucking kidding me?" he asks, his voice deceptively calm. "Do you know why I turned you down yesterday, Lauren?"

I shake my head, my eyes wide and pinned to his.

"Because it would be a conflict of interest. I can't be your lawyer because I'm your friend, and I want to be a whole lot more than that."

If I thought I was stunned before, it's nothing compared to this. My jaw drops as he closes the gap between us. He doesn't touch me, but his face is mere inches from mine. His eyes are on my lips as I bite them and watch him. I'm completely thrown by this turn of events.

"You have the most beautiful lips, Lo."

"What?" I whisper.

He takes a deep breath as he lays his thumb gently on my lower lip and pulls it from my teeth. "I want to taste these lips."

It's whispered so softly, I can barely hear the words. I can't tear my gaze away from his mouth and I take a deep breath, inhaling the musky scent of him.

I've forgotten Jack and his threats, the lawsuit.

Everything.

Ty clears his throat and backs away, watching me carefully. "Cary will remain your lawyer, but I want to know what the hell is going on, Lo. I can help."

I blink and continue to stare at him, completely dumbstruck.

He wants me?

"And another thing, Lauren. You're not settling. Fuck Jack and his lawyer."

Made in the USA
Charleston, SC
04 September 2014

33147845R00150